CW0088080j

# THE BAKER PAPERS

# THE BAKER PAPERS

## A Novel

EDWARD HAWKE

SECKER & WARBURG
LONDON

First published in England 1986 by
Martin Secker & Warburg Limited
54 Poland Street, London W1V 3DF

British Library Cataloguing in Publication Data

Hawke, Edward
  The Baker papers: a novel.
  I. Title
  823'.914[F]        PR6058.A87/

  ISBN 0-436-19144-X

Photoset in 10/12pt Linotron Plantin by
Deltatype Ltd., Ellesmere Port
Printed and bound in Great Britain by
Billings Ltd., Worcester

26 Nov.        Monday

When I was a kid people used to give you diaries and say stuff like
'You ought to write down everything what happens so's you can read
all about it in years to come' and I always meant to only I never did.
Anyway, I reckoned if you keep leaving it much longer, mate, then
you'll be too bleeding old to start. Funny thing, we was talking about
diaries and that down The Anchor and John reckoned he'd got hold of
this book called the secret life of Fanny somebody, all about this nun
and what she got up to with a load of monks—he's going to bring it in
when his old man's finished with it. So somebody says to him he ought
to write one and he says, 'What? And tell you buggers my secrets?'
    'You'd have a job keeping anything secret in this town,' says Tina.
    'Ah—no nuns for a start,' says John. 'Here, I reckon you'd make a
good nun though, Tina.'
    Well, that's just his talk I guess, but I was glad when she gives him a
look and says, 'Pooh! No chance, John.'
    'Got the figure for it,' he goes on. 'Hey—what about you and your
Marilynne as a pair of nuns, eh?'
    We all had a good laugh but I reckoned much more of that and I'd
have had to say something. Still, I reckon Tina can look after herself.
    'Trouble with Taunton it's so frigging boring,' says Janette.
    Trouble with her, more like.
    'Cheer up, playmates,' says John, 'payrise next year.'
    That's something to look forward to anyway. Really wanted Tina
tonight but she didn't want to. It's high time. I like her and that but if
she won't let me have it soon then there's no bloody point, is there?

29 Nov.        Thursday

Forgot about this diary till today. Nothing's happened anyway. My
old man was moaning breakfast time about getting waked up when I
got home last night.
    'That was Anna,' I told him.
    'No it wasn't,' she says.
    Course it was—that Dermot's car makes more noise than a lorry.
    'MGBs are supposed to make a noise,' she says. 'Anyway, he's
thinking of getting a TR7,' she says in her posh voice. I bet she fancies
herself in one of them.
    'Big deal.'
    'Now, now,' says Mum, 'don't argue all the time.'
    Decided to grow a moustache, Tina reckons it's a good idea.

**30 Nov.  Friday**

Bloody cold—had a job getting the car to start but then they say 1100s are always like it. Tina in a mood tonight. Got those massive tits of hers out—magic! I reckoned here we go—hand up and you're in, mate, then she won't do nothing else, will she? Really pisses me off it does. I don't know what she reckons she's playing at.

'Come on, Tina,' I said.

'What?'

'You know.'

That was that, I couldn't think of nothing to say.

**2 Dec.  Sunday**

Christ, I hate Sundays—they're so boring. It's boring even if you're feeling OK and I'm not. I feel awful. I just sat around all day up here mostly, listening to records. Had to go down for tea—was going to listen to the Top 40, but oh no, we couldn't have it on because me old man don't like it. Bloody Sunday tea drives me mad too—cold bloody joint, always bloody cold joint. Anna asked our Mum why we always had to have cold joint and Mum said well, it had to be eaten up and there wasn't nothing wrong with it, then *he* says, 'Want to think yourself bloody lucky, my girl,' and she gives him a look. You have to laugh sometimes—she can handle him all right. So she eats crisp-breads and he piles on his bloody Branston Pickle—gets through a jar of that a week he does, even has the fucking stuff on his sandwiches in the week. It's incredible. Anna reckons he eats like a pig. Then Mum says to Anna she's sure she's not getting enough to eat. Dad says, 'She'll eat when she's hungry all right.' Anna pulls a face at him and then her and Mum start talking about diets where you don't eat nothing but fruit and rice and all that. She keeps telling Mum to go on one and Mum always says she will but she never does.

Anna kept going on about how Dermot took her to this posh place last night and how they met his boss and his wife and all that and how she's got some fashion show to do at the Tech next week—on and on and on . . . It drives you spare after a bit. Least somebody's happy—not me. Our old man said this Dermot makes him feel like an errand-boy. Had a laugh at that, then he got stroppy as usual. He just can't take a joke, that's his trouble. Mum says she reckons Dermot's very nice, then she went on at Anna because she said the dress she wore last night was 'too revealing'. I'll say—left her tits half hanging out, and it's been cold here lately and all.

I went on up to my room—they asked me where I was going but I couldn't be fussed to answer. I don't want to talk to nobody today, I'm that pissed off. Wish I could go to sleep but I bloody well can't.

I mean take last night, was I mad. . . I get round her place like we'd said and that little sister of hers says oh, Tina's gone out with Janette. I was bloody mad I can tell you but Tracie said it weren't her fault, then she said she didn't know where they'd gone to and she shuts the door in my face. She's a right little bitch, that one. So anyway, I went on round to the party on my own and who's there but Tina. So I went right up to her in front of that Janette and asked her what the bloody shit she was playing at, and she tells me I don't own her and just stuck her nose in the air and told me to piss off and anyway her and Janette weren't staying *there* all night, so I asked her where they were going then and she said, 'Mind your own business.' Then Janette pipes up and says, 'Why don't you clear off out of it?' and I said I didn't want her advice thank you very much, then they just went on talking. I stood there like a fucking pratt for a minute or two, then I went off. So that's that. Looks like it's all over with Tina, and it really pisses me off. What's the bloody point?

Don't know what's got into her. I've thought about it—come to that, I've not thought about nothing else since I got back, and I don't know, I just don't know. Like I say, looks like it's all over with her. Well, she can go and stuff herself for all I care, that's what she can do. Straight, I could have smacked that Janette round the mouth, the way she was stuck there looking at me like I was so much shit the cat brought in. Course they all reckon she can't never keep a boyfriend cos she's so bloody mean and on account of her having a rotten temper. Makes me puke.


3 Dec.        Monday

I hate Mondays and all. Everybody I know hates Mondays come to that. Our Mum says our old man's like a bear with a sore head of a Monday morning—thank christ he was on early turn. Thought a bit last night about moving out . . . I don't know, I don't feel like doing nothing right now and that's a fact.

Saw John in the car-park before work and he said Dawne was away on Sat. so he'd gone out with this other girl and had her back her place. Christ, it really pisses me off. Spent the whole morning thinking about Tina—well, I didn't see why I should go round to her but that's what I did do in the end. I had to know if it was all over with her or not so I called in her place after work. I'd been shitting bricks all day.

'Oh—hello,' she says.

Well, I didn't reckon on saying nothing like 'Are we still going out together then?' so I said, 'You doing anything tonight?'

'No.'

'Oh.' Then I said, 'Going down The Anchor?' and she says, 'Oh—yeah, more than likely.'

'Oh—sorry about Saturday.'

'All right,' says she, then we looked at each other for a bit.

'Pick you up later then, shall I?'

'OK.'

So that was that. Rushed my tea and got hiccups—still, made Tina and Tracie laugh like it was the funniest thing in the world and she was in a good mood tonight. I just took things easy. Felt her tits again but she wouldn't let me get my hand in and said something like 'Steady on, lover' and I didn't take it no further. I reckon she must have had it before—it stands to reason, don't it? If she's still a virgin, then I'm fucking Mickey Mouse. This is getting nowhere fast though. I've just got to have her soon. Christ, the smell of her and the feel of her great tits in your hands is enough to drive any guy wild I reckon.

Don't ask me why I always get like in a state about girls, I just do and that's that. I keep thinking of that fucking Lynn and how the little cow was seeing that other guy on the side, so I says to her she'd better decide between the two of us and she says oh, that's no problem and the bloody door was right behind me. Girls really piss me off sometimes but you still want them, don't you—I'll bloody say you do, I do at any rate, but it's a fucking nightmare sometimes all right.


4 Dec.          Tuesday

John told us today Dawne's broken off their engagement. Well, I guess that's his own fault for two-timing her but he says he couldn't care less and did I want to buy an engagement ring off of him which at least she give him back even if she did chuck it at him. Anyway, so now he's going out with this Jacquie who's a typist down Dashiel Street. Good luck to him I suppose—I wish I knew how he does it though. I mean he don't look much, our Anna reckons he looks like he's been run over. If you had a quick look at him you'd reckon he was a funny-looking little sod. He's got the chat though, that's what it is I guess, he's always had it.

Bloody spots on my chin—that stuff hasn't done no bleeding good neither. Tina reckons that Acostan stuff is good so I'll get some of that next time I'm in Boots.

5 Dec.    Wednesday

That daft bugger Collins says to me today why hadn't I shaved this morning. So I says to him I was growing a moustache and he pulls a stupid face and says oh, he'd reckoned I'd forgotten to shave.

Thought a bit about Xmas today—suppose I ought to give Tina something. It's all so bloody expensive though. I don't know how to take her sometimes. I mean we're going out, right? Then she pulls that stunt the other day. I just don't know where I stand sometimes. Maybe it'll be better when I've screwed her. Guess I ought to give her something, some of that Musky Nights perfume they advertise on the telly all the time would be all right, Anna's got some of that and it smells OK. Course what I don't want is for me to get Tina something for Xmas then she turns round and hasn't got me nothing—I'd look a right pratt then.

Went down the pub dinnertime—Tina not there though. John's been round to the travel agents to get some holiday brochures cos he reckons him and this Jacquie are going on holiday together next year. He's a bloody fast worker I'll say that for him, but not in the office. Anyway, he reckons he's going to get Jacquie to go to a nudist camp with him this year, then he asks if Tina and me'd like to make up a foursome but I was ready for that one and I said that the sight of him in the nude would put me off my dinner.

Reckon I might get Tina the new Blondie album for Xmas—records are so bloody expensive though and I'm not made of money.

6 Dec.    Thursday

Anna's fashion show last night. We had a re-run all through our breakfast. Our Mum went along but not our Dad—he reckons it's all a load of rubbish—so Mum went and sat next to Dermot, lucky her. 'Up there wiggling her arse about,' says our old man and Mum says that's how models are supposed to walk, it's how they're taught to walk, and she tells him to take more of an interest in what his kids are doing.

Saw him on deliveries this morning looking bloody miserable as usual, but then that's nothing new, is it? 'Remember me?' I said to him and he says, 'No.' I ask you!

Anyway least that disco was good tonight. Quite a few people there were really into the latest disco scene and Tina said why didn't we have a go but it was beyond me. She said all you had to do was just express yourself so I told her she could give a solo demonstration if she wanted to but she didn't. She dances pretty well and the band were OK and all—The Lingams they're called and I know the drummer a bit, he used to be in our scout troop. Wish I could play an instrument. John said his brother's got an electric organ and he reckons it's dead easy but I don't fancy the organ and they're pretty dear, though his is on the HP from Debenhams. Then those bloody squaddies started a fight near the end but they soon got slung out by the bouncers. They're a load of bloody trouble those squaddies, but some of them are real hard and do all this unarmed combat stuff and all that.

Had a good kiss and a feel of Tina on the way back. I give her bum a feel and I wanted to get her jeans off but she wouldn't let me. I said something about why not or something like that, but all she said was not yet so I suppose that's not too bad—I mean it must mean that she's thinking about it, mustn't it, eh? Well, I bloody wish she'd hurry up and say yes, I'm dying for it. This is fucking daft, I'll have forgotten how to do it soon.

7 Dec.      Friday

Well, that's it I reckon. Tina told me tonight she's going up to London for the weekend to see Marilynne. Everything started off OK—we went to the party and we had a pretty good time. We kissed a fair bit and I says to her what are we going to do this Sat. then and she says oh she's sorry but she's going somewhere. Oh ah, says I, where to? Up to London if you must know, says she. Oh, says I—who with? Well, I thought it was another bloke right away. None of yours she tells me, then later I got it out of her she was going up to see their Marilynne.

'Why didn't you tell me sooner?' I says to her.

'Well, I've told you now—if it's any of your business.'

Made me sick—I asked her why didn't I come. Oh, she says, no room and anyway it'd be just girls and all that, wouldn't it?

'What am I supposed to do tomorrow then?'

'How should I know?' she says.

I like that. Well, I didn't know what to say next, then I said, 'I'll give you a ring, shall I?'

'If you feel like it.'

Makes me puke, it really does—the way she was talking it seemed like she couldn't fucking care less, then I suppose I was a bit huffy with her for the rest of the time so she got ratty.

'Have a good time,' I said to her when I left her at her place.

'Oh I will,' she says.

I just sort of kissed her on the cheek and that was that. I mean if she wants to play silly buggers then so can I.

Since I got in I've kept on wondering if it's all over with her. She's not said but I don't know. Have to wait till she gets back now I guess. It was all going so good too. Only the other day she says why don't I get one of those green and white transfers for the car and I'd said I would but I haven't got it yet, and now she goes off to London like that. Well, I keep telling myself she can do what she likes I suppose, but all the same I wish she'd told me about it, the way it was it seemed like she didn't want me to know and if I hadn't asked her then I don't reckon she'd have told me a bloody thing. Well, if there is another bloke then that's it if I want to fuck her or not. I'm just not going through that again, it's not worth it, there are plenty of other girls around and I don't reckon they all go around two-timing guys.

Can't say that I feel like going on with this diary neither.

## 9 Dec.        Sunday

Went out last night. I wasn't going to but I haven't stayed in of a Sat. night for years and I wasn't going to start now, so I said 'Stuff Tina' and went on down The Anchor and I really meant it and all too. Dave King was there and he'd brought along that transfer he'd said he'd get for me—don't look as if I'll be needing it now. Then along come Trev and Kev and we had a swift pint and talked a bit about when we was at school and that time Trev set fire to the stairs—by mistake he reckoned. They said they was going over to Ilminster to this disco at The Laurels and why didn't I come along.

'Ought to be a bit of spare all right,' says Trev so I thought to myself why not, Tina's out enjoying herself in London, so I said I'd go. Course, they wanted me to drive them over—ought to have known it.

'I ain't got no transport right now,' says Trev. 'The buggers took me licence away.'

Yeah, I heard about Trev's case—he'd been doing 70 on his bike down South Road the wrong way and they'd banned him from driving. They'd tried to get him to blow in the bag and all but he was too pissed to stand up let alone blow, then he spewed up in the panda car and he reckons the coppers beat him up for it. Kev's bike was off the road, so like a pratt I said I'd go along. Wish I hadn't now.

Don't know where they get their money from—the dole I suppose—but they were pretty flush. Trev said the people down the Job Centre are a load of right fucking pratts and they're all too worried about their own bloody jobs to worry much about him. They asked him the other day if he could carry heavy weights but he saw through that one and told them he had back trouble on account of coming off his bike a couple of months ago. It's the Social Security people you've got to worry about he says, they're the buggers who go round snooping and checking on you and all that. Kev said he was thinking of getting a job on the oil rigs and he reckoned you could pick up three hundred quid a week and have every other week off. John said he knows a guy who's been in the North Sea—fell off a ship he said.

Anyway, they kept on telling me to go faster on the way over there and when we got there they hop out of the car and they've got a pint down before I'm hardly in the bloody door, then they're off chatting up these girls.

All the girls was lined up waiting for a bloke to come along. I don't know, I didn't feel much like it tonight, I danced with a couple of them but afterwards they just said thank you in that bloody daft way they do and one of them didn't even bother to say that, so come the end I was feeling bloody pissed off and no mistake.

Karla and Nicola the girls were called Kev and Trev were with—nice-looking though. Hell, I'll say they were, specially that Karla, with those nice big tits bursting out of her top and one of them split skirts on which was dead tight across her arse. Christ, I fancied her all right.

'What you staring at?' she says to me straight off and the others laughed so I said, 'Oh—nothing.'

'He hasn't had it for a month,' says Trev and then they all laughed like anything.

There wasn't much I could say after that. 'Well,' says Karla, 'he can't have me,' and then Trev gives her bum a feel for her. Made me puke I can tell you. I told them I had to be going.

'Can you give us a lift, mate?' says Trev. 'Kev's a bit pissed.'

Looked like they all was—wished I was. I felt really out of it, then we had to have all this bloody whispering and giggling about where they all wanted to go, then when we did get in the car they all wanted to go in the back but I wasn't having that lark, and in the end Trev come in front and Kev and the girls went in the back and Karla reaches over in the front and puts her arms round Trev and she tells me to keep me frigging eyes on the road.

I felt really awful, we just went round in bloody circles cos I couldn't get no proper directions out of them where they lived except both of them said they lived on the council estates, then I must have taken one corner too fast after they kept on telling me to go faster and Nicola banged her head on the door—served her fucking right that did.

'Stupid fucking sod,' she goes. 'Ooh, I've hit me bleeding head.'

'Tough,' I said and she starts getting stroppy.

'Ere, watch out, Andy,' says Trev, 'that was the coppers back there.'

I got the wind up good and proper till he starts laughing and tells me it's all a joke and there weren't no coppers after all. Bloody daft thing to say that was and I told him so but all he did was laugh.

So we get to that Nicola's and her and Kev go off round the back and Trev went for a piss up against this lamp-post, that made Karla die of laughing and she tickles my ear and says, 'Cheer up, mate— soon be Xmas.'

'Yeah,' I said. 'Great.'

'Yeah. What's your name anyhow?'

'Andy—Andy Baker.'

'Oh! Andy Pandy!' Then she starts giggling. Christ, I really wanted her like crazy but what could I do?

Ten minutes later Kev and Nicola come back and he falls over the dustbin, this window opens and somebody shouts out, 'What's all the fucking noise about down there? Is that you, our Nicola?'

Course all she does is giggle and say no. Daft little cow.

Same thing at Karla's house. Her and Trev went off and Kev went to sleep in the back. They were gone so long, in the end I got out and went in and called out that I wanted to go, and there's Trev trying to screw Karla up against the wall, he's got her skirt pulled up and kept saying, 'I can't find the door, I can't find the bloody door,' and her top was up and I could see her tits sticking out.

'Fucking hell, mate,' he says, 'can't you piss off for a minute? I'm busy.' And she's looking right at me and she says, 'Perhaps he wants to watch?'

'Not bloody likely,' I said quick and I just had to go back to the car and wait. Bloody nerve, jammy fucking bastard.

Awful drive back too—I went too fast and even Kev woke up once and said, 'Slow down, mate, I don't wanna die before Xmas,' then he belches and goes back to sleep.

And that weren't all. It was gone three when I did get back after helping Trev to unload Kev and then dropping him off, then I had to go and scrape my fucking car on the lamp-post outside of our place. There was this MGB parked up a bit—Anna and Dermot of course, it had to be. They come back to see if I was all right.

'No harm done, I hope,' said Dermot in that voice of his like he's chewing a Mars bar.

'Oh no,' I told him, 'I'll buy a new lamp-post in the morning.' And he grins at me.

'He's drunk,' says Anna looking down her nose. Suppose I was. But I'll say this much for that Dermot, at least he offered to help me inside, but I said I could manage on me own.

Well, that was yesterday and today's not much better neither. Woke up in a cold sweat and remembered that scratch on my car. It's not too bad I suppose, I'll just have to see Dave King about it. More fucking expense—I'll be bankrupt soon at this rate. Then our Dad starts in on me.

'Were you drunk last night, Andrew?' he goes. I keep on telling them to call me Andy like everybody else does but they never listen.

'Dunno,' I said, which was about true.

'Scratched your bloody car I see—that'll cost you a pretty penny.'

'Oh dear,' says Mum, 'you ought to be more careful. After all, what about your job? What would they say at work about your getting drunk?'

'He'll just have to learn the hard way, that's all,' says my old man.

I didn't answer. In fact I stopped listening.

'You listening?' he says to us.

'You what?'

'I said you listening to me?'

'Nope,' I said, then I walked off. Straight, I can't take much more of this.

'Little buggers,' he says to our Mum, 'walk off when you're speaking to 'em now they do.'

Pisses you off it does—well, he does. Our Mum's OK, she fusses like some old hen, but him—well, just lately he's got really bad, he *always* knows best he does. You can't tell him nothing.

Then our bog got blocked—what a fuss that was. He didn't want to get Dyno-rod out—too expensive he said, mean bugger. So he had a go at it himself, poking these old chimney rods down the manhole. Well, he's like the bloody Incredible Hulk when it comes to DIY, but he won't leave it alone. I don't know why, he just thinks he can do all these jobs and he never can. Our Mum says she lives in fear of what he's going to bugger up next only she don't put it like that.

Anyway, course he got the rods stuck. There he was, the original nine-stone weakling heaving on these fucking rods like he was Superman, then crack! over he goes—shit on his hands and grass on his arse. We was all killing ourselves—me and Anna that is, our Mum said she couldn't bear to watch him. In the end we got Dyno-rod out. He'd cracked the drain, brought the whole lot in he had. They had to dig it up, and best of all was them wanting paying on the spot—forty quid! And him with only a tenner on him and them not wanting to take a cheque, but they had to in the end. So now we got this huge great hole in the lawn and the smell of shit everywhere. And I'm pissed off—suppose Tina's coming back tonight. Can't say I care much. Well, I suppose I do, it just pisses me off, that's all. Don't know if I ought to ring her or not, she hasn't rung me. I'm just all mixed up today—shitting spots again, it's worry I reckon. I keep thinking about that Karla last night. Christ, was she something . . . Then I keep thinking about Tina—I want it so much it hurts. One thing's for sure, I'm going to get everything sorted out with Tina tomorrow, and that's a fact. I mean I'm not going to hang on forever, am I? No, stuff that for a lark. Right. If that fat little bitch is messing me about then I'll chuck her. Sod it, that's what I say.

## 10 Dec.    Monday

Saw Tina after work. She wasn't in the pub dinnertime but there's that Janette and she looks up and says was I looking for Tina? I said not specially, then she says that Tina didn't come to work today due to her being sick. I didn't know what to do then, but if she was ill I didn't want it getting back to her that I knew about it but I hadn't gone round, and she'd be bound to tell her, just what she would do that is. So I got round there and Mrs Butler shouts up the stairs for Tina and I reckoned she must be in bed or something but then she comes down in her clothes and she looks fine to me.

'Oh—hello,' she says to me and I reckoned to myself here we go then.

'They said at work that you was ill.'

'Oh that!' she laughs. 'I was just too tired to go in, that's all.'

Well, I didn't know what to say.

'You wasn't worried?'

'Oh—well, I only wondered, you know . . . Have a nice time?'

'Oh, it was great, yeah.'

'Oh. Good'

'Well, thanks for coming round,' she says and I'm waiting there like a pratt for her to tell me to piss off.

'Sure. No trouble.'

We stood looking at each other, then I looked at the wall.

'Doing anything tonight?'

'Oh, I'm too tired,' she says and I reckon well, that's it then, old son.

'Doing anything tomorrow night?' I said to her then, just to see where we stood.

'No—I don't think so,' she says like she's got loads of offers.

'Shall us go down The Anchor then?'

'OK then.'

So that's that. I don't know—she didn't seem that friendly or something. I wanted to kiss her but I didn't. Have to see how it goes I reckon.

Wondered what she was doing tonight. She wasn't down The Anchor anyway.

Apart from that nothing happened today—except for Kev coming round to see us at the office that is. Bloody nerve he's got.

'Bit of a laugh Saturday,' he says.

'Yeah.'

'You not going over Ilminster way tonight are you, mate?' he says bold as brass.

'Sorry.'

'Oh—then you couldn't run Trev and I over could 'e?'

I'd like to run him over all right. I told him no way and all he did was to keep going on about those girls and how he reckoned that Nicola was the best fuck he'd had for a twelve month, then when he's gone old Collins come in and tells me not to let people in off the street 'just for a chat'. Typical. Tried to find Dave King to see about my car but no luck.


11 Dec.        Tuesday

Saw Tina tonight, she's got herself a pair of those new skin-tight jeans, shiny purple ones—she looks like she was poured into them.

'Do you like them?' she asks me. 'Everybody's getting them.'

I said yeah they were great, but if you ask me I reckon she's a bit too big around the hips and bum to wear them that tight, course I didn't say so to her. They make her big arse stick out like anything.

We went on down The Anchor and loads of people had a good stare at Tina's arse, I guess I ought to have known. She pretended not to notice but girls always do, don't they? I reckon she loved it, I could tell, and there's John having a good old look and all. Well, he'd better not try it on, that's all.

We met a few people down there and they all said, 'Ooh! I like your jeans, Tina', and she does her little smile and says, 'Oh yeah—I got them in London', and then she can go on about what she done up there and all about her Marilynne and how this super bloke she's living with is some sort of company director or other and is really nice, so then I said, 'Still working in the Wimpy, is she?' and Tina looked daggers at me and says as a matter of fact Marilynne's hoping to break into modelling soon. With her knockers she could break into the Bank of England, no sweat.

We didn't have a bad time tonight though. We got a bit pissed and then she reckoned she couldn't get into the car so she asks me to help her and I messed around a bit and had a good old feel of that bum of hers—christ, that felt good, just like a huge melon it was. I tell you, I could have pulled them off her right there and I could feel my prick starting to come up—'Here!' she says. 'What you playing at back there?' So I says to her oh, I'm just testing the fit of her jeans for her. Then I asked her what she wanted for Xmas and so she giggles and says, 'What have you got to give me?' I kicked myself afterwards because John or somebody would have come out with some clever answer like 'Six inches' or something like that, but I didn't know what to say and I just said, 'What do you want?' and she looks right at me and starts giggling. It was a laugh I guess but that's all it was—I didn't come no nearer to having her. I suppose she could be shy. That's the way I look at it anyhow, I don't reckon she's a prick teaser—I keep thinking she might be, but if she is then that's it. I'll finish with her if she don't let me have it soon. It's just a waste of time else, isn't it?

John asks me today if I'd heard about Kev and Trev. I said heard what and he said they got picked up by the police last night on Trev's bike out on the Ilminster road. They'd chased them for a couple of miles at 80, sirens going and all, but couldn't risk stopping them, then they'd come off the bike near Hatch and gone in a hedge. Trev's got a busted leg but Kev's just bruised. Course they was pissed and John reckons they'll get sent to prison more than likely the pair of them. Well, I don't like laughing at other blokes' bad luck but I couldn't help saying as how I reckoned they had it coming. John said he'd done

80 round there and how you had to really watch it though because it was a bad corner and it served them right.

Got hold of Dave King. He said he could do the car for me no trouble for about twenty-five quid as a special favour to me like, which is good on him I reckon cos I don't know him all that well. Seeing him meant I was late back for work after dinner and caught a packet from Collins. I don't know what gets into him sometimes but he can get really ratty.

'It's irresponsibility, Andrew,' he says to us. 'If you're to get on, you'll have to guard against it, you know.'

Still, it was gone three—Dave talks and talks and talks. He said he'd heard Kev had a busted collarbone but Trev wasn't hurt.

## 12 Dec.    Wednesday

Thought some more about last night. I reckoned that maybe Tina's a bit shy. John always says that women are funny when it comes to lights out time. I just can't think what she's scared of. Christ, I really hope she's not a prick teaser. If that's the case I'll have to do something about it pretty quick or else I'm just wasting my fucking time. I like her though and I want her—and she must like me or else she wouldn't go out with me then, would she? No, nobody's forcing her to go out with me, are they? One thing's for sure, I'll have to work this thing out before too long or else I'll go up the bloody wall.

Put up that transfer but then I had to leave the car with Dave—he said it'd take at least till Friday.

## 13 Dec.    Thursday

Had to walk to work today—bloody freezing morning too it was. Got there a bit late but no sign of Collins, thank christ. Still, soon be Xmas—have to make up my mind what to get Tina I suppose.

Saw Dave dinnertime. He said he hadn't had time to do the car yet so I told him to get a move on, but you don't like to keep on at people too much when they're doing you a favour, do you? Somebody in the pub said Kev and Trev had busted arms but were OK apart from that. Anyway, we'll see in the paper tomorrow.

## 14 Dec.    Friday

Cold again today—somebody said something about snow. The paper said Trev had a busted rib and bruising and Kev was only scratched, they're both out now but the bike's a write-off.

Dinnertime—my bloody car still not ready, I knew what it'd be. Dave said he'd do his best to have it ready for us by tonight but it weren't of course, he said the paint was still wet. The transfer's come off but he said he'll put another one on for me at no extra cost. So then I had to go round to Tina's on me way home to tell her.

'I've split me new jeans,' she says to me soon as she comes to the door.

'Oh—sorry.'

'Right up the back.'

She reckons they must have had something wrong with them, but if you ask me they was just too tight for her. She says she's lost the price ticket so she can't take them back, then when I tell her why I'd come she just rolled her eyes and went off in one of those not-speaking moods.

'Well, that's it—we just can't go, that's all,' she says.

'Nik's got a car, hasn't he?'

'You said you'd drive—he likes to have a drink.'

'Well, so do I—and I can't drive if I've no car, can I?'

'Huh!' she says, then starts to ring up Tara.

'Andy's gone and done something to his car,' she tells her.

'I have not,' I said.

'Oh shut up,' said Tina to me and then she went on talking to Tara.

'Oh gawd!' says Tara—I could hear that much. In the end she said she'd get Nik to use his car.

'Keeps it in a glass case, does he?' says I but Tina don't say nothing. Then she tells me Nik'd pick us up at her place so I better dash home and rush my tea and then dash back again. I said why couldn't they pick me up at my place but Tina said that'd be too far out of the way. Made me puke, I felt like not going after that, don't ask me why I bothered. As it turned out it wasn't too bad though because Anna's Dermot give us a lift. When he got to our place she wasn't ready as usual and he'd left his lighter at home so he said he'd go back for it and he asked me if I wanted a lift, then I got to Tina's place early after all that and she wasn't ready and I had to wait in the front room and her Mum and Dad was having a row in the kitchen.

The party wasn't too bad I guess, and I had a bit more to drink than if I was driving when I try not to have more than five or six pints or so, but I reckon I drive better when I've had a few anyway.

Course Tara was going on about being a personal secretary to this estate agent and that—going on, I'll bloody say she did, even Tina was getting pissed off with it. Straight, I can't stand stuck-up people, they just get on my nerves.

When we got back I decided to see how far I could get with her. I was feeling really merry so when we're kissing I has a go at unzipping her skirt.

'Not in the bloody street,' she says.

'Let's go inside then,' says I quick as a flash.

'It's the wrong time of the month. Anyway, me Mum and Dad are up.'

'When's the right time of the bloody month then?' says I and she gives a little smile and says, 'Wait and see.'

'Come on, Tina, you know what I want.'

'Oh yeah, I do—but you ain't getting it tonight.'

Shit—it fair makes me puke. I feel like puking anyway, I reckon I must have drunk too much. My bloody head's spinning—and I could swear that bleeding wardrobe's moving.

## 15 Dec.       Saturday

Made up my mind to have it out with Tina tonight, really level with her. Keep thinking of the tits on her . . .

'Tina,' I says to her.

'Yeah?'

Well, that was it, I didn't know what to say. We just kissed a bit, that's all. She's got a really great mouth. Makes me puke.

## 16th Dec.       Sunday

Must do something about Tina's Xmas present tomorrow—reckon I'll get her the Blondie album after all. Going to see *Quadrophenia* tomorrow. I haven't been to the pictures in quite a while—not at their prices. My moustache is really good now—my old man reckons it isn't but balls to him. It's a sight better than his is. Tina said it tickled a bit.

## 17 Dec.       Monday

Course, I'd gone out and got that Blondie album at dinnertime to give her for Xmas, then when we were talking about the film and the music and all she just happened to say she'd just bought the same album, didn't she? No idea what to give her now—reckon I'll have to change the LP for another one and give that to Anna and then get some perfume for Tina.

Anna wants to know what we're going to give our old man, had a laugh with her about that set of screwdrivers we give him last year. She said why not get him a pair of handcuffs or an Incredible Hulk T-shirt.

18 Dec.        Tuesday

My bloody car still not ready—it'll be a week soon. Every day he says, 'It's coming on. Leave it with me.' What can you say? I'm getting really pissed off with all this walking to work. I caught the bus a couple of times but I hate buses and you have to wait hours. Wish I still had my bike but I sold it when I got the car. Only got thirty quid for it too, and it was a bloody good one and all with drop handlebars and a derailleur.

Knocked off after dinner and went on round to The Griffon with John to have a look at the Xmas decorations. He's finished with Jacquie now and he's got off with this girl called Stephany who works for the DHSS and he says she's a right little cracker.

Our office party tonight. Last year we had that sword swallower from Creech who didn't go down too well, so this year we had a couple of strippers from Bridgwater called Sharron and Anjella, housewives they are and they're really something. Saw everybody there having a good eyeful, Collins and all. Anjella comes down into the audience and asks old Mr Brooks to unclip her bra for her. Everybody roared and poor old Brooksie's sitting there with hands shaking like a leaf and nearly choking on his Castella, then she gives him a little kiss on his bald head and bounces up and down in front of him—right in front of his nose . . . Man, what tits she had on her though! Good job he didn't have his cigar in his mouth at the time. Anyway, John goes and sings out, 'Brandy for Mr Brooks! Large brandy wanted for Mr Brooks here!' Honestly, it was the best laugh of the year I reckon, we was all killing ourselves. Then Stephany said she reckoned she could do as well as those two any day and I reckon she'd have showed us only she had an abortion last month and she didn't think it'd be good for her. I could fancy her myself. Got a lift back with John. How he missed that guy on the Parade I don't know.

19 Dec.        Wednesday

Felt a bit sick this morning. Anna went to Dermot's office do tonight which was a dress-up dinner at some posh hotel with him in a dicky-bow and her in a long dress. She was full of herself because some colleague of his said to him he reckoned she looked like Debbie Harry, likely story. Then there's the post office Xmas do tomorrow—Anna said they have mailbags on the table instead of tablecloths and our old man tells her not to be so stuck up. Nice one!

Got some of that Nubile perfume in Boots for Tina and changed the Blondie album for the new Lene Lovich for Anna. I can't stand buying perfume. Take today—there's the perfume counter with all those girls with loads of make-up and the long red nails and little badges with their names—Miss So-and-So and so on. Course I go up hoping to have a quiet look on my own and that one come over and says, 'Can I help you?' Then when I'd picked one out she asks me if I want to smell the bloody stuff so I just stuck the bottle up my nose, but she smiled like they do and said, 'No, not like that,' and puts some on her arm and makes for me to smell her, so I just took a quick sniff of her and said, 'I'll take it.' Then she said, 'Are you sure?' so I said, 'Yes thanks—that's fine,' then I couldn't find enough money and almost had to go away and get some more, but I found a quid in another pocket. I felt a right pratt and there's all these other Miss Whatsits pretending not to see me. When I got back to the office John said, 'Oh, you shouldn't let that worry you, mate—just kiss their hands like I always does.' Yeah, yeah.

Tonight was Tina's office party, which was good but not so good as last night. No strippers, only a comedian from Cothay who was quite good I suppose. Didn't get nowhere tonight neither. I'm getting fucking sick of this. She just giggled and said 'Get off!' in that daft voice. It's not every guy who'd stand for it I reckon.


20 Dec.      Thursday

Last full day at work today. I'm pissed off. I want Tina so bad it's making me ill. If she won't let me soon then I'll finish with her I reckon.


21 Dec.      Friday

The office shut down after dinner—met a few mates in the pub. They said Kev and Trev were up for trial on about a dozen charges—no licence, no MOT, no insurance, drunk, dangerous driving, ignoring warning to stop, ignoring traffic lights, speeding, damage to litter bin

and hedge, foul language to the police, and so on and so on and so on
. . . John reckons they'll get ten years.

After the pubs shut went around town with Tina and John and
Stephany and some other people. Went to a party tonight. There was
that band from Pitminster called The Groins. No luck with Tina,
pissed off again. I'll have to stop this diary. Wanting Tina so much is
making me really depressed, really think I'll stop this diary now.


22 Dec.          Saturday

Forget it—magic! MAGIC! Well, I wasn't waiting no longer—'What
about it then?' I says to Tina.

'What about what?'

Right, let your fingers do the talking I reckoned.

'Hey,' she goes. 'Ooh!'

Man, she's got some tits on her but I didn't have no time to waste on
them, I had the horn so bad I reckoned my zip was about to burst, me
and all.

'I ought to call you Handy Andy,' she says and her voice is all husky
and sexy so she's really turned on by now and I can't get her knickers
off quick enough.

'Careful! Don't rip them,' she says. I just stuck my tongue down
her throat and my hand up between her legs. Magic! She shifts her
bum around a bit and her legs open up nice and sweet and she grunts
when I stuff a finger into her.

'Oh christ, Tina!' I says and she's good and wet down there, really
juicy, she's taking little bites out of my neck and she's digging her
nails into my back. Well, I work her up a bit more, then it's out with
my stiff prick and straight in and she grunts and groans as I put it up
her, she grabs hold of my arse and she comes up to meet me—and it's a
good hard screwing. You can't beat it, when I come off it felt like I was
dying, it was that good. Magic!

I can't sleep for thinking about it, how good it was and all, just the
greatest thing in the whole world I reckon. Funny thing, screwing
always makes me feel hungry, so while she's getting her knickers back
on I asks her if she fancies a takeaway.

'If you're paying,' she says.

'It's on me'—and I give her nipples a little rub for good luck.
Magic!

23 Dec.    Sunday

Tina's going to relations tomorrow so I nipped round after dinner to give her the perfume. Everything's different today—I'm on top of the world. I wasn't going to stand no more of that nonsense. If she hadn't let me have her last night I reckon I'd have broken it off.

'It was good last night,' I said to her because I wanted to let her know how good it was.

'What?'

'You know . . .' As if she didn't!

'Oh—that. Yeah—great.'

'What you think I meant then?'

So I give her a little hug—well, a big hug really. Man, she's really something.

'Magic,' I says to her and she makes that little noise, really turned me on. Well, that's women for you!

Give her the perfume and she give me one of those gold chain necklaces. I thought about getting one of those for myself so I was really pleased with it. Then I kissed her again when I left and I told her she had a beautiful body. I just whispered it to her softly like and she smiled and says, 'Thanks love.' Magic!

'What are you so cheerful about?' says our Mum when we was having our tea.

'Oh, nothing,' I said to her.

'Oh—thought you might have got your car back.'

Well, I'd forgotten all about that so I phoned Dave up right then and told him to bring the car back. He said it wasn't ready but I was waiting for that shit, so I told him I didn't want to wait another year and if he didn't bloody well bring it round I'd have a word to say to his boss. Anyhow, he brought it round an hour later, the door's mended but not painted, so I told him I'd pay when the job was done and he started getting a bit stroppy. In the end I give him a fiver just to get shot of him.

24 Dec.    Monday
Xmas Eve

Anna had another do tonight so she spent the afternoon plucking her eyebrows and shaving her legs, then she had a long bath in that green stuff she always puts in. Bit bored tonight so I went down The Anchor and met John and Stephany for a few drinks. John tells me I'm looking pleased with myself so I just said, 'It's Xmas, isn't it, mate?'

Then he says, 'Tina giving it to you regular, is she?' so I told him, 'Regular as clockwork, John,' and he grinned. He reckons he knows all there is to know about sex, he goes on a bit but he can't help it.

Wish I could have seen Tina, I really want her again. It was so good I just can't stop thinking about it.


25 Dec.       Tuesday
Xmas Day

Everybody up earlier today—don't ask me why, all we do then is sit around waiting for the dinner to cook and watching the telly and that's a drag and all.

Got a record token from our Mum and Dad, some of that Grope aftershave from Anna. Dad got Mum some perfume which she likes and she got him a sweater and some Manikins. Anna got a bracelet from them and the record from me and Dermot give her a shawl for evenings made out of some special wool. She give him a clock worked by water—at least that's what she said, I'll believe it when I see it. Then me and her got a 50p postal order from Auntie Beattie in Hull who nobody's ever seen since 1969 and she's sent us 50p for Xmas ever since we was born and hasn't never kept up with inflation. Me and Anna got our old man a Boots gift voucher in the end and our Mum a thing for making yogurt which was Anna's bright idea and she got it down Debenhams I think it was. She likes yogurt. Cost enough anyhow.

First to get here was our Nan and Auntie Beryl, then Auntie Dorothy and Uncle Stan and the twins Ingrid and Mari giggling all the time. 'We like your moustache, Andy,' they say and then Auntie Dor says, 'Ooh! Don't it make him look grown up!' Anna took the twins up to her room to show them some stuff and they came down with their faces all made up. Then Uncle Les and Auntie Kath turned up. Lucky their Wayne couldn't come—I remember when we was kids he was a right pain in the arse, keeping on all the fucking time about what good marks he got at school and what did I get for this and what did I get for that, and his Mum and Dad used to keep on all the time about how he was going to go to university but he never did, then they kept saying as how he'd decided not to but work his way up in the office instead which was far more sensible anyway. To hear them talk you'd reckon he ran that place where he works. 'I'm in insurance,' he goes round telling everybody. He's a right loudmouth. I remember that time we were twelve and I hit him in his big gob—shut him up for all of ten minutes that did, then he said he'd get the police on me.

'We told him you'd be disappointed, but what can you do?' says Auntie Kath. That's right—they wouldn't tell him nothing because they reckon the sun shines out of his arse.

'Oh, I like your moustache, Andrew,' says Auntie Kath, 'it's a bit like our Wayne's.' Christ!

Uncle Stan asks me 'How's work?' just like he always used to say 'How's school?' and our Mum leans over and says, 'He's doing very well, Stan'—just like I was a bloody kid or something. Then Les starts sounding off about how well their Wayne's doing and I switched off. You have to hand it to Anna though—Auntie Kath says to her, 'Your young man works in an office, doesn't he, Anna?' and Anna looks at her and says, 'He's an architect, actually!' That shut her up.

And there's Mum fussing about all the time and asking everybody if they've got enough to eat. Well, that's a mistake for a start because the people in our family'll eat for a pastime. You put it in front of them they'll bloody eat, including Nan, and they like a drink and all. Still, no point in being miserable all the time, that's what I always say.

Anna kept on about us having to have paper serviettes and Auntie Kath says she got some lovely ones down Boots the other day with hunting scenes all over. Then we all thought Nan was dead—we couldn't get her to wake up after tea and I could see what everybody was thinking and Auntie Beryl says 'Oh Gawd' and our old man tells her to shut it and starts slapping Nan's face. Then she wakes up and asks him what the bloody hell does he think he's doing? 'You was asleep, Nan,' he says and she looks at him and says, 'Course I was bloody asleep—till you started hitting me. You all look as if you'd seen a ghost.'

Come eleven o'clock and Dad was eyeing the clock. Come midnight and them still here he looks in the fire and says, 'Well, everybody, that's the end of Xmas for another year then,' but still they didn't budge. I fell asleep and dreamed of Tina. In the end they went at half twelve and took Nan and Auntie Beryl with them, after finishing the lager. Some drag.

26 Dec.          Wednesday
Boxing Day

Got up early to ring Tina. Everybody else still in bed so I went out and had a look at my car. Looks like Dave hadn't done such a good job as I'd thought. I don't know. Ten o'clock and still nobody about—I couldn't wait no longer to ring Tina but I reckoned she must be out because it rang and rang for ages, then her old man says, 'Who the hell's this?'

'Is Tina there, please?' I said and he snaps, 'Who's this?' so I said 'Andy,' then he says, 'What's the bleeding idea ringing and waking buggers up this bloody time for?' Then he took ages to get Tina and I thought he must have gone back to sleep, but then he comes back and said she's in bed and told him to tell me to ring back later. So I rang back at half twelve.

'Hello, love,' I said to her.

'Oh,' she says, 'what do you want?'

'Can I see you?' I asked her and she says, 'I can't today—sorry.'

'Why's that?'

'I just can't,' she says.

I wanted to know what she was doing so I just said, 'You going out then, are you?'

'Yeah—something like that.'

Right, stuff this for a lark I reckoned, so I just said, 'It was great the other day.'

'Oh—yeah. Look, I can't talk now—ring me tomorrow.'

And that was that. I ask you! She didn't say nothing to me about going out.

Went down the pub and saw lots of people but they were all with other people and they asked me where Tina was and so on and in the end I wished I'd stayed home. It pisses me off.


27 Dec.      Thursday

No holiday for our old man today—he was bound to be in a good mood so I didn't bother getting up for breakfast. Didn't bother to ring Tina neither—I thought about it some more last night and reckoned I was fed up with her blowing hot and cold so I thought maybe I'd let her stew for a day or two, then she won't think I'm running around after her all the time which I'm not in any case. Afterwards reckoned I ought to have rung her and kept on meaning to but then it was too late.

Went down The Crown and got pissed. John had a bottle of some foreign liqueur which was pretty strong stuff. He said it was six times as strong as a double scotch and we was all well away come the end of the night and I'd cheered up a lot. I thought to myself well, I've had Tina now and I want her again, but if she wants to play silly buggers then that's OK by me and I can afford to wait, sooner she realises that the better. Drove the wrong way down Billet Street on the way back. Must have made a bit of a row when I come in too because our Dad come out to the top of the stairs and shouts, 'What's all that bloody noise about?' but I was ready for him so I said, 'Go to sleep, matey, or the post office'll grind to a halt!' Then he comes charging downstairs with Mum following on, saying he was going to clip me round the head if I didn't learn some manners.

'You're pissed again,' he says but I didn't answer him. I just stared at the daft bugger and went on to bed.


28 Dec.        Friday

Our old man waiting to bawl me out when I got down today.

'This has got to stop,' he says. 'You're just bloody irresponsible.'

'What has?' I said to him.

'What? Don't you backanswer me, young man.' Yap, yap, yap—he's all wind that bloke, and there's Mum with her hassled look on and Anna with her nose in the air. I just said, 'What's for breakfast?' and he says, 'Breakfast? It's bloody dinnertime!'

'Must have overslept,' I said.

'You're a bloody little fool,' he says. 'When are you going to grow up?'

Straight, I can't stand much more of this, they're really getting on my tits at this present moment in time.

'Don't you walk out when I'm talking to you!' he shouts but I didn't wait around, no way.

Looking in on Tina this afternoon—well, I reckoned she'd waited long enough. Soon as she opens the door she says, 'Why didn't you ring us yesterday?' so I just played it cool and said, 'Oh, I didn't have the time. I had to go out.'

'Huh! You had time to go down The Crown all night.'

'How do you hear that?'

Mind you, talking behind people's backs is a bloody national sport in this town. Then we just looked at each other for a bit. I could see she was put out. I reckon I could have blown it there and then if I'd kept on at her so I said, 'There's a party tonight.'

'I know—I told *you* about it.'

Then we looked at each other again.

'Right—we going then?'

'Where?'

'To the party.'

'I'll think about it.'

'Sorry about yesterday.' Don't know why I had to go and say that, it made it look as if I'd been in the wrong. Ought to have kept my big mouth shut.

'All right,' she says.

Still, I reckon she got the message—she could see I wasn't taking just any old shit.

Had a good time too, she was good fun tonight. No chance for a fuck at the party but we almost had it off in the car—had a good old feel anyhow. Reckoned it was maybe best not to seem too interested, but to tell the truth I was so near to coming I don't know how I stopped myself. She's got really big tits on her. Maybe she'd have gone the whole way but I didn't want to balls it up so we left it at that. Pisses me off a bit. We fixed to see each other tomorrow so that's OK. Reckon maybe I should have given it to her tonight. Still, it won't hurt her to wait a bit.

## 29 Dec.    Saturday

Had Tina again tonight—that's a relief. Looked like it was going to be a bad day to start with though—had a row with my old man breakfast time. He started his old when I was your age stuff again so I threatened to clear out. 'Good riddance!' says he. 'Bloody kids, you wouldn't last five minutes without your mother to feed you and do your washing.'

'That's all you know then.'

'Oh, do stop it, you two,' says our Mum in the end. I don't know how she puts up with him—and he's been worse lately. Might be the drains like Anna said. The guy next door asked if we'd had some manure delivered but our Dad knows better than to shout at him because he's a karate expert. Anna keeps using those spray things everywhere but they don't seem to work, more's the pity.

Anyway, had a really great time with Tina tonight. When me and her gets back I starts fooling around with her and having a good finger when all of a sudden she puts her hands up her skirt and starts fiddling about. Well, I reckoned she was trying to make me stop so I said to her, 'What you doing?' and she just says. 'Getting me bloody knickers off of course—what's it look like?' Just like that. Well, I'll say I didn't need to be told where to take it from there . . .

'Allow me,' I says.

She was really ready for it and all—and she wasn't the only one neither! She's got a really nice cunt on her, just how I like them, it's no fun if the girl's so tight you have to be a bloody acrobat to get it in.

'Easy baby,' I said—and I didn't keep her waiting none. I really give it to her—and she's that good too, it's really great with her. Then afterwards when we're getting our breath back she says, 'We can't go on like this,' and I said getting the wind up, 'Like what?' and she says, 'Well . . . without using nothing. I don't want to get a bun in the oven, do I? I'll have to get some pills.'

'Right,' I said. So that's that all nicely taken care of, no trouble. I'll go to sleep happy tonight, with sweet dreams and all.

Come to think of it, I don't know what I was so worried about. Well, I wasn't never that worried I reckon. Sometimes girls can be funny, can't they? You got to know how to handle them. Still, everything's nicely sorted out now. Her getting the pill—well, that's doing it properly. I'm not that keen on the old balloons and she isn't neither and her suggesting it—that's a nice surprise, it shows she's done some thinking about it all, don't it? It just goes to show that you can never be sure of what people are thinking in their heads half the time. With her on the pill, everything's fine. I've got no more worries, have I? No, sweet dreams for me tonight . . . Wish I hadn't ate so much though, hope I'm not going to puke.


30 Dec.        Sunday

New Year's Eve tomorrow. We're going to the office party, hope it's as good as last year's. Nothing much doing today—didn't see Tina but I thought about her a fair bit. Feeling great today. Nice weather—they reckon it'll last for a few weeks.

Uncle Ken and Auntie Audrey 'just looked in', as they always say, this afternoon—bang on bloody teatime as usual, no wonder he's seventeen stone and she's not far behind. Our old man was all for pretending we was out.

'Ooh—funny smell,' says Auntie Audrey.

'Yeah,' says our Dad, 'it's the drains, Audge.'

'You want to watch you don't get the council round after you, leaving your drains open like that,' says Ken. 'Health hazard that is, I shouldn't wonder.'

So then we had the story all over again, our old man's side of it that is, and when they've gone he says to Mum, 'I'll get on to that drain tomorrow.'

'You won't, Brian,' she says.

'No,' says Anna, 'don't want the whole street down with typhoid, do we?' And then she does a sweet little smile and sticks a bottle of scent up her nose.

'Bugger ate all the ham.'

'Well, Ken's a big man,' says Mum to him.

'Greedy if you ask me—you don't get to be that size else. Like an elephant he is.'

'Must cost a lot to feed,' says Mum.

'What—elephants?' says I for a laugh but they wasn't listening. I give up. It's a drag. Went to bed early and played some albums.

31st Dec.          Monday

New Year's Eve

Bit of snow this a.m. Saw John and a few mates for a drink dinnertime—it's nice to have a drink with just men every so often. I really like Xmas—pity John didn't have another bottle of that booze. Got home half three and went to sleep. My old man looks all serious and says, 'I'm getting really worried about your drinking, son,' but I went on to sleep. Tonight him and our Mum went to some do. Funny thing about him—well, not so funny really—is when he's had a few he gets even more gloomy. Me, I just get happy. There's nothing wrong with being happy, is there?

Happy tonight—or rather last night cos I'm writing this today or is it tomorrow? Anyway, the party was really great—lots of booze and good music and with Tina I felt great. Sometimes she can be a bit flighty and she can be moody but tonight she was just great to be with. Magic!

1 Jan.          Tuesday

New Year—snow all over the bleeding place when I got up, must have been four foot deep.

'Here, it's been snowing,' I said.

'Give the boy a medal,' says our old man.

'Happy New Year to you too, mate.'

'You what?'

I guess he's uptight cos he's got to work tomorrow—I'd like to see the bugger try and ride his bike in this lot.

'Grab a shovel,' he says.

'Who—me? What for?'

'You can give us an hand to clear the front.'

'No thanks, I'm trying to give 'em up, thanks all the same.'
Course that sets him off.
'You could have helped,' says Mum when he's gone out.
'Turn it up, I'd sooner watch him.'
Anyway, then we have him and Mr Sims from over the road seeing who can clear his path first—no contest.
'You done a good job there, Bri,' says our Mum, glad he hadn't bust nothing.
'Ah—showed him a thing or two,' he says rubbing his back. He reckons it's disc trouble because of riding his bike. Anna reckons he's hypocaustic.
'Right, I'll just put me shovel away, then we can have our dinner,' he says looking pleased with himself for a change, so he goes out the back door and next thing we know there's this horrible yell—the silly bugger'd gone and fallen down the drain.
'Whatever have you done, Brian?' says Mum looking all worried.
'Fucking drain!' he's shouting and he's banging his shovel on the ground like he'd gone off his head.
'What's he having a fit about now?' calls Anna down the stairs.
'He's fell in the drain,' I said to her.
'Oh my Gawd,' she says and goes back to washing her hair.
He had snow all over and reckoned he had shit on his feet, twisted his ankle as well he said.
'I hope the neighbours didn't hear all that swearing,' says our Mum.
'Fuck the neighbours—I broken me leg.'
'After you worked so hard too. Shall I call the doctor?' but he reckons they're overpaid and says he doesn't like to encourage them.
Heard later on the news the town was cut off for a bit. Phoned Tina—she's pissed off like me, her Mum and Dad was having a row.
Our Dad went to bed early with Mum fussing about after him and then she took him up some of that hot lemon stuff but he said he didn't like it.

2 Jan.    Wednesday

Rang up work but they said it was shut till next week—extra holiday, I like snow. Then Sims comes round looking for help in clearing the road cos the council are only going to do the main roads.
'What do we pay bloody rates for?' says our old man. 'They want to get some of they bloody unemployed to do it.'

So there we were. 'If you don't help you don't get no dinner,' he says to me.

'Your shovel's in the shed,' says Anna.

Then we get back in and Mum says there's been a power cut so the bleeding dinner's not cooked.

Dermot come round tonight, he'd borrowed a Range Rover and put chains on the wheels. He would. So Anna got all dressed up in her fur coat and off they went. Loaned my old man's wellingtons after making sure there was no shit on them and went down the pub. No one there except that tramp in the corner and after a bit I got pissed off, what with him trying to cadge fags all the time and telling me about how he got beaten up by the Salvation Army because he told them he don't believe in God, and I come on home. I don't like drinking on my own and I was buggered if I was going to buy him one. Really pissed off not seeing Tina—said I'd go round tomorrow. It's a drag.


3 Jan.       Thursday

Still no sign of the council near us. My old man walked into work and they spent the whole day playing pontoon out the back but he wouldn't play for money. Got round to Tina's. She's got a bloody cold now—flu she said. She was in bed so I tried to join her but she said she was feeling too ill and she'd ring me. I guess she did look a bit rough. Fucking snow!


4 Jan.       Friday

Snow melting a bit. They say the council cleared some roads but not ours. Course that Mr Luckes of No. 32 tried to go out in his car but he skidded down near the bridge and went into somebody's hedge. Postmen having to walk everywhere on foot—my old man pissed off. My car battery's flat. Balls.

Tina still ill—rang her today. Christ, I really need a screw.


5 Jan.       Saturday

Tina still ill. Went down the pub tonight, saw John and me and him chucked snowballs at that tramp.

'Gerroff, you little bleeders!' he shouts. 'It's wet!'

'Piss off or we'll throw in some soap!' says John.

That shifted him . . .

Pissed off today. Got Gerry to charge my battery for us.

## 6 Jan.    Sunday

I hate Sundays. We was all looking forward to a good dinner, then the fucking power went off again.

Anna went out with Dermot in the Range Rover again tonight—she says he's thinking of buying it. Yeah, yeah.

## 7 Jan.    Monday

Reckoned I might stay off sick today but I'd only get bored. Got in about ten and not many people there.

'Did you have a nice Xmas, Andrew?' says Collins and I reckoned he'd been drinking but he couldn't have been that time in the morning. Nothing to do so he said tidy the files which took about five minutes.

John says he's going to move into a flat soon with this Katya and then he'll give a party. Right now he says things at home are bad on account of his old man having fallen in love with one of his Mum's best friends, so his Mum's cleared out.

Went on home at half three, nothing else to do.

## 8 Jan. Tuesday

Heating broke down at work—that union bloke Douglas come round and told us all to go home because it was too cold to work and it weren't allowed. Nobody argued with that. Anyway, on account of the heating still being busted we all went off home again and I called in at Tina's on the way back. Only her and her little sister in the house so I thought to myself, 'Hello! Here we go then,' specially when she says she's feeling better but her cold's gone down on her chest. 'Let's have a look then' I says to her and I was just getting her tits out when her bloody sister barges in.

'Oh, sorry!' she says and goes out giggling her head off.

'You'd best go,' says Tina. 'Our Mum'll be back soon. She's only nipped out for some of her pills.'

That giggling Tracie let me out and says, 'If you give us a fiver then I won't tell our old lady what you and Tina been doing up in her room.'

'Get stuffed.'

'If I were to tell our Dad he'd just about kill you.'

Little bitch. I reckon she was joking but Tina told me once when their Marilynne had a guy up in her room with her then Tracie somehow got hold of the bloke's jeans and hung them up out on the line. Anyway, I didn't give her the money, have to hope she don't say nothing—Tina's old man's got an awful temper.

Didn't go out tonight. No point. Pissed off.


9 Jan.      Wednesday

Tina better today though her voice is a bit husky—very sexy I told her. Went down The Anchor but she was still feeling a bit ill so she went easy on the vodkas. Asked her when she was getting the pill and she said she'd be going to see the doctor next week. Reckon I can leave it to her now. Really wanted it tonight but she said we ought to wait. I said I'd get a johnny but she reckoned it wasn't the same and I agreed in the end.

Not much snow left. Heard that Kev and Trev come up in court next Monday.


10 Jan.      Thursday

Flat battery *again*. Rang up Gerry and he said it most likely needs another charge. Asked him how come and it turned out that all he'd done the first time was to stick it on a four hour booster charge instead of trickle charging it which was what it really needed. That's the bloody last time I get *him* to do anything. In the end I loaned a charger off of Steve Wright but all this made me late for work again and I ended up getting a bollocking from old Collins. He said if I was late again this week it would be a very serious matter. I told him about the car but he just sticks his face in mine and snapped, 'We don't pay you to have your bike repaired in our time.' I could swear he'd had a few. Then he said, 'I would have thought better of you, Andrew.' That pissed me off—I've always got on pretty well with him before.

Tina's better, thank christ. Snow almost gone, you'd never know we'd had none at all. Our bloody drain still not repaired though—our old man moaning as usual but he cheered up a bit when he found out Sims has got a chill from being out in the snow.

11 Jan.     Friday

Got to work early. No one there. Heating on the blink again—
Douglas reckons if it goes on then it could mean a strike.

Anna not ready when Dermot come round tonight—as usual—and
our Dad couldn't clear out quick enough so he had to talk to him.

'Are you pressing ahead with automated sorting procedures, Mr
Baker?' he asks and our old man looks vacant. 'Ah,' he says after a bit.

'Will it increase productivity though? Or merely replace man with
machine?'

'Should do,' says Dad.

Then Mum asked, 'Are you designing anything nice at the
moment, Dermot?' and he starts to give us all a lecture on something
or other—don't ask me what. Should have called him in when our
Dad was doing his front wall, couldn't have turned out no worse
anyway—when the first one he put up fell down he swore blind it was a
hit-and-run driver, then the one we got now, you'd reckon you was
going up a hill till you see it's higher one end . . .

'We've got the drains up at the moment,' says Mum.

'Oh really? I don't really do much with drains, Mrs Baker.' He
wouldn't.

Went to a good party tonight anyway. Plenty to drink. Douglas says
next year we ought to be able to have three New Year's parties at least.
Saw Collins and his wife. John says she's having it off with the guy
next door, that's why he's been hitting the bottle. John reckons he's
pissed as a newt by half seven every night.

Tina told me Tracie's been dropping hints to their Mum and Dad
about when I come round last time but she belted her round the head.
That's the way to treat her. That's the trouble with living with
parents—no privacy.

John says him and Katya are going to look at some flats next week.

Got home at three o'clock.


12 Jan.     Saturday

Went down The Anchor tonight—and who should walk in but Trev
and Kev! Out on bail and not a mark on them.

'Fucking coppers,' says Trev, 'they'd never have caught us if the
bike had been OK.' Then he tells us all about being in the cells and
Kev says how he tried to escape but they caught him nipping out of a
window. Kev says he reckons they'll get probation again because the
judge is a soft old bugger. Then somebody asked about the break-in

down at Boots the other day and Trev said, 'Ask no questions, tell no lies,' and he rubs his finger on the side of his nose. Kev says if anyone wants any cosmetics and stuff like that on the cheap then he could put them in touch. Trev's got engaged to Karla, the jammy bastard.

'Think they're somebody, don't 'em?' says John when they'd gone, but he wouldn't say it to their faces because he likes to keep in with them. Then he told us all that joke about this couple of poofs and a cucumber which made everybody die. John says his cousin Neal got picked up by a queer when he was a kid and it turned his mind and he's been like it ever since, poor sod. He reckons they ought to castrate poofs at birth.

Got home at 12.45. Wrong time of the month Tina said. 'It's true,' she says so I reckoned play it cool, mate—we cuddled a bit and I held her close. I reckon I've got a really good thing going with Tina, no sweat. Everything's fine, just fine.


14 Jan.      Monday

Anna says she's got some more modelling to do next week. All the people studying fashion at the Tech and so on there have shows of what they've dreamed up a couple of times a year and course she's got in on it. Don't ask me how her typing's coming on—she says Dermot could get her a job in his office any time she likes. Maybe he don't write many letters. Anyway, so we had to have all this fashion stuff right through breakfast again. I sat there yawning so Anna says not looking at me, 'Do you think he's trying to say something?' in that voice.

'Why don't you grow up?' I says to her. 'And get a job.'

I don't reckon she's ever going to get a job. Course she says she's going to be a model, or an air-hostess—yeah, yeah. Anyway, she's got these huge purple patches under her eyes and our old man looks up and says, 'Dermot been blacking your eyes for you then, has he?' so she snapped something at him, then he lost his cool. People always turn and look at our Anna when she goes by, course she loves it or else she'd never do it. We told her to go in for Carnival Queen next time round but she said only little tarts went in for that and last year they only had five entries anyway and one of them was aged thirty and had four kids so it'd be no contest. Yeah, yeah.

Big row at work when I got in. Somebody had stuck an empty whisky bottle on Collins' desk and they'd put 'Fill 'er up, missus' on the label.

'Do you know anything about this, Andrew?' he says to me as soon as I open the door. He's all red in the face and his breath smells something awful.

'About what?'

'About this, you—' he says, poking the bottle under my nose.

Well, I didn't know what he was on about, did I? We had a talk about it in The Grapes in the dinner hour and John reckoned maybe it was one of Collins' empty ones he'd forgotten about and he wrote on it to remind himself to get some more in. Anyway, he spent the whole day in his room and wouldn't answer the phone or see nobody, then when it was time to go home he wouldn't say goodnight to nobody. He just walks past me—well, if he wants to play silly buggers . . .

When I got home Mum said I couldn't go in the sitting-room because Anna was just slipping into some of her fashion show stuff, then our old man was in one of his moods because he'd been out on deliveries and got chased by this dog he reckoned was as big as a donkey. When we all laughed he got even more stroppy. He can't take a joke, that's his trouble.

15 Jan.        Tuesday

Collins still in a huff today—he's made so much fuss about that whisky bottle that the Dept Head is looking into it. Collins just glares at everybody and says nothing. Course nobody's admitted doing it so the Dept Head reckons it must have been the cleaners. Douglas said Collins better not start making allegations or else the union could become involved. Barry was outside the door when Mr Collins was seeing the Dept Head and Collins was keeping on that the bottle ought to be dusted for fingerprints. John reckons Collins' wife is going to leave him soon.

Saw Tina tonight. She's going to see the doctor tomorrow and get the pill. Don't want to be fussed buying johnnies all the time, though I guess I could get them from the machine in the bogs down at The Volunteer. Somebody's put 'This chewing gum tastes awful' on the machine in felt-tip! I can't wait much longer.

16 Jan.        Wednesday

When we was all having our coffee break Collins comes in and says, 'All right, I'm going up to the police station now so if anybody wants to own up now it'll save everyone a lot of bother.' We was all too surprised to say a thing and just looked at him so he says, 'Right then,' and goes out and slams the door! 'He's so pissed he can hardly stand up let alone find the police station,' says John. He reckons Mr Collins is going to crack up soon. He come back after dinner and spent the whole afternoon in his room and Frann didn't know what to make of it because when she collected his dictaphone tape to type up all that was on it was a load of queer noises and once him saying 'Bloody woodworm—making all that noise,' least that's what it sounded like. She let us all have a listen to it but nobody could make the noises out, but John reckoned old Collins was having a wank. Frann says Collins doesn't half look odd at her sometimes so she tries never to turn her back on him and Samantha said she reckoned that Collins looks like some murderer she's seen on the telly.

Barry said the Head of the Dept had been telling Collins to pull himself together and Collins kept saying, 'They're all against me, they're out to get me, the bastards.'

Got home. The builders hadn't shown up and Dad was hopping mad so I was glad to get out a bit early. My windscreen transfer off again. Bought a can of spray paint on the way home to do my car door with. I reckon I could do it as well as anybody and at half the price and all. It's got a coat of primer on it so it ought to be all right.

Tina great tonight—she was really dying for it. So was I—I'll say I was. The doctor give her the pills so she had one with her tea, then we had it off in the car in a lay-by out Henlade. Best yet . . . She's getting better all the time. I wanted her to take everything off but she said what if anybody come along and anyway it was too cold. She's got really good tits on her, she likes them rolled around while she's being screwed so's her nipples get really stiff. She said afterwards she really enjoyed it tonight. So did I. I've never felt so good with a girl. She said it's fine now she's got the pill because she was a bit worried before in case she got put up the spout. Well, I can understand that all right but I reckon she was maybe a bit shy and all. I'm sure glad we've got it sorted out anyway.

Had a good laugh and all. Tina's a big girl and she gets cramp sometimes—tonight she yelled out which put me off my stroke but then we just had a good giggle about it and carried on where we left off. She said it wouldn't happen if I had her from the back and that'd be better for touching her boobs as well. Me, I like it from the front but I'll try anything once. Magic!

Got home around one.

17 Jan.          Thursday

Met John in the car-park this morning. 'You're looking bloody cheerful these days, mate,' he says to me. 'Sex life OK, is it then?'

Well, some guys mightn't like that sort of crack but John's a good mate of mine so I told him things were pretty good between Tina and me right now.

'On the pill yet?' he says.

'Oh yeah—course, long time.'

'You're all right then,' he says and we had a good laugh about it, man to man. He's going out with this Dianna right now so I asks him what she was like in bed. He would have told me pretty soon anyhow.

'Cracking—loves it,' he says.

She's a pretty good looker, that Dianna, John got her on the rebound from this guy she's been living with who's a chef down the Castle Hotel. Then John and me had a good talk about technique, course I don't really think he's done all the things he reckons he has but there we are.

'You ought to get your own place,' he says and told me him and Dianna are going to look at a flat next week if she can get the time off.

'It'd be good having your own place,' I said.

'That's right—get Tina to go in with you.'

That's a good idea, it'd be great I reckon.

When I got home Anna's gone off early so our Mum's going on about that Doormat again.

'Wonder if our Anna and Dermot will get married?' she says while we was having our tea and Dad nearly choked on his sausage.

'Well, he's a very nice respectable boy—so well bred.'

'Only wants her for one thing,' says Dad and our Mum snaps at him and tells him not to be so vulgar.

'What's he want with her then?'

'Maybe they're in love,' says I.

'I do hope so,' says Mum and puts that soppy look on her face again. Wedding of the year that'll be, if it ever comes off.

18 Jan.          Friday

Didn't see Tina tonight so I had a think about me and her. Well, I've been going out with her for quite a long time now and it seems sort of natural. Anyway, I feel OK with her and now we've got our sex life sorted out it's really good all round. I really like her and I reckon she likes me and all. Funny thing was, tonight I wondered what it'd be like to get married to Tina . . . I don't know why, I was just wondering, that's all. I wouldn't mind living with her, it'd be good I reckon. Don't think I can stand it here much longer anyhow.


19 Jan.        Saturday

Me and Tina had a row tonight. She was in a funny mood and I was pissed off with my car door. I'm not very good at DIY, I must get that from my old man I guess, it always looks easier than it is. First go, I got paint all over the front tyre. Then our Dad comes out and says, 'Not like that,' which is just the sort of bloody daft thing he would say. It's always harder to do something when somebody's looking at you—specially when it's him. 'You're making a right balls-up of that,' he says next.

'Oh yeah? Why don't you stick to drains?'

That got him mad and he went in and I got on with the job. Took me about two hours but it don't look right. It looks OK till you get up close and you can see all these ripples and bumps in the paint. Then I opened the door and found that some of it had somehow got in on the fucking seat. It really pisses me off. Then Steve Wright come along and said he reckoned it'd be better to get a new door. He had his wife with him—she's really lovely, great pair of tits on her, not as big as Tina's though.

Really pissed off about my car—and the bleeding MOT's due soon and all. Anyway, went out to a party with Tina tonight and I bloody well wish now I hadn't.

'What you done to your door?' she says to me as soon as I picked her up.

'Painted it of course—what's it bloody look like?'

Well, I was still mad and the last thing I wanted right then was daft bloody remarks like that.

'I can see that.'

'Well, then.'

She didn't hardly say a word to me on the way there—just to make me feel stupid I guess that was, so I carried on as if she wasn't there. I suppose I was meant to say I was sorry and all that but you know what it's like, I didn't see why I should, she'd been just as snappy with me.

'What's eating you?' she asks me later so I said, 'I could ask *you* that.' She didn't answer me. Don't ask me why she gets these moods—even with a few drinks inside of her she wasn't much better. It was terrible really, like we were bloody strangers or something. We danced around a bit but I just felt pissed off and she had that look on her face all the time. Then she starts talking to these people I didn't know and I was just standing around like a pratt. Christ, I was mad with her. Then she was huffy all the way home—and no sex neither. I wanted it really badly tonight and all. I stuck my hand up and she says, 'Leave off, leave me alone.'

'Look,' I said to her, 'what's wrong with you tonight?' but she wouldn't answer. So that's that. Reckon it's all over with Tina—bugger it. And for another thing, writing it all down don't make it no better neither, it just makes it worse. I don't reckon it's my fault anyway. I said I'd ring her but I don't know if I'll bother to or not. I keep on wondering if maybe it's another guy. I'll fucking kill her if it is.

### 20 Jan.        Sunday

Can't be bothered to put nothing down for today, I'm too pissed off with everything.

### 21 Jan.        Monday

John told me him and Dianna have split up and he's gone back to Jacquie and Dianna's gone back to live with her chef. I told him I reckoned me and Tina was most likely splitting and that was a mistake and all.

'You wanna get somebody else quick,' he says to me. 'Don't let the grass grow under your balls, mate.'

'Show her who's boss,' he said. Well, that's John for you and if it's over it's over but I just want her to be a bit more reasonable, that's all. I don't know. To tell the truth, I didn't know if to ring her today or not—as it was I met her in the pub. She was a bit cold and somehow I just couldn't ask her what she was doing tonight. I said I'd ring her and she said OK. I don't know, hope to christ it's not all over. Makes me puke—everything was just great too.

### 22 Jan.        Tuesday

Saw Tina again dinnertime today and all she says to us is just 'Hello,' then she said she had to go and meet somebody. Wonder if it's another guy? John said he'd seen her in the record shop with a few people but he couldn't see who she was with and nobody else had seen her. So I don't know if it's another guy or not and it's fucking well driving me spare not knowing. Wonder what I'm supposed to have done? Huh! What *I've* done—that's a good one, I don't reckon I've done nothing. She can be a real little bitch when she wants to be, sticking her nose in the air like that really makes me mad. Reckon I ought to chuck her and that's a fact. But somehow I don't want to. All I want . . . well, all I want is for her not to get into these daft fucking moods of hers and then everything'll be OK.

Course John says to me, 'Who cares? There's plenty more to choose from.' Then he said there's a party tomorrow night and there should be plenty of spare so why didn't I come along and let Tina stew in her own gravy for a night or two. I told him *I'd* decide what I did about Tina. I didn't get stroppy with him or nothing, I just told him straight and I reckon he could see I wasn't kidding. Sometimes he gets on your nerves, that's all.

Anyhow, tonight I thought a bit about what he said and I wasn't too keen, but now I reckon I will. Why not? He reckoned that Sharron Rendall from Education fancies me and she might be there . . . Her old man's got this baker's shop—John said you'd be all right for doughnuts if nothing else and I had to laugh. Should have rung Tina today—all day I kept telling myself 'Ring her tonight' but I didn't. Shit. I can't make her out sometimes.

23 Jan.        Wednesday

Bloody fuss at breakfast. Mum says she reckons I'm looking miserable and then Anna pipes up and says, 'Oh, that's because he's split up with his Tina again.' I give her a good talking to but all she said was 'See what I mean?' and rolls her bleeding eyes.

The builders come today—about ten of them so I heard. The drain's fixed but they haven't half made a mess of the back lawn—looks like a field. Our Dad was hopping wild as you'd expect, he only done that lawn last year.

'Look at my fucking lawn!' he shouts and our Mum tells him to be quiet because the neighbours might hear him. They really make me puke with their stupid little problems all the time. Anyhow, fact is I saw Tina tonight.

I went on early and there's Sharron and she's on her own for about twenty minutes so I went right on up to her and asked her to dance, but here's let-down number one because she says she's waiting for her boyfriend. So I just said, 'Suit yourself,' she says, 'I will,' and I went off, not having no time to waste. Let-down number two happens when Tina turns up with a couple of her mates. Soon as she sees me she looks the other way and starts giggling away with her friends like she's having the time of her life, so I went up to the first girl I could find and asks her to dance. Turns out she's nothing to write home about but I wasn't fussed. I could see Tina looking out of the corner of her eye so I tried to get real friendly with this girl and when there's a chance I put my arm around her and grabbed myself a slice of arse. Course she turns out to be some stuck-up bitch who says to me, 'What the bloody hell do you think you're doing, you animal'and she pushes me away so I'm left in the middle of the room like a pratt on me own. And course all the time I could see Tina was looking, then making out she wasn't, and giggling and that with her friends. I felt a right fucking pratt. I suppose I was meant to go over but I didn't—I saw John and Jacquie so I went to talk to them but I kept my eye on Tina without letting her see. I wanted to know if she was meeting a bloke or not but she just stayed talking with her friends at the side and hanging round like girls do, when these two guys come up and ask her friends to dance so there she is all on her own trying not to look spare. I pretended not to notice but she just looked at me and then looked away so I started to laugh at one of John's jokes, that one about the cucumber again. 'Well,' says John all of a sudden, 'can't stand round all night', and off he goes to dance with Jacquie so this leaves me on my own on one side and Tina on her own on the other, but I was buggered if I was going to go over. She looked over once or twice but I didn't do nothing, just looked back. I guess this went on for about an hour or so—anyhow, we found ourselves a bit nearer and I don't suppose we could help talking. But I wasn't going to speak first, then we started at the same time so it was all right. 'Nice party,' we said and she said 'Yes' and I said 'Yes'.

'Yeah,' I said. 'Want to dance then?'

'Might as well.'

'Suit yourself,' I said, not standing no more shit off of her.

'Come on then,' she said and goes off.

So that was that. Guess you could say Tina and me are back together again. I didn't say nothing about Saturday and she didn't neither. We started kissing away like nothing had happened and it was all so good it didn't seem to matter. We were both pretty stoned come the end and I felt a bit rough, so I knew I wouldn't be able to get the horn if I wanted to and I sure as hell wanted to so we kissed a bit, that's all. Can't remember much else—think I said I'd come round or something, anyway there we are.

I reckon she'll be a bit more sensible from now on now she's seen I won't take just any old shit.


24 Jan.    Thursday

Woke up feeling really awful—couldn't go to work, no way. Our old man said it was 'Bloody disgraceful, kid your age' and Mum looked sad. 'Shall I get the doctor, Andrew?' she said but I just said I'd stay in bed. They don't know nothing about it. About twelve phoned up work and John told us Tina'd been looking for me and he told her I'd run off to South America with Arlene Cridge. Told him to get stuffed and to tell her that I was ill and I'd get back to her, then he phoned again after dinner to say he'd told Tina and she said she'd look round tonight. Christ, I feel really bad.

Got up teatime but not very hungry. I've never had an hangover like this before, I feel as if I've been run over and when Tina come round I found out why. She said some daft cunt had been putting some stuff into the drinks last night and two other people had gone down sick as well. She said it was supposed to be some aphrodisiac from Hong Kong but instead it just made people ill.

She let us feel her tits but I wasn't up to it. If I ever get hold of the bugger who spiked my drink I'll kill him.

'Hope you've learned your lesson,' says our old man. I felt like killing him and all. As it was, I couldn't be fussed.

Reckon I'll have tomorrow off as well—it's hardly worth going back on a Friday and like Tina said it's not every day you're poisoned, is it?


25 Jan.    Friday

Well, here I was in bed feeling better but I was pissed off, till I had this great idea. I had the horn and I started thinking of Tina . . . Now if Tina could come round while our Mum was out shopping . . . well! There's an idea—had me feeling even better. Rang Tina up at work, got told she's home ill. Had me worried—she was all right yesterday—so I give her a ring home. My lucky day—she just felt like a day off and she said she'd come round when our Mum was gone out. Nice one . . . Our Mum out, Tina in—magic!

'Nice room,' she says.

'Bed's nice and all.'

'Looks it.'

We just stood there a bit and she has that little smile on her face, then she sits on the bed and looks at us.

'Christ, Tina—I don't half want you.'

I'll fucking say I did.

'What you waiting for then?'

Well, I jump on board quick as a flash just as she's getting up, but I needn't have worried cos she's just slipping her jeans off.

'You didn't half look funny,' she says, 'just like jumping in the pool.'

'The water's lovely,' I said and reached out for a nice big handful. Magic!

She's all tit and bum that girl. I knew her tits was big but somehow you just got to see them in daylight, ginormous they are.

'Come on,' she says and her voice is all low and sexy. Anyway then I just stripped off and let her have a good eyeful, and there's her lying on the bed with her tits all over and me getting the horn—magic!

Anyway, all that waiting and looking couldn't last for ever—in fact it didn't last no more than about ten seconds I reckon—and we just sort of fell on the bed with me grabbing for her tits and her hand going down between my legs straight off. Then it was on the job, her on her back with her legs in the air and me giving her six of the best right up. I tell you it was bloody lovely, really great.

'Here,' she laughs, 'you been in bed with girls before then?'

'Ask no questions, tell no lies,' I said giving it to her hot and strong.

'Ooh!' she goes. 'I can take plenty of that!'

Well, she got plenty and she loved every minute of it. Fantastic! You can't beat women I reckon. Then after we just lay there thinking of how good it was and looking forward to the next time.

'How long before you're ready?' says Tina touching me up gentle like.

'Don't know,' says me feeling all sort of relaxed. 'Pretty soon I reckon.' Then I heard the front door.

'Christ!' I says. 'It's our Mum come back!'

So that was the end of the afternoon for us, more's the pity. We went on down to say hello to our Mum and have a cup of tea. I reckon we got our clothes on in record time—magic!

26 Jan.        Saturday

Went to the disco down the Shire Hotel, saw Anna and Dermot in the bar—she had on one of her long dresses and her new shawl because

Dermot was taking her on to some fancy place or other. Our old man asks her if she's going to Buckingham Palace but she didn't answer him.

Had a good time tonight. We bopped around a bit—it's better when I've had a few. Great time. Bit of a fight when that punk starts in on this squaddie then two of his mates pitched in—could have got really nasty but Big Dez wades into them, grabs one in each hand and lifts them clean off the floor! That little punk says he'll get Dez for that so Dez just sticks his huge fist under this guy's nose and says, 'Yeah? You wanna try?' Course soon as they're outside they start all over again but that's their affair and in the end the police turned up and broke it all up. John says last Thurs. there was a gang fight in the High Street, mods v. punks, just like years ago when the mods and the rockers used to go in the park every Saturday night after closing time and rip up the flowers and then each other. There was about twenty on each side last Thursday and it took I don't know how many coppers to handle it. Two of the mods got pieces taken out of their legs by the police dogs and all.

Tina reckons I ought to get an ear pierced so's I can wear an earring, they're really fashionable right now. She says she's thinking of getting hers done—there's a woman in a place down by the market who does it for a quid or two.

Didn't have her tonight. I didn't push it, I reckon I don't want to come on too heavy with her all the time, just let her go at her own speed. Really good with Tina right now.

27 Jan.    Sunday

Sunday again—it always seems to be bloody Sunday in this house and they're always a drag, specially when Nan and Auntie Beryl come over. They got here and straight off you could tell they'd been having a row, most likely about who's going to have the house when Nan dies. Then she goes to sleep and Beryl tells our old man how she reckons they ought to stick her in a home. I come on up here and played some albums. Talked to Anna for a bit, she said she was pissed off with Dermot on account of him not wanting to get his ears pierced. She reckons if I have mine done then I ought to get it done properly or you can get christ knows what and go deaf. Then we went down for our tea and Auntie Beryl was off again. She never used to go on like it—I remember the time she said something to Gramps and he looks at her in front of everybody and says, 'It's bloody bad enough having you in the same house, Beryl, let alone having to listen to you.' And she starts crying and says 'Oh, Dada!' and goes off and locks herself in her room. Hard old bugger he was, we kids were always scared stiff of him and our Dad says the old man made his life a misery when he was a kid.

We had one of those turkey rolls left over from Xmas, so Nan keeps on wanting to know where the bones have gone to.

'There aren't any, you old—' says Beryl.

'How can you have a sodding bird without bones?' Nan says.

28 Jan.     Monday

Really pissed off with that transfer on my windscreen this morning—it falls off every time you shut the fucking door—so I got some of that Superglue from Boots and did it in the dinner hour. Seems to have worked OK and it looks pretty good. Then Tina's going to learn to drive she says dinnertime and like a berk I had to go and offer her a few lessons, didn't I? Not sure if my nerves can stand it . . . She says her old man give her a lesson once back in the summer but he only blows his stack before she's got it in gear. I know somebody like that. I remember our Dad's lessons—great they were, all two of them, then he jacked it in for good and I had to fork out for proper ones from a driving school. Course it was a family outing, him in the front shouting and Mum and Anna in the back saying things like 'You almost had that bloke on the bike' and stuff like that. I ask you . . .

Went down The Railway tonight for a change, bit of a dump but the beer's cheap.

29 Jan.     Tuesday

Bloody transfer down again. I don't know . . . John reckons you can't stick things like that with that Superglue anyhow. For over a quid a little tube I reckon it bloody well ought to stick anything. He told us that story about the woman and the bus seat all over again, then he said the same thing happened to a woman in the public bogs.

Collins in today for a change, heard him singing in his office after dinner, then he comes out and starts asking me about some job I was doing two months ago—I couldn't make head nor tail of what he was going on about and his breath was like a fucking flame-thrower. John says his wife's gone off with somebody else, not the guy next door after all cos he's gone back to his wife, but the bloke across the street.

Collins' new secretary Madeline says she went in with his post but that he was asleep and she didn't like to disturb him cos he looked so peaceful. Everybody's talking about Collins these days and every time he comes along they all clam up and look embarrassed so I reckon he must know something. John reckons he could be a schizophrenic in which case he could be locked up if he's not careful—he saw this programme all about it on the telly and the way Collins looks at you sometimes he's a dead ringer for some of the loonies in the programme.

30 Jan.    Wednesday

Suppose we'll have to put up with the fashion show all through breakfast tomorrow. Worst of all, Tina said she wouldn't mind going but I put my foot down and she got huffy. I'm not paying two quid just to watch our Anna poncing about and that's straight.

She's had her hair done twice this week instead of once and she's got it in these strings all over, so our old man tells her she looked like a gyppo and she told him where to go and the quickest way to get there.

Saw John down The Anchor tonight and he told us all about Kev and Trev's trial. Found guilty of course, not much doubt about that from the start. They said not guilty so their lawyer refused to go on because he told them they had to say guilty. The judge give them a right bollocking about it and sent the pair of them down and fined them and banned them for five years, which he reckoned was letting them off light, so then Trev pipes up and calls him a silly old cunt and gets another talking-to and told to shut it or else he'll be had for contempt in the court. Then all Trev's relations starts shouting out that the police are victimising them and the judge tells them not to talk so fucking daft and orders everybody to get out of the room or else they'll be sent down and all. Mind you, Trev's family are a pretty rough lot and they say what his old man don't know about locks just isn't worth knowing. Kev's old lady and his sisters Britt and Jayne wasn't so noisy and they just cried all the way through. The judge said he'd never seen nothing like it. Still, like John said it'll make the roads round here a bloody sight safer for the next five years.

31 Jan.    Thursday

The weather forecast for today said we might be in for some more snow. Had fashion for breakfast. I didn't listen much but looks like it went off OK and Anna was clapped like anything. She says her photo's going to be in the paper tomorrow because the photographer was there and he promised her. Our Mum's gone and ordered three copies. Bloody cold today—enough to freeze your outlying areas as the bloke on the radio said. Hard to get the car started, bloody battery must be on the blink again. Collins in today but he didn't come back after dinner and Judi said she saw him in his car and he was sleeping like a baby with his thumb in his mouth.

1 Feb.    Friday

Those papers Mum ordered didn't arrive so she sent our Dad down to the newsagents. He didn't want to go but she said he wouldn't get his breakfast if he didn't go and why didn't he take more interest in what his children were doing in life. Then when he got back Anna's picture wasn't there—not on her own but just in a group and she was at the edge and you could hardly see her. It didn't give names neither, just said 'Students of the Technical College flashing their fashion flair for February' or something like that. Anna was pissed off—this other girl was right in the middle with her dress pulled up and giving a huge smile and Anna said that was Tessa Spearing and she was a right pain and everybody hated her because she was always pushing in where she wasn't bloody wanted.

'Who's going to pay for all these bloody papers then?' asks the old man, so Mum had to fork out. Mean cunt!

Trev and Kev got their names in all right though. He read it and said, 'Bloody little hooligans,' and he's in favour of bringing back corporal punishment and hanging, he reckons there ought to be a referendum about it and he knows which way he'd vote and no mistake about that. 'I'd pull the switch,' he says and I bet he fucking would and all.

Then Anna says she's thinking of becoming a fruiterer. Course nobody knew what she was on about so she said it meant eating just fruit all the time and Dad says, 'Not in this bloody house you don't. Think you're a bloody monkey?' and our Mum says she'd be on the bog all day. So Anna says, 'It doesn't have to be in this house,' and he says, 'Huh! Moving into the zoo, are you?' and she said, 'No need—I already live in one,' then they had a row. Surprise, surprise. Christ, it's becoming really boring. I went on to work to get out of it.

Wanted to have it off with Tina tonight but she said she didn't feel like it, so I tried to get her in the mood by touching her up—she always gets feeling randy when you work her tits a bit—but she wasn't having none. And neither was I, more's the fucking pity. I was talking to John about sex today, well, he's always on about it—anyway, he reckoned five or six times a week was about right which puts me and Tina way behind. Some guys John says, and I've heard this and all, only need it about once a week which don't seem much to me but there we are. He says men want it more than women unless they're nymphos so sometimes you got to go without, just make sure it's good every time then maybe they'll want it a bit more—unless you can get a bit on the side. Anyway, I can't complain that Tina don't like it, thank christ, so I guess there's no real problem. But I reckon any guy whose woman only lets him have it once a week is on to a bad scene and really ought to put his foot down.

2 Feb.      Saturday

Weekend at last. The weather forecast reckons it'll be an early spring.
    Had it away with Tina tonight, which made up for last night. She's a right little cracker when she gets going. I remember I used to really fancy slim girls but I reckon it's better when they've got a bit of meat on them. It's just great getting hold of Tina's jugs—she says they're forty inches and I believe her. I had a skinful and when we passed our usual lay-by Tina says, 'Aren't we stopping tonight?' So I pulled up quick and we shot back, so there we are . . . Course in the summer I reckon we can get out and go into the field—I must get hold of an old blanket or something to put in the car for when the fine weather comes. Be prepared, like we used to say in the scouts when the guides come along.
    It was a bit short tonight. I took a long time getting the horn and then it didn't last long, we tried it with Tina bent over the seat with her arse up in the air but it kept slipping out so it was a bit of a letdown and I couldn't keep my knees on the seat. Still, she got what she was after and I'm not a one to say no. I don't reckon any bloke is, come to that. I felt a lot better after, must have cleared my head. Had a scare when she grabbed hold the handbrake though! Magic!

3 Feb.      Sunday

Tina in a huff with me today. I'd said I'd take her for a driving lesson up on that old airfield, but when I went out to the car after dinner to go over and pick her up the bloody thing's dead. Tried to borrow my old man's car but he wouldn't lend it me, the mean bugger.

'That's that out then,' says Tina with that look on her face. I told her I was sorry but she didn't want to know—anybody'd think I done it on purpose the way she went on.

'We can go for a walk,' I said.

'What—in this weather? Not bloody likely.'

'What about your old man's car?'

'He wouldn't let you use it.'

So that was that. She went in and I had to come home. Feeling pretty pissed off tonight. When Tina's in a bad mood, she's really in a bad mood. She ought to get together with my old man.

Spent the afternoon ringing up any of my mates who could loan me a battery-charger, in the end I managed to get one off Alun Chant and put the bloody thing on charge. Had one hell of a job getting the nuts undone to add to it, then up pops our Dad and says, 'And who's paying for all these calls then?'

Well, by then I'd had just about all I could take of today so I said to him, 'You are, arsehole' and walked off.

When I got upstairs he's got his voice back and he starts shouting and that gets our Mum out and she's ratty cos she's been in there listening to her Jim Reeves records and crying her fucking eyes out. I just ignored him—I reckon that's the best way.

Teatime he starts off again so I took mine over by the telly. Nothing on, only a lot of old religious programmes and buggers singing hymns. Pissed off today and no mistake.

## 4 Feb.       Monday

That sodding transfer fell off again this morning so I ripped it up. Got to work to see Collins being carried out—he was pissed and fell down the stairs. Serves him right. So now Singleton's taken over for the time being and he spent the whole day going round shifting everything about and putting everybody's backs up, he's even moved into Mr Collins' office and they say there was enough booze in the filing cabinet to last a normal guy a fortnight and Singleton took a couple of bottles home with him. John says Collins has gone out Tone Vale to be dried out—long spin and short rinse he reckons. Kari's organising a collection for Collins—John says they better get him a Peter Dominic's gift voucher and she laughed and tells him not to be so cruel, and cos he fancies her he put in 20p and calls us a mean cunt for only putting in 5p.

Saw Tina at dinnertime. She seemed in a good mood and as there weren't many people around in the pub we did some shopping. Bought a couple of albums in the record shop, then Tina looks at me and says she's got to go down to Marks & Sparks to get herself some new knickers. I went along of course but I soon wished I hadn't because she kept on holding up these pairs of knickers and asking me if I liked them, there was a load of people in there and all.

'What's wrong?' she said. 'I want your advice.'

'I just don't like lingering around the lingerie counter, that's all,' I said, which I reckoned was pretty good but she didn't get it and all she said was 'What don't you like about it?' Then she says, 'Do you fancy pink?'

'Are you going to buy anything or not, Tina?' I says to her.

'All right, all right—you're fast enough getting them off.'

There was this old bloke stood behind us having a good laugh so I just said to her that I had to buy some socks and I'd meet her outside, so off I went. I could have belted her . . . And that old bloke too. Then when we met up in the street she says, 'Don't you want to see what ones I bought then?' and starts taking them out of the bag.

'I'll see them tonight—on you,' I said and she just says, 'You'll be fucking lucky, mate' and giggles. That's the last time I go shopping with her. Tonight I said to her, 'Got your new knickers on then?' and she says, 'Don't be so crude.'

I reckon I'm going to have to take a firm hand to her. Sometimes I wonder where it's all going to end, silly little cow.


5 Feb.          Tuesday

Bit of a giggle at work anyway today—John tries to get off with Kari but she's not having any, is she . . . He gives her all his usual old chat and she just looks at him and says in that posh voice, 'You must be bleeding joking', then he comes back with a face as long as his arm and starts telling us as how she's a stuck-up little bitch all right and what the fuck are we all laughing about? So we tell him the door was open and we could hear everything! He looked like he'd shit himself. He was real mad too—tells us all where to go and walks out and slams the door, then he was all right again later on and he reckoned it was a bit of a laugh too and that's all he did it for. Who's he think he's kidding? He says this Kari's got her eye on Mr Singleton because he's on the Executive Officer, 3B grade, and Singleton's got a wife and two kids but he likes a bit of something extra on the side and John says anyway everybody knows Singleton's missis is always having affairs with other guys.

Didn't see Tina tonight, don't know what she's doing.


6 Feb.    Wednesday

Jan says she saw Singleton and Kari coming out of The Castle after dinner and he put his arm round her so somebody told John and he said Singleton was welcome to her. He reckons you'd have to have one of they American Express cards to get her open.

Anyway, John and Jacquie have split up because she found out he'd been trying to get off with Kari. He spent the whole day trying to find out who told her and he says he's going to belt whoever it was when he finds him.

'What if it's a girl what told her?' I asked him.

'Then I'll belt her too,' says John but he won't. I don't suppose he'd belt a guy neither. I remember at Xmas when somebody pissed in his lager and John swore he'd kill whoever it was so that big skinhead Ace comes up and says, 'It were me, John—just for a little giggle, eh?' and John says 'Oh—well, that's all right then, Ace. No hard feelings.' I reckon if he'd tried anything on then Ace would have killed *him* . . . Then John buys him a drink. Funny thing is, I know who'd really done it . . .

Bought a new windscreen transfer at dinnertime and it looks OK—touch wood. Tina likes it anyhow and so do I. She watched telly last night and her Mum and Dad had a flaming row and then Tracie comes in with lovebites all over her and the three of them had a good old bust-up.


7 Feb.    Thursday

More bad news for John today—two lots in fact. Jacquie's got engaged to a guy called Leon who works in the VAT office and then Adge comes in and tells us John got carved up good and proper in his car last night when he tried to mix it with this bloke in a white Lotus. Had to come I suppose. John reckons he's a great driver but like Adge said, 'He ain't never gonna break the sound barrier in a MK2 Cortina even if it have got spotlights—might break his fucking neck though.'

So last night he's had a drink or two and he tries it on with this Lotus out on the Wellington Road. First off, he nips in front at the lights and the other guy hoots his horn at him, then John tries some of his fancy burn-up stuff—you know, really winding it up through the box—but this Lotus just keeps up with him, then where the road narrows down a bit and one of them's got to give way he just speeds off out of sight—but at the last moment, so John has to brake like mad or else he'll go off the road, then he swerves a bit and goes up on the verge. Sounds like John was really shown up on that one. Adge said it was pure magic. So when John gets in I said to him, 'Hear you been doing a bit of racing, John', and he snaps back at us, 'You wanna watch your fucking mouth, Andy.' Well, I'm not going to take that sort of shit from him, no way, so I said, 'Says who, John?'

'I say,' he says.

'Stuff you, mate.'

'Look, mate—I'm not fooling about. OK?'

So I said something else and he starts off again getting real stroppy. Anyway, Adge quiets him down so I didn't have to do nothing but I reckon I could handle him. We all had a drink in the pub dinnertime as usual and John tells us it was him what chucked Jacquie and not her what chucked him. 'That's right, John,' we said to him and he looks as sick as a parrot.


8 Feb.     Friday

More fuss at work today. Janey said Kari took an overdose last night and tried to kill herself on account of Singleton telling her he didn't want to go away with her and leave his wife. She was in one hell of a state when Janey saw her and was threatening to do christ knows what but Janey didn't take much notice, and next thing Kari phones her up and says she'd taken a bottle of tablets but not to do nothing because she just wanted to end it all and Janey could have her gold ring and her shawl and all her LPs, then she put the phone down. Anyhow, Janey and her boyfriend nipped round and broke it just in time . . . Janey says Kari kept on calling Singleton a 'callous bastard' who had just used her and didn't love her at all and to leave her alone because she wanted to die. Kari's down the hospital now and off the danger list and when Singleton turned up for work as usual nobody would speak to him. And Kari sent a note to his old woman so she cleared off to her mother's and took the kids with her. Janey and some of the other girls went down the hospital dinnertime and took Kari a nice bunch of big lilies and some non-fattening chocolates. They were all late back and Singleton asked why as if he didn't know, but they just ignored him. Some of the girls were so uptight they were talking of lynching

Singleton—or castrating him. Good job they weren't around when
John says it serves the poor bitch right for getting involved with
somebody like Frank Singleton who's broken more hearts than he's
had hot dinners.

When I told Tina about it all she said she's already heard and men
could be real bastards and she'd be buggered if she ever did that just
because of a man. She didn't fancy having it away tonight so I didn't
push it.

10 Feb.          Sunday

Next Thursday is Valentine's Day—better get Tina a card I suppose
or I'll never hear the last of it. Screwed her last night I'm glad to say. I
was really ready for it and all. We went to the party out Bicknoller and
slipped off upstairs but all the bedrooms were in use so we nipped in
the bog and had it standing up because the place was so small, or at
least we started off standing up but in the end we fell on the floor and
Tina cracked her head on the bog and that give me a fit of the giggles
and she got a bit stroppy, then she's giggling and all and, man, I
couldn't get the knickers off her quick enough. Just as well we had it
then because we were too pissed up to manage it later. Some people
were smoking grass and we had a few drags though it's never done
much for me—well, not that much anyhow. This guy called Griff,
who's a student out at the Tech was passing round the pills—some
speed I think it was—but we didn't have none. Anna reckons he takes
so many pills he rattles!

'I don't like them,' says Tina so I asked her if she'd ever had them
but she was too smashed to answer. She says grass gives her a nice
swimmy feeling inside and makes her all randy—that's how we ended
up in the bog. She's got a fair old bump on her head. Neither of us
could stop giggling and Tina goes all glassy eyed too like she was going
to pass out but she didn't. Really great night, magic. Bloody sight
better than today anyway.

'Where was you last night?' says our old man when we was having
our dinner.

'What's that to you?' I asks him and off he goes.

'If you don't stop keeping on, I'll move out,' I told him.

'Huh! Where the hell'd you go to?'

'Plenty of places.'

'You wouldn't last five minutes,' he says, then Mum says she's read
somewhere that drinking too much at my age can dissolve your brain

when you get older. Bollocks! Thought about getting a flat but then fell asleep. It's really good with Tina just now, last night she was a real giggle. She's great to be with when she's like that and that's how it ought to be after all—what I mean to say is life's for the living and if you just sit about all the time moaning like my old man does or worrying about everything like our Mum then there's no point to it. I'd really hate to end up like them. Anna reckons our Mum lets him walk all over her but he can't help it, she says he's a male chauvinist and she's never tried to widen her horizons so it's half her fault but it's too late now.

11 Feb.        Monday

Weather's a lot warmer these days so what with everything we were talking about holidays in the office. Don't know where our Mum and Dad are going. I remember the last time I went with them—well, I don't reckon I'll never forget it. We all went to Teignmouth and it rained most of the bleeding time and I was bored out of my mind. I'd as soon go to prison for a week along of Kev and Trev.

The people in the office all seem to fancy Greece or Malta this year. I like a bit of sun, must talk it over with Tina sometime—looks like we'll go together somewhere, least she said that'd be OK. Double room of course. It'll be just great, suppose I'll have to put 'Mr and Mrs Baker' on the forms. John's got off with a new girl called Cherylle and he's been on about his nudist camp idea again. He says there are these places in France where all you can see for miles is sand and thousands and thousands of tits and bums and pricks flopping up and down and the night life has to be seen to be believed. I don't reckon he'll go through with it.

I quite like the sound of Greece though, if we can afford it. The people in the office say there are some really nice beaches out there and the food's good and all, it's not all this pongy foreign stuff full of garlic and onions. Our Dad didn't like all that when they went to Majorca and I agree with him for once. Still, they only had to put up with it once before they found half a dozen places round the corner doing proper food so he was OK then and they even had some Branston Pickle but he said it didn't taste the same, and Mum reckoned they couldn't make a decent cup of tea to save their lives. I've heard foreign food does really awful things to your guts and course your shit always turns black, that happened to me last year and we didn't even eat none of their Spanish stuff. Anna says she likes it of course, so she can show off with how many foreign words she knows. They all seem to mean stew anyway. Still, that's Anna for you. Hope Dermot don't think that she's going to do all the cooking in this Spanish villa or he's in for a shock—you can't live off fruit for two weeks. Or lettuce. Not unless you're a fucking rabbit.


12 Feb.          Tuesday

Dashed out this morning to get Tina a Valentine's card—I'd forgotten it before. Got her a good one in Boots which says, 'With your assets you'll never be left behind.' Made for her. Then before I knew what I was doing I went and put 'From Andy' on the inside, then had to go and get another one because you're not meant to sign them. Tried rubbing out on the first one but it just made a hole. Managed to post the new one by dinnertime—ought to get there in time.

Saw her dinnertime and talked about holidays. She went to Spain once with some friends but this year she really fancies Tenerife or the Canary Islands. We had a good laugh when I said why not the Budgie Islands! She says she'll have to go on a diet—hope those tits of hers don't shrink but maybe she can do with a few pounds off round the middle. Come to think of it that might make her even bigger up top. Anyway, Tina's got a friend who's the manageress in a travel agents and she's going to go in sometime and get some brochures.

Talking of Valentine's cards, John's got his new girlfriend this one he sent off for from some mag with this bloke on the front and when you open it his prick pops up! Then he goes round showing it to the girls in the office and they all laughed like mad. He said it cost a quid though because they were only making a few of them and it was first come first served.

'Here, remember that school trip to Normandy?' says John to us. I'll say I do.

'That were a laugh, eh?' he says.

It sure was, what with almost getting sent home on the way out for buying booze and fags on the ferry and then nicking stuff from shops when we was there and getting chased by those French kids for chatting up their girls. Then coming back, when everybody else was buying stuff like models of the Eiffel Tower to take back to our parents, John went and got that little model of a bloke standing in a bog and when you pressed a button the door opened and the little bloke turned round and pissed out a great stream of water at you! When the RI teacher saw it he blew his stack and told John to take it back but John said he couldn't remember where the shop was. Anyway, John's old man couldn't stop laughing when he saw it and spent the next week showing it to all his mates. John and me often have a good laugh about it even now and he always says he wished he'd got six of them because all his old man's friends wanted one for theirselves and he could have made a small fortune.

13 Feb.       Wednesday

This ginormous Valentine's card come this morning for Anna—guess who? Dad said it was bloody daft to send things that size through the post because it only made more work for the postmen. Course Anna was tickled pink. Nothing for me—guess mine'll come tomorrow on the day.

Kari come home from hospital today. She would have been out much sooner only they discovered she had pneumonia, but she won't be back to work for a fortnight and she's got a transfer to another department so Singleton's got that new secretary called Mandi and by the sound of it she's not going to stand for any of his horny old stuff. Now his wife's gone he's really desperate they say, so he tries it on with this Mandi at half ten and she straight off slaps his face for him! Jan says you could hear that slap half way round the building. So Singleton's been in a rotten mood all day, snapping at everybody—the way he snaps at you he ought to be called 'Jaws' like John said. Wonder how he's had so many women but then they seem to go for these guys who look like they have been run over by a bus. He really fancies himself what with his tinted glasses and all. Most of the girls won't speak to him now—he said something to Jan this afternoon and she looks at him and says, 'Had any good slaps lately?' We was all killing ourselves and he didn't know what to do.

Big news teatime—Anna says she's got what she calls a 'modelling assignment', paid and all. Seems somebody come round to the Tech from the shirt factory looking for some girls to model their latest shirts at some promotion and our Anna got her name down and that Tessa Spearing wasn't there so nobody told her about it and she missed out. Beats learning to type any day of the week. Don't ask me how come they want girls to model guy's shirts. Anyway, Anna says they just got to wear these shirts over black tights with nothing else and pose around for a few photos. Mum kept on telling Anna to be careful she didn't bend over or nothing and course then our old man has to pipe up and say that's just what *was* wanted anybody could see, and Anna sniffs and says if he wants that sort of thing then he ought to get his old mac on and nip down the newsagents. Then Mum tells Anna to be sure to wear a bra and not to open too many shirt buttons and Anna says it's not like that at all and anybody'd think she'd signed up to do a centrefold for *Men Only* or something and Mum says she hoped no daughter of hers would ever lower herself to *that* sort of thing. Anna's going to get ten quid for this little lark and says there's no telling what it could lead to. Yeah, yeah.

Then when Dermot comes round to pick up Anna our Mum gets a hold of him and asks him what he knows about it and was he sure that it was all quite decent and you know. Course he don't know much about it, only what Anna told him, but he says, 'Knowing Anna as I do, Mrs Baker, I have no doubt she would not undertake anything which was in the slightest way indecent or immodest.' Then when they'd gone she said, 'Dermot's such a well-bred young man, a proper gentleman', and Dad says, 'Huh! They're the worst' like he always does and Mum gives him a dirty look. I reckon she'd like to marry Dermot herself sometimes. It'll be pictures in the paper and all that Anna says. Still, I guess it's better than having a sister who's an ugly cow. You feel pretty sorry for girls who are ugly sometimes—not being able to get a bloke and they say they get really frustrated. There's that Paula Fudge in our typing pool who'll go out with anybody and who lets them have it and all John says, because she's so desperate. He reckons he banged her up in the stationery cupboard when he went to get a biro and she was so grateful she give him forty fags and kept bothering him for a fortnight. They say he'd have his own Nan if he got half a chance.


14 Feb.        Thursday

Tina off sick today so I rang her up to see if I could come round, but her Mum was staying in all day with one of her headaches, worse luck.

'Can't you send her out for something?'

'Don't be daft,' says Tina. 'We can have it tonight.' And we did and all—Magic!

Then she says she's got the Valentine's card all right.

'How do you know it was from me?' I said for a laugh.

'Well, who else would it be from? What do you mean?' I saw right off she was thinking I meant something about her and other guys so I had to be pretty quick to calm her down which I did pretty well. When I rung off I realised she hadn't said nothing about sending me a card and nothing come to me today neither. Have to see tomorrow I guess.

Tonight she told me her Mum had found her pills in her bedroom. Her old lady tried to get a bit stroppy and Tina said she even started saying she wanted to talk to me about it but Tina told her straight to mind her own fucking business. Then her Mum said she didn't mind long as Tina knew what she was doing and Tina said it wasn't up to her to mind or not and course she knew what she was bloody doing or else she wouldn't have had the pills in the first place then, would she? It isn't as if it's a new thing in their house neither because their Marilynne went on the pill when she was fifteen, though her Mum only found out eighteen months later when she found her on the job with some bloke up in her room—turned out he'd come round to do the windows—and there was one hell of a row when their old man come home Tina says, and he was going round to clout the bloke till he found out he was six foot three and a Hell's Angel.

This Hell's Angel used to nip round to their house whenever he fancied a bit with their Marilynne and they'd just go on up to her room and her old man had to keep his trap shut or else this bloke would have shut it for him. He'd just say, 'Hello, matey, OK then?' to their Dad and go off upstairs and their Dad'd usually go off down the pub for the night. I remember him a bit—he had this great big scar on his cheek where some Mod razored him in a fight on Clacton beach, he said they had to scrape the Mod off the floor after he'd finished with him. He had this fantastic 650 and then he went off to work on the oil rigs.

Tina and me had a good laugh about it.

'Here—what you doing with your hand?' she says.

'What's it feel like?' says I.

'Careful.'

'Lift your bum up then.'

So she did. Pity about her tights—said I'd get her another pair.

'Don't bother,' she says. 'Don't know what I'd end up with.'

She's got a great sense of humour—great time tonight, magic!


15 Feb.        Friday

Anna got herself three pairs of fancy tights yesterday for her modelling show, two quid a pair she said! They're supposed to be special ones like real models have to have. So ten quid minus six quid leaves four quid profit—hope she don't have to buy the shirt as well . . . Mum said she reckoned the shirt people ought to provide everything but Anna said that wasn't the way these things were done, and Mum says to her to be sure to wear knickers as well and Anna told her not to keep on so. It's not everybody got Anna's expensive tastes—poor old Dermot. Still, Anna says he's rolling in money. Nice for him. Then Anna says she's taking up yoga. She already goes to some exercise or other but that's mainly for people who've just had kids and want to get back in shape and she only goes because one of her friends just had one and don't like to go on her own.

Carina come round to pick up Anna and she's really nice. Anna says the father of her kid went off with some Italian girl just before the wedding and Anna says Carina's really depressed just about all the time. I could fancy her all right. Dermot's got an expensive Jap camera with loads of lenses so he's going along to this show and take some pictures of Anna for her. Mum's going, Dad isn't. Lot of fuss in our house about it all. Anna's trying to make something of herself our Mum says. Anyway, she's been a lot better here lately, I'll say that for her.

Still no card from Tina. She said she didn't feel like going out tonight so I didn't see her and went down to The Grapes for a drink with a few of the lads. Big news down there though—John and Cherylle have gone and got engaged! It's not official yet so they're only telling a few people. They're going to look for a ring next week so for now Cherylle got John to tie a bit of string round her finger. We all had a good laugh when he tied it on for her, then he had to stand a round.

'It's expense all the bleeding time,' he says. 'Still, isn't every day you get engaged, is it?' More like every week in his case. She said she'll wear the bit of string and not take it off till they've got a proper ring, then she wanted him to let her put a bit round his finger but he said it'd look daft and anyway he was allergic to string so she give him a bit of her hair instead, then she cried a bit and everybody said 'Ah!' Like I say, she's a really nice girl.

16 Feb.        Saturday

Tina's Valentine's card come at last. Took long enough. It's got this big pink heart on the front and says all this stuff about tender love and all that—really nice. Went round to see her but she was a bit blocked up in the head, she reckons it's the bloody flu. Big Marilynne's coming back tomorrow for a few days with the bloke she lives with who's a company director and is really nice. She says she hopes she'll be better by then so's we can all go out together for a drink. Tina says this bloke of Marilynne's has got an XJ6 or something, anyway it's a great car. Hope she's better tomorrow. 'You know what's the best thing for flu?' I said to her.

'What? One of they hot lemon things?'

'Sex of course,' and I give a little smile.

'Christ!' she says. 'You're all cock you are.'

Well, I reckon that's the nicest thing any girl's ever said to me.

'You'll catch it,' she says when I go to kiss her, so I kissed her hand instead and give her tit a rub—really good.


18 Feb.        Monday

Had a really great time yesterday—best Sunday I've had for years. Tina rang us up about dinnertime and said she was feeling a bit better so if I wanted her and me and Marilynne and Angelo (that's her bloke) would all go out somewhere tonight. I said OK so I drive round and there's this whacking great XJ outside with spotlights all over the front and fur seat covers and tinted glass—the lot. Some car!

Angelo's a Cockney but his old man's Spanish, he's about thirty-five and he's really smooth. He had on this flash pinstripe suit and open pink shirt with a great chunky gold pendant, his chest don't half look like a hearth rug and all. He looks like he can handle himself—does weight-training Tina says. Anyway, he's really together. Tina says his bracelet and watch and rings and stuff are all real gold. When I got there he says to me, 'How you going, mate? I've heard a lot about you,' real friendly, and even their old man seemed to like him, he's that sort, gets on with everybody, even little pricks like Mr Butler. Course I thought Tina meant for us to have a drink down the pub but Angelo and Marilynne say they could do with a steak so off we go for a meal. Marilynne's all poshed up and Tina's got her new split skirt on and her heels. Me, I was just as normal but Marilynne said that'd be OK.

'What about some entertainment?' says Angelo.

'Dunno,' says Marilynne. 'Not much to do round here. It's not like London, Ange.'

Then she says we could go up The Webbington and have a really good blow-out. I'd already had my tea and I had to say I only had five quid on me but Angelo flashes his wallet and says, 'That's OK, Andy—it's on me, eh?'

Well, that's generosity for you! He'd only met me ten minutes and here he is offering me free meals but Tina said she got some cash and we'd club together to pay our whack, but no he was definite, he just says to her, 'Forget it, girl, it's on me. No trouble—put it down to expenses. What's The Webbington then?'

'It's not much, Ange,' says Marilynne and Tina says how would she know cos she's never been there.

'I've heard,' says Marilynne.

Me and all. That Jason Potter reckons you can generally pick up a bit of spare—either housewives out in a group or else divorced and looking for a good time. They have some pretty famous singers and that as well there sometimes, not bands so much but older guys like Tony Trichinopoly and people like him, and they once had Engelbert Humperdinck there before he made it big, but I'm not into that sort of music personally.

'Right,' says Angelo, 'we'll give it a go.' So next thing we're in the XJ and cruising off up the motorway at 100 plus. Great cars those Jags—they can really motor. He winds it up to 80 on the slip-road and just puts his foot down and off into the outside lane all the way and even at the ton there was hardly any noise or nothing—terrific acceleration and all. He had it up to 130 once when he was showing this Stag a thing or two, he had one of them but they're rubbish. He's a great driver.

When we got there that shit on the door says we got to have ties on—big problem I thought, but Angelo says no trouble cos he's got his luggage in the boot so he unpacks a bit and gets out a couple of ties, one for him and one for me but it's a bit hard to wear a tie with a T-shirt, but again no problem—he pulls out this really lovely shirt and just tells me to slip it on with the tie.

'Say no more, mate,' says he. 'Let me have it back later OK?'

Well, I said OK then and I dived behind the car to slip it on and Tina starts fiddling with my belt and saying, 'Hurry up, Andy, I'm starving,' and Angelo and Marilynne have a good laugh and he sings out, 'Not now, love—save that for later.' I was killing myself with laughing. Then there's no problem with the guy on the door this time, so we're in.

Really nice shirt—Italian he said—slimline and made to hug your body. Angelo reckons that the Italians are the only ones who know how to make shirts proper and he can get them cost price from a guy he knows and if I wanted he could get me half a dozen at about fifteen quid each. I had to say no but he's a pretty useful guy to know I reckon.

Really plush place—plush prices and all. 'You get the first round,' says Tina so I did and I was sure glad Angelo got them in after that—

over four quid for a round! And that barman was a pratt and all.

One thing about Angelo, even though he's got cash and knows all about wine and food and all that, there's nothing stuck-up about him, he can talk to anyone, like when I offer him one of my No6 he offers me one of his French fags instead, he smokes them all the time. He's got this great gold lighter too.

I reckon, looking back on it, we made a pretty good party. I could see loads of people having a look—well, they had to when big Marilynne starts laughing to see where all the fucking noise was coming from. We had a few drinks and then it's off into the restaurant for the meal—steaks and huge ones too with lots of good red wine. We all had avocado pears to start with which I never had before though Anna's always going on about them, with this funny sort of vinegar, I think it was, all over them. I sure have never had vinegar on pears before but it wasn't too bad I guess. Tina reckoned you always had vinegar on them.

'I'd rather have custard,' I told her.

'Trust you,' she says.

Then just as we're getting on to the steaks up pops this bloke in an evening suit on the stage and introduces the cabaret. There's these girls in black catsuits with silver trimmings who dance around a bit, a couple of local comics called Tom King and Jerry Something, this singer called Michelle Moonlight, then the ice cream and a couple of exotic dancers.

'Hello, hello,' says I when the first one's on.

'She's not much good,' says Marilynne and Angelo says she'd be lucky to get work in London only in some of the backstreet places. He's the chief executive of an entertainments complex, bit of stripping, bit of film and a bit of bingo round the back for the old folks—give the punter what he wants. Sounded to me like he knows quite a bit about the film business and all—he's met Fiona Richmond loads of times and he knows Michael Caine. When he went for a slash Marilynne told us he's got lots of business interests but she wouldn't say no more, then she said Tina and me ought to come for a weekend sometime and they'd show us around.

'I really don't know how I used to live around here, Tina,' she says. 'It's so boring compared to London.'

'Lovely meal though,' said Tina.

'Oh yeah—not bad for round here. Nice peas. But you'd think they'd know how to mix a Harvey Wallbanger.'

'What about a Tony Trembler?' I says. 'Eh?' Nice one!

Then Angelo gets in some cigars—Castellas. I reckon I could get a taste for them. It sure was good just sitting there smoking these big fat cigars and drinking Southern Comforts and with a good meal inside of you while the second exotic dancer was on—a dark girl she was with lovely little nipples and a cracking arse on her. Angelo gives us a wink and leans over and says, 'I could fancy that, eh, mate?' and I said so could I, no trouble.

'You'd fancy anything,' says Tina and we had a good laugh.

It wasn't till gone two that we left. Well, I don't know how much Angelo must have spent but he said it was no bother and he could claim it off his expense account and he paid for the meal with one of his credit cards because he doesn't like to carry too much of the readies around with him. That was some night—how the other half lives I guess. Marilynne says they usually eat out two or three times a week with business associates of Angelo's—don't ask me what he must be earning, hell of a sight more than me anyhow, but he's such a nice guy you don't really mind. Not like some of these buggers who don't work and just get it all off of their old man—Angelo come up the hard way, left school at fourteen and had to look after himself.

So there we are. Went straight to sleep when I got back last night and had a bit of an hangover this morning so didn't go to work and got up around two o'clock. Couldn't manage much dinner.

'Where was you to last night?' our old man wants to know. Typical.

'Out.'

'I know you was out.'

'Up The Webbington if you must know.'

Too smart for him by a mile. Anna and all. 'Sounds wonderful,' she said and gives a little smile so I give her one back.

Got Mum to do Angelo's shirt and took it back to him tonight. Tina had today off as well, Angelo and Marilynne'd gone out and Tina said she'd give him the shirt back when she saw them. They're going back to London tomorrow morning so won't see them again for a bit. Great time.

19 Feb.        Tuesday

Back to work, worse sodding luck. John said his brother used to have an XJ6. Saw Tina tonight—she says her Mum hopes Angelo and Marilynne'll get married but what she don't know is Angelo's still married to his second wife who's Greek or something and won't agree to a divorce, so Angelo's got his lawyer on to it and he's going to divorce her.

'He's really nice,' says Tina.

'Great bloke, yeah. Marilynne's well in there all right.'

'Yeah—little bitch.'

'What you say that for?'

She gives us a look and says that Marilynne's a fucking little show-off.

'Fell on her feet,' says me.

'On her back more like. You got your door fixed yet?'

'Don't reckon I'll bother, it don't look too bad.'

'Typical!' she says and pulls a face.

'No way I can afford an XJ,' I told her, just to let her see I knew what she were on about. Bit of a laugh really, women.


20 Feb.          Wednesday

Saw Tina dinnertime and she told me their Tracie's gone and run away from home. She just went off in the night—packed her bags and left. Their old man woke up about two and heard the door go and shouted out, 'Stop that fucking noise down there!' Then he went back to sleep. When they all got up in the morning Tracie's gone. Her Mum's dead upset and all that, but their old man's browned off cos Tracie's only fifteen and if she'd waited a couple of months till she's sixteen she could have gone and he wouldn't have had to report it, but as it is their Mum keeps on at him to get on to Scotland Yard. Course this starts a cracking row with her calling him a rotten father to his kids and him telling her the kids learned it all off her in the first place. Tina says she couldn't stand no more of it so she come on to work, then I had to hear all about it. Her Dad went down to the police and told them his daughter had run away and the bloke behind the desk says what did he expect them to do about it? Nice one! Anyway, he said call back if she don't come home in three days. She didn't leave a note or nothing—just took her clothes and two quid out of the coffee jar in the kitchen window and all the milk money. Her old man wanted to get her done for theft. When I called in he looks at me black as thunder so I kept my trap shut.

Tina says Tracie's more than likely gone off with her boyfriend who's at the same school as her and plays in the town under sixteen football team, so their old man went round to Darren's house only to find he's gone and all so her Dad and Darren's Dad go up to the police station together where they get told that it happens all the time and to come back in three days like they was told before. Darren left a note at his place and said he couldn't stand his parents' bollocking no longer so he was going off to start a new life and he wanted freedom. We was talking about it in the pub and somebody said maybe they'd gone off to join the Foreign Legion, and another guy said once you're in that you can't never get out and if you try then they peg you out in the sand and let the ants have you and it's when they start eating your eyes that it's worse—or your prick like John said.

Tina says she's never seen her Mum so upset—she's had to go down the doctor's and get some valiums to tide her over and keeps going on about getting the radio to do a message to Tracie telling her to get in touch if she's all right. Her and her old man stopped speaking to each other about it, not that they ever been very friendly Tina says. She reckons they might split up and her old man leads their Mum a right dance and why she puts up with him she'll never know.

Told my parents about it just for something to say and my old man said, 'Bloody kids, like a millstone round your neck they are all the time,' but our Mum shushes him and tells him not to talk so daft. Wish I hadn't said nothing.

Anna's big day today—course I had to hear all about it. Sounds like it went off like a house on fire. I got back a bit early because Tina wanted to get back to see her Mum so we couldn't fuck tonight which made me puke because we haven't had it lately and I'm dying for it, but Tina said I'd just have to die till tomorrow night and she'd make it up to me then. I squeezed her tits and whispered in her ear that I'd look forward to it. Anyway, I got back only just after Anna and our Mum and Anna was upstairs having another bath because it's hot under all the lights.

'You ought to have seen Anna, Andrew,' says our Mum. 'But there, you'll see the lovely snaps Dermot took.'

Well, I thought of asking how she knew they were lovely but I didn't.

'Yeah—right ho,' I says just to shut her up.

Looks like it didn't last all that long—sounded more like a quick flash to me, here are our latest shirts modelled by Anna, Pati and Sandra, then Anna and the other two danced about a bit and then they all sat around drinking white wine and eating little cheesy biscuits with Anna trying not to bend over and Dermot being well bred all round the fucking place.

And our old man went after all. He swore blind he never would but he got dragged along and Mum somehow got him into a jacket and tie so he wouldn't show them up too much.

'Get a good eyeful?' I asks him and he says, 'You watch your bloody lip, boy.'

Nice! Went on up to bed when Mum starts saying how beautiful Anna was and how she couldn't really believe that she was 'her little girl' . . . Christ!


21 Feb.      Thursday

Anna off again breakfast time, you'd think she was Miss World to hear her talk. The advertising and promotions executive from the shirt factory took a note of her name and said he could have sworn Anna was a professional model because she was so much better than the other two. I said I was glad it all went OK and maybe she ought to get her black tights framed for a souvenir, but course she had to take that the wrong way so I said, 'All right, all right, don't get shirty about it,' and she took that the wrong way and all and stuck her bloody nose in the air.

'He's very pleased for you really,' says Mum and Anna just says, 'Oh is he?'

Then when we was having our tea the bell goes and in comes Dermot. 'Do carry on, Mr Baker,' he says to our old man. 'Don't let me disturb you.'

He said he'd got a mate of his who's a professional photographer and got a posh studio to develop the pictures extra quick as a special favour to him so he'd dashed straight round and here they were. Great.

'Oh, that's ever so kind, Dermot,' says Mum. 'They're lovely.' Then she had to go and offer him the last bit of blackcurrant cheesecake—and the bugger ate it and all.

But I got to admit they weren't half bad. All Anna, mind—you couldn't hardly see the other girls. She's got a good pair of legs, I'll give her that, specially in one of them where she was bending down sort of and you could see her arse—or most of it. Mum didn't like that one much but she said she'd take five copies of each all the same, which ought to set her back a bit as there's about three dozen in all. Even our old man said he reckoned they'd come out well—but that was only because Dermot was around.

Didn't have Tina tonight. Was I mad . . . I'd been looking forward all day, then when we got down to it or so I thought she says she's a bit sore down there and didn't feel like it after all.

'What about what you said last night?' I said to her.

'What did I say last night?'

'You promised.'

'Oh well,' she says just like that, 'you can't always have everything you want in this life.'

Shit! She said she'd wank me off if I wanted but that was all. I told her to stuff it.

'I'm past wanking,' I told her.

'Oh, I dunno, it comes in handy.'

'Yeah, yeah.'

'Don't sulk.'

'I'm not,' I told her and I didn't say no more. Shit, I'm pissed off.


22 Feb.          Friday

Still no sign of Tracie so she's now an officially missing person. Tina says her Mum now reckons it's all their Dad's fault. Tina even got roped in to go up to the police with them because her Mum said she wouldn't go with just her old man. When the copper says it's not likely Tracie'll be found if she don't want to be her Mum breaks down and says, 'It's all his fault.'

'Oh yes,' said the copper, 'what's that mean?'

'Always going on at her he was.'

'No I bloody weren't,' says her old man.

'Yes you was—telling her she was a little madam and all.'

'Is that true?' asks the copper.

'Flighty,' says Mr. 'Got it from her mother. See for yourself.'

Then they started rowing and a woman copper has to be got in with a cup of tea to calm her down. Tina didn't know where to put herself, then the copper wants to know why her old man said 'got'.

'Got what?' says Mr.

'Got it from her mother.'

'I dunno.'

'I see.'

'He hated her,' says Mrs.

'Did you?' the copper asks him.

'Course not—it weren't me what told her to go.'

'Who said that then?' asks the copper and Mr nods at Mrs and says, 'Ask her.'

'Did you tell your daughter to go, Mrs Butler?'

'I never—on me mother's grave I never did.'

'Yes you did,' says her old man. 'You said to her she'd better learn herself some respect or else clear out. Anyhow, your old lady was cremated.'

'I was upset, that's all—I never meant it.'

'I see,' says the copper. 'What *did* you mean by it?'

'Nothing. We was just having a little row, that's all.'

Then he started asking how often they used to have little rows and all that and Tina's old man starts getting mad and says, 'What you trying to say?' but the copper just says, 'I'm trying to find out the facts, Mr Butler.' Tina says her old man reckoned that copper was a right pratt when they all got home again.

And the radio told Tina's Mum that they can't put out any old appeal or else they'd be flooded with them. The daft cow tried to phone up Jimmy Young. Tina says her Mum's scared now in case Tracie's got picked up by a sex maniac or something. If you ask me, we ought to worry about the sex maniac . . .

Tonight I says to Tina straight, 'I really want it, Tina,' but she says she's still a bit sore. 'What you been doing?' I says to her. 'It's probably sore because you don't use it enough.'

'Don't be so fucking crude—you're all the same,' she goes.

'Who is?' I asked her.

'Men,' she says.

'Oh?'

'Yeah,' she says. 'You'll just have to wait.'

Makes me puke it does, straight.


23 Feb.        Saturday

Bit of a giggle this morning. Come and have a meal, says the bloke from the shirt factory to our Anna last night, there's something I'd like to discuss with you. So it's posh dress on, shawl and all and round he comes in his Spitfire and she's put Dermot off and her Farah Fawcett-Majors smile on and off we jolly well go, don't we?

Anyway, then it's come back to my place and we'll talk about your possibilities. Oh ah? says Anna—ended up with her catching hold of the coffee pot and telling him to keep his hands to himself or else she'll put out his fire for good. Even our old man had to laugh at that one. Mum said she ought to tell the police. I reckon Anna can look after herself OK.

Anyway, thank christ me and Tina had it off tonight—at last. That's women for you, all cold one minute and hot the next and when Tina's hot she's really hot. I can always tell when she wants it—you can tell it in her eyes—so tonight when I see this look coming into her eyes and this little smile on her face I knew it'd be OK. And I was right and all. Just work her tits a bit, that always gets her going, it's a cinch. Then it's out and in we go. Great! It was good and all, really great— then it always is if you wait a bit but who can wait, that's the point. I really want to do it with her in bed again, and the sooner the better. Maybe we ought to get a place of our own—that'd be great. Anyhow, our relationship's really great at the present moment in time. You don't get on all the time but then who does? She's funny sometimes but then they all are. Magic!

And guess what? Darren's back. He turned up on the doorstep this morning, the pratt missed meeting Tracie at the bus-stop so he hung around till the morning, then hitched up north on the motorway to try and get a job on the oil rigs, but there weren't many oil rigs in Preston so when his money ran out he'd gone to the police and they said if he was still there when they come back after tea break then they'd have to hang on to him. He said he hadn't seen Tracie since Tuesday night when they planned the whole thing . . .

So Tina's old lady got herself into an even worse state than before and started saying Darren had abandoned her and he was as bad as her husband.

Mind you, that Darren's a bit thick—all his brains are in his feet they reckon, and when he was a little kid they say he went into the shop and asked how much was that 10p Fruit & Nut in the window so the bloke said 12p and Darren says he don't have enough money on him. Her Mum says she wouldn't be surprised at nothing that Darren did and course his old woman's on the listen cos they're round there and she says, 'Oh yeah, and what's that supposed to mean then?'

'Nothing,' says Mrs Butler.

'If you've got anything to say about our Darren, then you say it.'

'You know.'

'Huh! He's a good boy—till he met your Tracie anyway.'

'Oh yeah, what's that mean?'

'Just look at her—out till all hours running round after boys.'

'Yeah, that's right,' chimes in Darren's Dad. 'Led our Darren on she did, making eyes at him all the time.'

'Here,' says Tina's old man, 'you stay out of this.'

'Oh yeah—what you going to do about it?'

'You never mind what I'm going to do, mate. You look out to your wife.'

'You insulting my wife?'

'I'm saying nothing.'

'You'd better watch it, mate.'

'Little tart she is, that's what she is,' says Mrs Darren.

'You calling my Tracie a tart?' says Mrs Butler and Mrs Darren just gives her a look and turns her head away.

'I'm talking to you, Mrs,' says Mrs Butler.

'Your wife's got a big mouth on her,' says Mr Butler to Mr D.

'You'll have something on you in a minute, matey.'

'Oh yeah?'

'Yeah.'

'C'mon, Frankie,' says Mrs D. 'Don't waste your sodding time on such people.'

'He's asking for it,' says her old man. 'An' he'll fucking get it in a minute an' all.'

'If you got any allegations about our Darren,' says Mrs D. 'we'll get the law on you. You can't go round doing that, can they, Frankie?'

'No, the buggers can't. They got enough problems with a daughter like her as it is.'

'He's abnormal, your Darren, I reckon,' says Mrs Butler. 'Still everybody knows that.'

'Ah,' says her old man, 'Tell 'em about the tin of striped paint he tried to buy down Woolworth's.'

'That's a sodding lie!' says Mrs Darren. Anyway, the front door's open by now according to Tina and most of this is going on out in the garden so there's quite a crowd building up and then somebody must have called the law because a panda car rolls up before they've all finished.

'Come in and calm down,' says the copper to them.

'I'm not never going in there again,' says Mrs Darren.

'Don't you worry about that,' says Tina's Mum. 'You find out what that boy's done with my Tracie, that's what you can do,' she says to the copper.

'That's libel and slander that is,' the other woman shouts. 'We can have you up for that.'

'Go on then,' Mrs Butler shouts back at her.

'Right, we will,' says Mrs D. and her hubby looks all stuck-up and says, 'I'll have a word with me solicitor in the morning.'

Well, by now the coppers is fed up and this big sergeant tells them they're acting like a lot of bleeding kids and they'd better grow up bloody quick, then he orders Mr and Mrs off home and Tina's old man and woman in house and that's that.

Anyway, I must have laughed a bit because Tina says, 'And I don't know what you think you're frigging laughing at.' So that was me in the doghouse for tonight I reckoned—but no! Like I said, girls are funny. Maybe it's just my charm . . . Anyhow, I know Tina well enough by now to know which are the right buttons to press, they're fucking big enough by christ . . .

## 24 Feb.      Sunday

Auntie Vi and Uncle Len come round this afternoon. They're about the best of our relations I guess. He says Trish wants him to go on to 'The Generation Game' with her. I reckon they'd do well too.

Course we had to have Anna's photos handed round again. There can't be many people down our road who haven't seen them by now.

'Hello, hello,' says Uncle Len when he gets to the one of Anna's arse, 'this is a bit of all right.'

That's what Steve Wright thought and all, he offered to take a few of Anna himself—what sort was pretty obvious she says, but she just told him she wasn't interested. Just now a lot of people seem to be calling on Steve and his wife and I did hear they're into wife-swapping and all that. Anyway, this big black guy spent the weekend with them a week or two ago, and we all know what they say about black guys being the best lovers—keep going all night they say, lucky buggers! Same goes for black girls John says. Our old man reckons this spade was out doing a rain dance in the garden.

Didn't see Tina tonight.

## 25 Feb.      Monday

Tina says her old lady's getting into a right state about their Tracie. She reckons Darren did away with her because he's subnormal, which he isn't—not quite anyhow. Tina says the coppers come round again yesterday to ask them a load of questions and Tina's Mum says to them, 'You want to ask that Darren what he's done with her,' then they have to warn her to keep her trap shut and after they'd gone she starts crying and won't stop so her old man goes off down the pub. Well, Tina's worried so she calls the doctor in who says it's her nerves, but she's had them for years so she could have told him that. Her usual doctor's just got kicked out for having it away with one of his patients in the surgery and his receptionist who was in love with him but he chucked her so she told on him, so Mrs Butler's got to get this new one filled in on her medical history which is about as long as the phone book. Tina says she's never been the same since Tracie was born and her old man gets really frustrated because she'll only let him have it once a fortnight if he's lucky. Poor sod! She says she can hear them at it through the wall and she wouldn't be surprised if they split up soon.

No sex tonight—I was feeling really randy and I told her so too.

'Oh yeah?' she says in my earhole. 'What is it you want then?'

'You know what I want, Tina,' I says to her feeling her tits.

Then her voice goes all husky and she whispers to me, 'Tell us then.'

'Tell you what?'

'Tell me what you want.'

'I want you course.'

'What's that mean?'

'Eh? What the fuck you think it means?'

'Oh . . . that,' she says.

'Yeah—get 'em off.'

'You want it then?'

'Yeah, course—we been all through that.'

'Say it,' she says, but I'm getting a bit fed up and I'm just about ready to burst.

'I want to screw you.'

'Sorry. I got a pain.'

'For christ's sake, Tina—I'm desperate.'

'Oh dear.'

Then I lost my rag.

'Don't go on so. Go over behind that bush and have a toss.'

Well, stuff that for a lark. I was mad—in fact I was so mad I couldn't think of what to say next.

'It's cold,' says Tina.

But I still couldn't think of nothing to say. 'Tina . . .' I said but it was no good.

'Do my bra for me,' she says. Well, what else could I do? It was no good going on at her, no good at all, she'd only lose her rag. No, I reckoned the best thing I could do was just shut up about it, not stay there whining.

'Hope you're not too disappointed, Andy.'

'If you got a pain, you got a pain.'

'Sorry—I'll let you know when it's gone away.'

'What sort of pain is it?'

'Oh—women's pains. You know.'

That's just fucking typical, there's not much you can do. Nothing *I* could do anyhow so I left it at that and we come on home.

26 Feb.        Tuesday

Girls are moody, everybody knows that. Tina's moody sometimes, they all are. You just got to live with it. Pisses me off though—she's got a bit to learn I reckon. Take today—I asked her if she'd got any holiday brochures yet because it was about time that we got round to making our minds up where we're going.

'Are we going together then?' she says.

'If you want,' I said. Well, I could see I could have made a big scene about it but no, I just kept things cool. She was only fooling, that's all.

'I'll think about it,' she says.

That made me mad a bit and tonight I says to her, 'I'd really like to go on holiday with you, Tina.'

'Oh yeah?' she says and smiles at me. Reckon I handled that one really well.

At work they reckon Collins'll be back next week. Singleton's been off for an interview for some job in South Wales. I don't reckon there'll be a collection for him. Still, he's having it off with this girl in the Motor Tax Office now but John says she'll eat a little 'un like Singleton for breakfast.

Tracie still missing.

27 Feb.        Wednesday

Had to buy a new shirt and some shoes today. Tina said why not get an Italian shirt like Angelo's but I couldn't afford that so I went to Marks & Sparks as usual and to Curtess for the shoes. Nobody knows why we have to wear a jacket and tie for work. You won't catch me in a suit though. I remember when I started work out goes Mum and gets me a tie—I told her not to bother but she said no, it was a special day of your life your first day at work and you had to look just right for it. I told her this wasn't the 1930s now and she just went quiet on me and said all the same she'd like to buy me one so I didn't stop her and I've worn it ever since, though it's a bit tatty now.

Bloody shoes cost me nine quid! And you're not meant to wear training shoes neither.

Heard today The Police are giving a concert at the Odeon in three weeks—must be quick to get tickets though. Tina says she'd like to go. This is going to be an expensive week as we're going to see *Apocalypse Now* at the pictures on Friday.

'How you feeling then, Tina?' I asked her tonight.

'Eh?' she says. 'Oh—not bad. Bit better, you know.'

'What about it then?'

Nothing about it, that's what. She got a bit ratty.

'Stop pawing me,' she says.

Right, I reckoned, fuck this for a lark. She'll come round in her own time. I just started the car and we come on home.


28 Feb.          Thursday

Took the morning off to get the concert tickets—told Singleton I was feeling sick, then when I get down there I found most of the other people from our office in the queue as well! Anyway, got the tickets even though I did have to wait for about an hour and a half—Marilynne said when she was down that her and Angelo are always going to concerts and most of the time he can get the tickets for free because he knows the right people. That must be really great.

I haven't been to a concert since Kate Bush come last year and I didn't know Tina then but she was there and all, it's a small world I guess. When I think about it, my life's a whole lot better this year than it was then when I was going out with that fucking Lynn. I remember I was really depressed for weeks after that, not that she was worth it—it don't bother me now. This year everything's really great.

Saw Tina dinnertime.

'What about our holiday then?' I says.

'Oh—yeah. OK then.'

Magic!

She's going to get some brochures off of her friend soon as she can. Told her to get a move on. Then when we're all having our tea Anna asks me where I'm going this year and I just said we hadn't decided yet.

'Who's "we"?' says our Mum. Well, I ought to have expected that.

Anna says, 'Going with Tina, are you?' and I didn't see why I shouldn't say so.

'I think you ought to have asked us first, Andrew,' says our Mum, so I said, 'What for?'

'Well, I think you ought.'

'What for?'

Then course Anna has to pipe up again and says, 'What Mum

means, Andy, is she wants to know if you'll be in the same room or not.' Trust her.

'All the same,' says our old man. 'Only think of one thing at his age.'

I said, 'That's our affair,' but Mum says, 'Not while you're living under our roof, Andrew, it's not.'

'What's that got to do with it? I'm not staying here for the holiday.'

'Well, I don't like it—anyway, I don't suppose for one minute the holiday people would allow it.'

'Allow what? We're not going off to rob a bank.'

'Oh,' says Anna, 'they don't care. All they want to do is sell the tickets.'

I was getting really sick of all this, trying to make me feel like a fucking kid and that.

'What do Tina's parents think of it?' asks Mum as if that mattered.

'It's none of their business.'

'Well, I think it is—they don't want another daughter going off the rails.'

'Huh! What's that mean?'

'What it means,' says our old man, 'is they wouldn't want you putting her up the spout, that's what.'

Mum told him not to be so crude but she has a laugh all the same.

'What would people say?' she says.

'What about?'

'I don't want to hear any more about it,' she says. 'It's just not nice, that's all. Look at Marilynne—having an abortion at twenty.'

'Well, she changed her mind about it when her husband pushed off so she had to get rid of it.'

Then Anna starts off about how women ought to be able to choose and our old man tells her they can always choose to keep their legs shut. She rolled her eyes and called him a chauvinist and you could see from the look on his face he didn't know what she was on about.

So that was that. None of their bloody business anyhow.

29 Feb.        Friday

Went to the pictures with Tina tonight to see *Apocalypse Now*. Good film! She said all the blood and stuff made her feel a bit ill once or twice but she thought it was great. I remember when we went to see *Jaws*, every time the shark come along Tina grabbed hold of me because she said she was scared—anyway, she gets randy when she's scared, I don't know why and neither does she. John says a lot of girls are like that. Tina reckons he's enough to scare any girl to death.

Talked about holidays after the film. Tina says she likes Malta or Spain but quite likes the look of Majorca or somewhere like that. I said we ought to hurry up and book or we might not get in.

Tracie's still missing but the police have been round asking questions again, specially their old man. They wouldn't say why even though he asked them, only they wanted 'to clarify a few outstanding developments'.

'Did you ever hit your daughter, Mr Butler?' says this sergeant.

'Who told you that?'

'Never mind that, Mr Butler—just answer the question.'

'Well, I never.'

'Not in the highway last August?'

'Who told you?' says Mr Butler and the inspector coughs and says they're acting on information received and more than that he's not at liberty to diverge.

'That's those people,' says Mrs Butler, 'that Darren's family.'

'Been behind our back, have they?' says Mr B. but the copper just says, 'Did you hit your daughter in the street last August, Mr Butler?'

'I don't know. I might have done.'

'Were you in the habit of hitting your daughter, Mr Butler?'

'Course I wasn't.'

'Why do you say "wasn't", Mr Butler?'

'Eh? What d'you mean?'

'You're talking as if your daughter was no longer here, Mr Butler.'

'Well, she's run away, hasn't she?'

'I don't know, Mr Butler—you tell me.'

Then he makes a few notes in his little book and says, 'So, why did you assault your daughter in the carriageway last August 18th, Mr Butler?'

'I don't know if I did. I can't bleeding remember.'

'According to our information, Mr Butler, you hit your daughter around the head.'

Course he wants to know who told the coppers but they're not saying, are they?

'You want to see that Darren and ask him—he's abnormal he is,' says Tina's old woman.

'We are satisfied as a result of our ongoing enquiry procedures that Darren is telling the truth,' says the inspector.

'Pooh!' says Tina's Mum. 'He wouldn't know the truth if it fell on his head he wouldn't. He's abnormal.'

Turns out Darren went to the wrong bus-stop but Mrs Butler won't listen.

'I'm sorry you're not cooperating fully, Mr Butler,' says the chief copper and gets up to go. 'We'll probably want to see you again—don't leave the town without informing us first.'

'Why don't you find my little girl?' cries Tina's Mum.

'Yeah,' says her old man, 'and why don't you catch a few criminals instead of buggering honest people around all the time?'

'No call for that sort of talk, Mr Butler—and as for criminals, you might be interested to know we catch a good few of them, specially them as least expects it.'

That's how I had it all from Tina anyhow. Seems she just sat there in the corner with her mouth shut and this young copper kept on making eyes at her, so she showed him a bit of leg first off and then when he grins she stuck her tongue out at him and looked away. Nice one!

Tina can look after herself all right I reckon. Ever since the M5 rape case she's carried this bleeding great knitting needle around with her and I reckon she'd bloody use it and all too, leastways she says she would. So I said to her don't some women get really turned on by the idea of getting raped, like I heard John say, but she said it might be true for some but if any guy tried it on with her then she'd poke his frigging eyes out for him.

1 March        Saturday

Went on round to Tina's place after dinner to see about our holiday. Big shock when I got there cos there's this police car outside and this copper on the gate. I was going in when he steps in front of me and says, 'Where d'you think you're going to, chief?'

'In here.'

'Do you live here then?'

'No, but my girlfriend does.'

'Oh yeah?' he says. 'Who's that then?' So I said, 'Tina Butler.'

'Come back later.'

'I'm expected.'

It turns out later this copper is the one Tina put down the other day. Anyway, he wasn't going to let me in till I kept on, then he climbed down when his sergeant come along and said it'd be OK. Then Tina come out and tells me to hurry on up and come on in. We went on up to her room and on the way I saw her Mum and Dad in the front room with these two coppers. I reckoned I ought to say hello or something so I just said 'Evening all' for a giggle as we went past, but the sergeant comes out and says they're making investigations and would we keep fucking quiet, then he shuts the door in me face.

'Huh!' says Tina. 'Investigations! They reckon our old man's knocked Tracie off, that's what he means.'

'What? Had it off with her?'

'No dumbo—done away with her.'

'Never! Who give them that idea?'

Tina's really fuming and she says 'Some fucking bastard's been telling the pigs our Dad used to knock Tracie about and all that.'

'Who'd say a thing like that?'

'Bloody Darren and his parents I expect,' says Tina.

We hung about on the stairs trying to listen in but we couldn't hear much, then we went into the front bedroom and started calling stuff out to that young copper and nipping back behind the curtains every time he looked round.

'He's the one who fancies me,' says Tina. 'Little bastard.'

'He'd better keep his bleeding eyes to himself,' I told her. Then she gets so mad about everything and all she opens the window and shouts down to him that the bog was blocked.

'What d'you expect me to do about it, love?' he shouts back.

'Well,' says Tina, 'you're a shit, aren't you?'

Then we laughed for all we was worth and slammed the window shut. He was really mad and he sticks two fingers up at us just as his sergeant comes out the door! That really served him right . . .

'Sorry about all this and everything, Tina,' I says to her when we get back to her room. 'Guess I'd better go.'

'Pity,' she says, 'I was feeling really randy just now.'

'Oh yeah?' I said looking up and she grins.

'Yeah, I was thinking about that copper downstairs and I got really wet.'

'You wouldn't!'

'I dunno,' she laughs. 'Depends what you can do about it, don't it?'

'About what?'

'About me feeling randy.'

So there we are—I did something about it all right . . . That's the second time I've had her in bed and it gets better all the time. There we are bouncing up and down and the bed's sounding like it's going to collapse.

'What about them downstairs?'

'Sod them,' says Tina. 'They got enough problems.'

Well, I had to laugh and we just carried on. It was great, magic. The coppers left about when I did and I bet they didn't enjoy their visit half so much as me. Mr Butler looked really shit scared and Mrs was crying all the time. Her old man told her to shut it but she kept right on and told him he was a thoughtless bastard.

'What a life!' says Tina to me as I'm going.

'Yeah—but it's got its good points.'

'Yeah,' she says and gives me a little feel through my jeans. 'See you, lover.'

Went down The Anchor tonight with Tina and John and Cherylle and a few people. It's really good with Tina right now. She's the best girl I've ever gone out with, that's for certain—by a long way. Magic!


2 March          Sunday

Not much doing today. Didn't see Tina. Had a drink with a few mates down The Nag's Head. When we was talking about holidays, Marcella said a friend of hers had a cousin who went to Tunisia and got bitten by this fly or something on her face and woke up next morning and her face was itching a bit so she thinks it's just a gnat bite and puts a bit of fly-spray on it and off she goes to the beach without thinking no more about it. Anyway, a few days later her face is a bit red where the bite was and a bit puffed up so she sticks a bit of suntan stuff on it, but by the time she's ready to come back home there's quite a bump on her face and it's itching all the time, then after she's been back a week her cheek's all red and swelled up like a golf ball Marcella says, so this girl's getting a bit worried. Next morning the itching's stopped but it feels like her face is all moving or something, so she gets out of bed and goes to have a look in the mirror and the spot's all ready to burst and she gives it a bit of a poke with her finger and it pops and all these maggots come tumbling out together with all this yellow stuff! We all nearly spewed I can tell you—the girl fainted and they had to get the ambulance for her . . . The worse part of it all is when she come round the shock had turned her mind and she was all raving and screaming and she's still like it now and they don't hold out much hope of her ever being normal again, and even though her face healed up long ago she just sits staring into the mirror touching her face and then going off into fits. Marcella said she hardly seems to know nobody now and her fiance's ditched her. One thing, none of us ever wants to go to

Tunisia if it's as bad as that out there. Then John wanted to know what happened to the maggots and Suzanne threw up.


3 March        Monday

Mr Collins back at work today. They said he'd been dried out but nobody reckoned he'd turn up. They were wrong though because there he is—first in, new suit, haircut, new moustache, the lot.

'Good morning, Andrew,' he says. 'How are you?'

'Oh—great, thanks.'

'Just come into my office a moment will you, Andrew, and tell me what's been happening in my absence. I need to have a grassroots opinion.'

'Oh yeah?' I said.

'Absolutely. Keep the men happy—and the women as well of course. I hear that the heating's been playing up again.'

So I told him about it. You know, he didn't look normal to me— he's twitching all the time like he wants to go to the bog and he's talking ever so fast.

'Oh yes, yes—can't work without heat and Mr Singleton's been transferred to the Rates Office at Llantrisant.'

'Has he?'

'Yes, the climate there should suit him. It's the coal, you know. Still, God is everywhere, Andrew. He is no respecter of places.'

Then he wipes his face with his hankie.

'Oh ah?'

'Yes indeed. Do you give much thought to, ah, God these days, Andrew?'

Well, I was stuck for an answer to that one.

'You ought, you know. Just between you and me, I've given the matter a lot of attention in recent weeks.'

'Yeah—great.'

'God has revealed himself to me,' he says.

'Oh—nice one.'

Christ, was I feeling daft stuck up there in his office.

'I have some pamphlets here,' he says fishing about in his new attache case. Then he hands me these little pamphlets.

'Er, how much?' I said reckoning it must be some kind of raffle.

'Oh, no charge to you, Andrew. Take them, read them and inwardly digest them.'

'Thanks.'

So I took a couple and went out.

'What you got there?' asks John. 'Dirty mags, is it?'

'It's called *Watchtower*.'

'Don't sound very interesting—what's it all about?'

We had a read and it was all this religious stuff, we couldn't make head nor tail of it. John had just asked which page the cartoons were on when Dani come in and looks over and says, 'Oh—you got some of them as well, have you?' We asked her what she meant by that and she told us Collins had been dishing them out to everybody.

'He's joined the Jehova's Whatsits,' she says.

'Blimey,' says John. 'I thought he was on the bottle again.'

'Oh no,' says Dani, 'they're not allowed to. They mustn't smoke or drink, or drink tea or coffee, or eat chocolate, and they can only make love once a month.'

'Christ! What's that in aid of then?'

'I don't know—that's their religion I suppose.'

'How d'you join that lot?' I asked her.

'Don't ask me. All I know is they're the ones who come round our house every six months and our Dad never answers the door.'

That rang a bell with me and I remembered they'd come round pestering our old man that time. Our Mum told him not to go to the door but he got caught going out to the car when they were coming back down the street. They told him his soul was in danger and he told them to go jump in the lake. Dani said that sounded like the same bunch and once you had them in your house you couldn't never get rid of them—bit like dry rot she reckoned.

'That's not what I call a religion. What you want to be is a Paki,' says John.

'No I don't,' says Dani, 'they smell.'

'No hang on—see they can have as many wives as they want and if you gets tired of one you just flog her down the market and get another one.'

'Typical!' says Dani. She's really into all this women's lib stuff. Then John looks at her and says, 'You'd be worth about two and a half camels I reckon,' and she tells him not to be so bloody cheeky, then she goes out laughing.

'What are you going to do with they books?' says John to me.

I said I didn't know and he said why not go down and put them through the papershredder. Trouble was, there was a queue of all these other people with stuff Collins had given them too and then the fucking thing broke down. One of them said Mr Collins was meaning to get up a vigilante committee against dirty books to try and get that place in Station Road shut down, then along come young Michelle Collins and she said her Dad was a real pain and you can't say or do a thing in their house without praying first so she's moved in with her current boyfriend. When her old man got converted her Mum went along with it too and threw out all her make-up and decent clothes so poor Michelle's ashamed to be seen with her now, then her old woman goes next door to see the guy she'd been having it away with and told him he was a tool of the devil and she was breaking it off. He said there was plenty more fish in the sea and she smacked his face and busted his glasses. ·

Played Battleships for the rest of the morning. Saw Tina dinner-time. She said they'd had a reporter from *The Gazette* round but her old man told him to hop it sharpish or he'd bust his arse, then they saw this guy go over the road and they reckon he was asking questions off the neighbours. Anyway, all the neighbours have stopped speaking to the Butlers and somebody sent her old man an anonymous letter calling him a murdering swine.

John reckons old man Butler'll do time but he doesn't dare say so to Tina's face because he knows she'd most likely have a go at him. He just said, 'Reckon your old man did it then, Tina?' and she said, 'Huh! Who knows? He might have done, the old sod.'

'You don't reckon he did, do you?' I said to her.

'He might have done for all I know. He's got a really nasty temper on him.'

'How's your old lady taking it?' John asks her next.

'All she's taking is valiums and moggies,' says Tina and she rolls her eyes. We had a good laugh at that one.

4 March          Tuesday

Got to work today to find a couple more of those little booklets on my table.

'Here,' I says to John, 'did you put these here?' I reckoned it must be one of his jokes.

'No—it were Collins.'

Then in comes Collins smiling all over as usual. 'Ah! You've found them then, Andrew?' he says.

'Oh—yeah.'

There's John grinning in the corner and Collins says, 'Here you are, John', and before John can open his mouth he shoves a couple at him and goes out.

'I'm buggered,' says John. 'How much bleeding longer's this going to go on?'

Then Max comes in and says he's just seen Collins with a huge box of the stuff. We had a swift look at what we'd got.

'Repent now and the gates of Paradise will swing open for you,' John reads out.

'Hope there's plenty of women up there,' says Max and we all laughed.

'The Lord will be there to welcome you,' goes on John.

'Wouldn't mind if Mrs Collins was there,' says Max. 'I could fancy her.'

'Well,' says John, 'that's what it goes on to say. See here—"And Mrs Collins will be there to welcome you and if you want the cups of her bra will swing open for you." '

'Par-a-dise!' says Max.

Then in come Shaking Stevens and wants to know what's going on.

'We've seen the light,' says John keeping a straight face.

'Oh yeah?'

'It's true—Mr Collins has converted us.'

'Huh! Perverted more fucking likely.'

And he does that dirty little laugh and tells us to get on with some work for a change. John reckoned he can't stop shaking because every week he goes down Mac's Books and stocks up on the hard stuff.

'Thought he had something wrong with him?' I said.

'Night starvation,' says John. 'His wife's in a wheelchair.'

Saw Tina tonight—told her that story about the girl's face. She said she'd heard the same about a girl who went to Israel.

'What about Malta?' I said. 'Might not be many flies there.'

'Oh, Marilynne says Malta's boring.'

'Where do you fancy then?' I said and Tina said Marilynne and Angelo had gone to Corfu with his business associate Michael and his wife Kris and it was really good there.

'We'd never afford it,' I said and neither would we. 'What about Spain?'

'I quite like the look of Torremolinos—it's nice and hot there. We can get a good tan.'

So there we are. We talked a bit more and in the end we decided on Torremolinos for now and she's going to have a word with her mate down the travel agents. Just hope we're not too late, that's all.

5 March       Wednesday

Went round to pick Tina up a bit earlier than normal—Anna was going on about something as usual so I cleared off out. When I got to Tina's there were these blokes round the gate and this copper keeping them back. Blow me if I knew what was happening—all he kept on saying was 'No statement for the interim period of time.'

'What's going on?' I said to this guy in a hat.

'They're digging,' he says to me out the side of his face.

'Eh? What's that again?'

'You know—looking for the body.'

Christ! So I goes along the fence and took a look over and there I can see these two coppers digging up the back garden. There's quite a few people round the front by now and I heard some woman say to the little bald-headed bloke she was with, 'He did it all right, the animal. That's what he is, an animal.'

'Yeah—stands to reason, Hilda.'

'Come on now,' says this copper, 'vacate the highway, please. There's nothing to look at.' But nobody moves.

'Come on, son.'

'I'm going in,' I says.

'Not bloody here you're not!'

Well, this was the second time I'd had all this sodding hassle so I pretty soon told him who I was and what I was there for.

'Did I hear you say you know the Butlers?' asks this other guy. 'I'm from *The Gazette*—we might be interested in your story, old son.'

'Oh yeah?'

'We might—if we can come to some arrangement.'

'Well, I ain't got nothing to say.'

'We could make it worth your while.'

Well, here's me with ideas of how I can get us a free holiday in Corfu so I says to him, 'How much?' and he leans over and whispers, 'Five quid maybe.'

'Get stuffed—five quid!?'

'Could be six—if you got a good story to tell. I can see that you're a smart lad.'

'Well, I haven't got a story to tell,' I told him, then I hopped over the fence.

'Here you!' shouts the copper. 'Where the fuck d'you think you're going?' but then Tina comes out and tells him who I am so I'm in at last, then we had it all again when we went to get out—amazing it was.

'Don't leave me alone, Tina,' says Tina's old lady.

'You got our Dad.'

'Don't leave me alone with him—there's no telling what he might do.'

'Oh yeah?' shouts Mr Butler. 'What the fuck am I going to do with half the town outside me bleeding gate, eh?'

Tina's Mum reckons her old man might have done away with Tracie after all—either that or it's all the neighbours and their lawyer says they'll never prove that no way, not in a million years. She looks really incredibly awful does Mrs Butler and she's moved into the spare room because she don't trust her old man no more and she sleeps in there with the door locked, and when her old man hears her locking herself in he shouts out it's to stop any rapists getting out if they decided to call round and nip in the window, the poor buggers. Tina tore him off a strip for that and they had a good set-to the pair of them.

'I've got to go, Mum,' says Tina, 'me and Andy's going out.'

'Oh—suit yourself then. If I'm not here when you get back perhaps you'll wish you'd stayed.'

'Silly old cow,' says Tina to me when we're outside. 'We ought to get her head looked at.'

'Still no news of Tracie then?'

'No.'

'How long have the pigs been digging?'

'Oh, since dinnertime. You should have seen it when our old man chucks a packet of runner beans at them and told them to plant those buggers for him!'

Well, I had to laugh.

'What they say to that then?'

'Told him not to be so hostile and made a few notes in their little black books, then the cheeky sods all come marching in and asked if they could have a cup of tea.'

'What did you say?'

'Told them to get knotted.'

Good for her I said. Then she told us how they'd called in this caravan thing, what they called a mobile command post with blokes inside of it who dished out tea and sandwiches to all the rest every half hour.

'Our Dad said it was like a bleeding Wimpy's,' says Tina, 'then he asked them if they'd got planning permission to open a cafe there.'

Went out The Bull Inn to a disco tonight. Trouble was, the whole thing ended up in a fight when that load of skins started making trouble. Tina and me hid under a table when the bottles started flying, then we nipped out through the bog window. When we got round the front there was these five guys kicking hell out of this bloke lying in the road but they all run off when his mates arrived. They chased the other guys up the road but they all got away except one—this guy's mates were all big rugby club blokes so they got hold of this little punk kid and smacked his head up against the wall a couple of times and handed over what was left to the coppers. One skin was nipping up an alley where there's this guy out walking his alsatian and as the skin goes past the dog takes a piece out of his arse, which slows him up quite a bit, and the cops get him as he's trying to dive over a wall into somebody's garden. It was just like something out of a Bruce Lee film. Me and Tina stood there along with a load of other people just staring like we couldn't hardly believe it, then the ambulance comes along and sees to the bloke in the road who's just lying there with blood coming out of his head and moaning a fair bit. Luckily this nurse who lives opposite had come out before and given him a bit of treatment.

'Ugh!' says Tina. 'Who'd be a nurse, eh?'

Too true, I'm not squeamish I don't reckon, but all that blood was turning me up a bit. It's funny though how you can't seem to do nothing about it except just look and they say you soon get used to it, like all those guys in Vietnam in *Apocalypse Now*, if you think about it too much you'd just blow your mind so you have to learn not to and just get on with the job.


6 March          Thursday

Bloody car broke down today. Last night it was running a bit hot, tonight it boiled over. We were on our way to a party at this place in Wellington, then after about two miles . . . splat! Steam everywhere . . .

'Radiator's boiled,' I said to Tina.

'I can bloody see that—what do we do now?'

'Have to wait for it to cool off.'

'How long?' she says.

'Don't know,' I said getting an idea, 'half hour maybe.'

'Gawd!'

'Here,' I says to her, 'I got a good idea.'

'Oh yeah,' she says, then she reaches over and gives us a feel. 'Christ! You off again?'

'On more like.'

We had a good laugh about that one, then we hopped in the back.

We had a tremendous screw tonight—it was really great. Tina's great, I think about her a lot. Come to think of it I think about her pretty much most of the time. I reckon I love her. You know, the more I think about it that's what I reckon—I love Tina. It makes me feel really good, I know that.


7 March        Friday

Collins come in with more leaflets today.

'These are 10p each,' he says, giving me more of the bleeding things.

'Thought they was free,' I said.

'Oh no.'

'No thanks then,' I tell him.

'Oh—but you've had them before.'

'Oh yeah, but they was free then.'

'They were all 10p,' he says.

'You didn't tell us.'

'Didn't I? Oh well, you've no need to pay me now.'

'I didn't know they weren't free.'

'Oh dear,' he says and goes out. I reckon he got the message.

Saw Tina dinnertime and talked about our holiday. She's seen her friend and they got a two-week trip to Torremolinos all in for just under two hundred quid each. Sounds OK—the brochure's very nice, near the beach, swimming-pool, bars, disco, the lot. Looks great. Lots of really gorgeous suntanned women lying round the pool. They've got a sauna and there's live entertainment there every night.

'What do you reckon then?' says Tina and I said I reckoned it looked great and I couldn't wait, so we're going down tomorrow afternoon to book it all up.

Tina says the coppers have dug up her old man's garden really well and they had him down the nick for six hours yesterday. He's got hold of this solicitor and he's told Mr Butler to keep his mouth shut till he's charged. It don't sound too hopeful for Mr Butler—wonder if he did do it? He's got a really bad temper that's for sure, but knocking off his own kid, well, that's something else, isn't it? John did a great impression of Mr Butler going mad with an axe and then Tina come in so he made out it was Collins not her old man . . .

Bloody car's still overheating. I've fixed up to see Nik Harris tomorrow morning about it, it can't go on like it is.

8 March          Saturday

Had a good laugh with those reporters outside of Tina's gate today.
Tina says they're there all night.

'Are you a friend of the family?' says that one to me.

'That's right.'

'Can you make a statement?'

Well, this time I'm ready for them so I says to him quiet like, 'I
know who did it.'

'Did what?' says him looking all interested.

'The murders of course.'

'Murders!' he whistles. 'How many?'

'Six'—and then I had to laugh and messed up the whole thing.

'Aw—get off out of it, you little sod.'

'Sorry, gents,' I said and kept moving right along. I told Tina when
I got in and she killed herself, then when she'd finished we come out
and she says to them, 'They're under the shed.'

'What are?' says this photographer.

'The bodies,' says Tina and bursts out laughing right in his face.

Anyway, there was even a mention of it on last night's news so I
reckon it must be pretty certain now Mr Butler did it though they
haven't found the body yet. Tina reckons he'll be nicked soon, but all
the coppers found in the garden was his seeds and some bits of old
china. They took it all away to look at.

Saw Nik this morning. The car was boiling like a kettle when I got
there—he says it's an hose and he'll get me a new one and in the
meantime just to keep topping up the rad and drop it into the garage
on Monday. It went OK on the way back and it was all right tonight
but we didn't go out of town.

Booked up our holiday I'm glad to say—last week in August and
first in September. I'm really looking forward to it. Double room of
course—Marsha says nobody minds who shares with who except
they're not very keen on two guys in the one room, not if they're queer
anyway. I reckon I'll be OK this year with Tina. I'm really looking
forward to it, I could do with a good holiday. Come to think of it, I
could do with eleven months' holiday and one of work. I don't mind
work too much I guess, but you get pissed off with it, don't you? I'll
bloody say you do—at least I do, what with Collins and those bleeding
leaflets just about everybody wants a holiday. Most people reckon he's
gone off his head. I mean take yesterday. I thought he hadn't seen me
but he gets us to come in his office and he goes on about work for a bit
and then he says, 'We must be good, Andrew.'

'Oh yeah—right.'

'If we are good then we shall get our just reward.'

'Oh yeah—payrise, you mean?'

'Heaven, Andrew,' he says with that look on his face.

'Great.'

'But if we fail to follow God's law then when we die . . .'

'Hell, eh?'

'When you die it is but a passing into new life. Death is not the end, it—everything just meaningless . . .'

Then thank christ the phone went so I hopped off quick.

Went down The Anchor tonight. Tina likes to get out of the house as much as she can these days because her Mum's depression's got a lot worse and she don't bother to do nothing no more and their old man goes down the pub when the police don't want him. So Tina gets most of her own meals—she won't cook her old man's though, so they keep having rows.


10 March          Monday

Got a letter today, turned out to be all this religious stuff from this place called The Garden of Eden Holy Holiday Village up in Norfolk somewhere.

'Dear Young Friend,' it said. 'Our Friend in Christ, Tom Collins, has given us your name as being one favoured by God who would be glad to take advantage of our Summer Youth Camp and Prayer Meeting Scheme this year. We trust that . . .' And so on.

'What is it, Andrew?' asks our Mum and I show her. Anna starts giggling of course and Dad says he's buggered. Wish he was. Bleeding nerve! Well, I'm not having any of that, so I ripped it up. And I reckoned I'd have a word to say about this to Collins soon as I saw him—first thing and all too.

Anna says she's going to Greece with Dermot to one of these holiday villas he's got an interest in—them and another couple she says, one of his architect mates and his wife.

'Oh ah,' says I. 'Same room, is it?'

No answer—typical.

Just made it to work but the car was really hot when I got there. Saw Nik dinnertime and he did it this afternoon, picked it up after work and thank christ it seems OK now, touch wood.

'Good morning, Andrew,' says Collins when he comes in. 'God bless you.'

'Thanks,' I said, then I had a word with him. 'I got some stuff through the post about holidays,' I said.

'Oh really? I was going to ask you whether it had arrived.'

'Well it has, ta.'

'Oh good—I thought you'd be interested. The holidays really do offer a most stimulating . . .'

'I've already fixed up my stimulating time, thanks,' I told him and John gives a little laugh.

'Oh? Have you?'

'Yeah, I've fixed up my holidays.'

'Really? Well, that's splendid. I knew you'd be interested.' Christ, are some people thick . . .

'Not that—in Spain.'

'Spain? But I thought— oh, well—'

It took a long time but I reckon he got the message at last.

'That'll teach him,' said John, 'bleeding meddler. You know, they reckon he wants to start having morning prayers in here.'

'Christ!'

'Straight up. No sweat.'

We had a good laugh about it and then he asks how Mrs Collins is going to cope now she's only allowed to have it off once a month. John said he'd be glad to help her out.

'Don't reckon she'll be able to hold out much longer—nor him neither.'

Then he says she ought to get hold of a copy of the rules because maybe it means only once a month with the same guy and she might be on to a good thing without knowing it. He can sure make you laugh can John—he's a good mate I reckon.


11 March        Tuesday

Big news—Tracie's back! Tina told us all about it dinnertime. Mr Butler saw the panda pull up outside and went to get his coat cos he thought his time was come, but next thing they know the coppers are bringing Tracie in the door. Course soon as her Mum sees her she breaks down and starts crying, 'My little girl's come back to her Mummy!' and Tracie says, 'Don't act so frigging daft in front of the bogeys,' but there's no stopping their Mum. Turns out she was working as a chambermaid at a hotel in Cleethorpes but when the under-manager pushed her over for the new cashier Tracie moved on and a copper spotted her dossing down in the bus station.

'Thank christ you're back, Trace,' says her old man. 'They buggers was all set to have me for murdering you.'

'So what?' says Tracie and sniffs at him.

'Little bastard.'

'Come to Mummy,' says Mrs B.

'What's up with her?' says Tracie to Tina and Tina says, 'She was worried, you little pratt,' but Tracie just says, 'So? I can take care of meself, can't I?'

Well, there we are—and there they all are. The chief copper told Mr Butler he'd better keep his bloody nose clean in the future and give Tracie a right telling-off and she just said, 'Balls to you, mate,' then him and all the other coppers pushed off. Mr Butler went out after them and so's the whole street could hear he shouts, 'And don't bloody well come back!' Next thing he comes in and starts trying to give Tracie a good leathering but she grabs up the poker and says if he comes any nearer she'll knock his frigging head off for him. Sounds to me like she don't much want to be home and Tina said Tracie hardly said nothing to nobody except as soon as she's sixteen she'll be off for good and then no frigging pig'll bring her back neither.

'Did that Darren touch you, love?' asks her Mum.

'Huh! That pratt? He couldn't touch a frigging brick wall if he walked into one he couldn't.'

'What did you do, love?'

'Worked, din I?' says Tracie, then they couldn't get another word out of her for the whole time, not even Tina who's normally pretty OK with her, together just the two of them. Tina asked her if she'd got put up the spout but Tracie just said, 'What's it to you if I have?' so Tina told her to mind her mouth or else she'd fetch her one round the head, then they didn't speak to each other for the rest of the time and their old man went down the pub. A couple of the neighbours come round and said they was ever so pleased to hear Tracie had been found and was all right, but Tina said in their hearing if they couldn't be fussed to speak when they thought her old man had done away with Tracie then they needn't bother theirselves now she was back, but her old lady had them in for a cup of tea and some almond slices all the same and kept on breaking down and crying and the neighbours said if there was anything they could do then just let them know. Tracie went up to her room, then she phoned up somebody in Hull called Franz who Tina reckoned was a merchant seaman. She says Tracie's a real pain and the sooner she clears out the better. There's been a whole lot of fuss about Tracie and her school—being absent and all—but it don't really matter because it's her last year and she's not taking many exams anyway. Well, when they asked her what ones she wanted to take she said she couldn't be fussed so they didn't put her down for none, then they thought she'd better do some or else they might get in trouble so now she's down for a couple of CSEs—Humanities and Craft I think Tina said. There's trouble in Cleethorpes too and the under-manager's got the police after him for having it away with Tracie who's under the age and for fiddling the insurance and tax forms so he could take her on to work there. He's done a flit over to Denmark or somewhere on a ferry boat. Then there's the bloke Tracie's supposed to have gone to bed with for five quid who's a big estate agent in Grimsby—he's in the shit and all. Not to mention Tracie but she's not worried, Tina says she could get sent to Borstal. Their old man's stopped speaking to her since she threatened him with the poker and just pretends she's not there and their Mum won't hear a bad word against her and keeps on buying her Fry's Peppermint Creams which she liked when she was a kid.

Tina's really pissed off. We had it away tonight and she said it cheered her up a lot—made me pretty chuffed as well, come to that. I do love her, I know that—well, I've said it before, christ knows I tell her often enough when I'm screwing her, it just seems to come out, and I've thought about it and I'm sure. I told her I loved her tonight just as I was coming off and she says, 'Oh christ! Yes!' Made me feel really good, she's great. Magic!

12 March        Wednesday

That Gill Smith in the computer section threw a fit this morning because she reckons everybody hates her. She's not far wrong neither, bossy old bugger. All the girls go on about her and how she's always rabbiting on at them all the time. Anyway, she was telling Josette how she'd done something or other wrong again and how many times did she have to tell her. So Josette turns round and gives her a bit of her own back—really tore into her the girls said—then Gill Smith starts breaking down and everything and moans about everybody having it in for her and calling them a lot of horrible little girls, but Josette just says to her, 'Oh, go and get stuffed, you silly old cow,' and next thing Gill Smith's up on the windowsill and threatening to jump out if anybody so much as comes near her.

'Nobody likes me in here,' she says and Josette says, 'Too bloody right,' which sets her off screaming and slinging the cactus pots everywhere. Then all the girls reckon she must mean what she says so they sent for the Dept Head who comes running up and tries to calm her down.

'Wouldn't you like to come to my office and talk it over?' old Lewis asks her.

'You don't care,' she says to him.

'We all care, Miss—um—'

'No you don't,' she sobs. 'You don't even know my bloody name.'

'Come now,' says Mr Lewis, 'it must be cold out there. Wouldn't you like a cup of tea?'

Well now, who should come along now but old Collins—John started calling him Moses so everybody calls it him now.

'Let me talk to the poor woman,' he says. 'Let me through here.' And he pushes his way in.

'Is anything wrong, Miss Smith?' he says.

'Everything.'

'Oh yes? Could you be a little more precise?'

'They all hate me.'

'Oh. Who's "they"?'

'All of them—everyone.'

'God doesn't hate you, Gill,' says Moses looking all serious.

'I'm all alone,' she cries.

'No, no, you're never alone with God. Give God a go, Gill.'

'Are you sure you know what you're doing, Mr—er—Mr Collins?' asks Mr Lewis in his earhole.

'Oh, quite sure, Mr Lewis. Leave it to me.'

'Well, all the same, we'd better call for the police.'

'Just let me talk to her. She's in shock,' says Moses. Then he says to her, 'Will you talk to me, Gill? You know me—Tom Collins—and you know Joan too, don't you now?'

'Oh yes, I know you—you're the one who's got religious mania. You don't like me neither.'

'Of course I do,' says Moses lying his head off.

'It's just not worth carrying on living,' she tells him.

'You're just depressed—come in and have a cup of tea, will you? A nice cup of tea?'

'Stuff your fucking tea! I might as well end it all here and now.'

'Oh no, you mustn't ever talk like that, Gill—it's very wrong.'

'Is it? Who says?'

'Oh yes, so very wrong. Pray to the Lord, Gill—pray.'

'I don't know how. I'm a Baptist.'

'Repeat after me . . .' he says, then he kneels down and starts praying. And next thing the silly bitch closes her eyes, sticks her hands together, tries to kneel down, slips off the ledge and she's left hanging on by her hands. Everybody goes 'Ah!' and some of the girls scream.

'I'm going to fall!' she shouts. 'I want to die!' Then these two coppers dash in and grab her and haul her back in through the window.

'Thank God!' says Moses. 'Oh Lord!'

'What's your bloody game, mate?' says one of them to him. 'You could have killed her.'

'That's what they bloody want,' screams Gill Smith, 'specially him.' And she has to be dragged off to the ambulance. Heard this afternoon they took her straight out to Tone Vale.

'Have the old electrodes on her head by now,' says John at teatime and he takes a bite of his doughnut. 'Stupid cow! It's only three floors up, she wouldn't have killed herself from there, no way—not in a million years.'

Dani come in and told us that Miss Smith's got a split personality and chronic depression and Josette was a bit churned up by it all so she had to take the rest of the day off. Moses had to go home and all—he were sent home John reckons.

Another hose went on the car today. Took it round to Nik's but they didn't have one in stock so he taped it up for me. He says when one goes then the other ones go and all so I might as well have the whole lot done and make an end of it but it was up to me.

Reckon I ought to think about getting a new car soon. Nik reckons on fifty thousand miles and that's your limit unless you're very very lucky, he said they've got this great Rover in at the moment going really cheap and what with the prices the way they are at the moment I'd be doing myself a real favour. Told him I couldn't afford to do myself favours like that, no way.


13 March        Thursday

Marilynne dropped home today. Her Angelo had some business in Bristol so he loaned her the Jag and she come on down for a few hours. My fucking car bust again. Well, stuff Nik so Maurice Govier took a look at it for us and he said he couldn't find nothing wrong except some silly bugger'd gone and stuck a load of tape round one of the hoses. Then he says why don't I take a look at this new Allegro they've got. I don't reckon I'll ever get it fixed. Anyway, Tina says, 'Isn't your bloody car fixed yet?' and I had to say, 'No—sorry,' then she just tossed her bloody head and pulls a face. Then Marilynne rolls up in the Jag and she says why don't we all go off out and have some fun.

'Good idea.'

'How do you know *you're* invited?' says Tina to me so I said, 'All right then, I'll walk,' but Marilynne says, 'Don't be fucking daft, you two.'

We went down The Anchor and met John and Cherylle and some other people.

Marilynne says me and Tina can go up to London for a weekend anytime we want.

'What about next weekend?' says Tina, so that's that. 'And you better get your bloody car fixed,' she says to me.

'Yeah, yeah—don't nag so,' I told her. I'm getting sick of it.

'Why don't you hitch?' says John. 'Or cut holes in the floor for your feet.'

Tina told him to piss off and I weren't far behind. Trust him. Then Marilynne says Angelo's thinking of ditching the Jag and getting a BMW. It's all right for some. John says oh yeah, a mate of his had a BMW—nice motors, so Marilynne looks at him and says, 'Oh, dinky model, was it, John?' His face was a picture.

Had to leave my sodding car in Parmisan Close up by those posh houses and walk the rest—it bloody well boiled again. Bleeding thing's boiling quicker'n a fucking kettle now. You can't go two miles. Got home at half one. One of these fine days I'm going to kick hell out of that fucking car.


14 March          Friday

Went to pick up my car and I'm just getting in and waiting for the bloody thing to blow up on me when this bloke pops out of the hedge and says, 'Do you mind not parking outside of my house?' so I said, 'What's it to do with you?' Then he starts getting stroppy about it.

'We pay our rates,' he says.

'So what? It's a free country.'

'What do you mean by parking here all night? I thought it had been dumped.' Charming!

'I broke down.'

'That's no reason,' he says but by now I was so totally pissed off with him that I just stuck two fingers up at him and drove off.

Bleeding nerve! You'd think he owned the sodding road.

Just made the car-park in time. I don't know what I'm going to do with it.

Played darts most of the afternoon. John's really into darts right now and he got himself a board down Bridge Sports at dinnertime so we tried it out, then he found an old pin-up picture and we stuck it on the cupboard door. If you hit a tit you got five points, a leg two points and so on, with a bonus of twenty if you got one right between her legs and first one to a hundred the winner. I won twice, John won three times and Marc Sully won five times, and John got a bit mad because Marc said he hadn't played for years, then Moses come in.

'Take that disgusting thing down,' he says to us.

'It's all right,' said Marc, 'nobody's looking. Have a go.'

'I'm looking—and so is God.'

'God?' says John with his mouth open.

'Well, I don't suppose that means anything to you, John—but I would have thought better of you, Andrew.'

'What's it got to do with him?' says Marc.

'He sees all, hears all, knows all and judges all,' says Moses ever so seriously.

'Stroll on.'

'Now don't add blasphemy to your other sins, Marc.'

'Pooh!' says Marc on his way out. 'You look out to your own sins, mate.'

Well, that's Moses put in his place good and proper but he kept on at us till we took the picture down. John said it must have reminded him of happier days.

Got our spring payrise today, didn't tell our Mum in case she asks for more keep. Anyway, I'm saving for our holidays.

Tina had the day off today. Her old man spent last night down the pub—with the barmaid her Mum says. So when he shows up her Mum went for him and tells him he can pack his bags and clear off out of it for good and live with his fancy woman for all she cares. Tina said to her when she quieted down a bit how would she manage without her old man's money coming in, but she just said she'd rather have his room than his company and anyway she could always take in lodgers. Then her Mum and Dad had some of what they do when they've had a bust-up, which is not speaking or when they do talking through Tina like. 'Tell your old lady *she* can go if she wants,' and then she says to Tina, 'Tell him nobody could ever have a worser husband than what he is.' Tina says it's a bit of a giggle sometimes, but then she got pissed off with it and stopped passing on the messages. She don't know why she stands it. Then Tracie's welfare officer come round but Tracie wasn't back from school yet.

'Hello, Mrs Butler,' says this welfare woman. 'Oh hello, Mr Butler. I don't think we've met—my name's Alexis Bargate.'

'Oh,' says Mrs, 'you've not missed much.'

'Bollocks,' says her old man and Alexis Whatsit says what nice weather it's been.

Tina said she was OK though and she was really together, she had on a nice denim skirt and boots and she had a really nice sharks-tooth necklace —our Anna's got one, Dermot picked it up in Spain off a little shark he knows.

They all had to sit and talk about Tracie till she got home and their old man couldn't keep his frigging eyes off this Alexis, but she could handle a little sod like him all right. This barmaid of his is really ugly and horrible—a real old shagbag Tina says. Mind you, her old man's always had an eye for the crumpet as he calls it so you can tell how old he is, but on account of being an ugly little cunt he usually don't get nowhere, but when he was younger he fair used to drive his old lady mad always chasing after other women and now he's older he's got just the same way again.

They're not doing Tracie for the bit up north with the estate agent because they can't prove nothing and he's got friends, so Tracie's got away with it this time but she's got to be supervised by the social people till she's sixteen.

'Hello, Tracie,' says this social officer to her ever so friendly but Tracie just says, 'What d'you want?'

'Only to have a word with you, Tracie. You know me—my name's Alexis.'

'Is it?'

'I've been talking to your parents.'

'Oh,' says Tracie and looks right through her.

'We're all very concerned about you, Tracie,' says Alexis.

'They aren't,' says Tracie.

'Oh, I'm sure they are.'

Then Mr Butler gets up and goes out and his wife shouts out after him, 'Off to see your slut, are you?' but for once he don't answer, just slams the door and the clock falls off the wall.

'Do you ever feel harassed by your family situation, Tracie?' asks the woman as if nothing had happened.

'Dunno.'

'Well, if there are hassles now, they won't last, will they?'
'It's boring.'
'Well, Tracie—you've got your whole life ahead of you, you know. When you leave school you can do what you like, form new relationships.'
'Huh!' says Tracie and then Alexis says how much she likes Tracie's hair and wants to know if she bleaches it herself.
'Do you want anything else?' says Tracie, then she goes out.
'How do you relate with Tracie, Mrs Butler?' says Alexis.
'She's my little girl,' says Mrs B. chewing her hankie.
'No problems? You have a good relationship?'
'Oh yes, very.'
'What about you, Tina?'
'What about me?'
'Do you get on with Tracie?'
'Not if I can help it,' says Tina to her just like that, then Alexis has a good laugh about it. You've got to hand it to Tina—she's bloody brilliant at saying things like that.
'Oh well, you're bound to have the occasional hassle.'
'Yeah,' says Tina, 'every occasion I see her we have one.'
Really looking forward to going up to London—hope to christ my car's OK, the last thing I want is for it to pack up on the way.

15 March          Saturday

Not much doing today—not compared to London anyway. Tina says Marilynne and Angelo got this really lovely flat with all this really modern furniture and everything all chosen by Angelo's ex who's an interior designer. She says we're bound to have a great time. I could sure do with a change—you get a bit bored stuck in the same place all the time, don't you? I always reckoned their Marilynne would land on her feet—still, I guess if she landed on her tits she'd bounce . . .
Went to the disco down The Avalon, haven't been there for ages and it hasn't changed much except maybe the kids are even younger. John said he wished he'd put on his short trousers and we left after a bit. That little mod— couldn't have been no more than fifteen—come up to Tina and says, 'Fancy a dance, darling?' Well, I told him to go and get stuffed, then he pulls out this knife and threatens to cut my balls off. Fucking little sod. Anyway, Dean Todd was on the door and he sees what's going on so he comes up behind this kid and grabs him and takes the knife away, then he says do I want to take the kid outside

but I said no, forget it. Not Tina though, she kicks the kid in the nuts good and hard! Straight up, magic—took his breath away anyhow. Then John tells him to watch his mouth in the future or else and we pushed off.

'That's what you ought to have done,' Tina says.

Well, I didn't like that, I told her I'd handle things my way, no problem. Felt like going back and seeing to that little cunt after that.

John and Cherylle split up tonight. They had a row and she told him to take her home, so he said she could walk so she did, then he went after her but she told him it was all over and give him his string back. John asked Keith Snook cos he works in the Legal Dept if he could sue Cherylle for the cost of their holiday, it's all fixed up and she said she'd pay him later and he didn't know if he'd get the money back from the travel people now, but he was pissed up by then.

'What you going to do then, John,' somebody says to him, 'become a poof?'

'Piss off,' he says.

Tina really had the hots tonight—when she come off it was like she was having a fit or something, really great, she's really good. Reckon I'll need new seats in the car soon, but we got that sorted—I put the front seats forward as far as they'll go and then she sits sort of sideways in the back with her legs on the seat and the door, sometimes she sticks one foot out the window and it's really great like that and sometimes she bends over the front seat and I have her like that. Like I said we've got it all worked out. Magic.

16 March        Sunday

Reckon I'll need a new fucking engine now. I let Tina have a driving lesson—don't think there's much of my gearbox left. Still, I was on the job when I said yes, I never thought she'd remember but she did, worse luck. Course she kept saying things like 'Keep your hair on' and 'How am I doing?' all the time. Well, she wasn't so bad steering the thing but as for the rest . . . Once she pulled up so quick that guy behind almost goes into us, then he shoots past, blowing his hooter and shouting and Tina gives him two fingers. I was dead embarrassed—there was these other blokes stood there on the pavement laughing and putting their hands up, saying things like 'I don't wanna die' and 'Spare me life, darling, I got a wife and two kids.' They got two fingers and all. I took over quick, reckoned Tina wasn't quite ready for the town yet and we went out into the country and I let her have another go. Course then she has to go down that little lane just like I told her not to, then we met that other car and I have to change seats sharpish and back up to let him through.

'I've aged ten years,' I told her and she just says, 'Don't act so bloody daft. Anybody'd think I killed somebody.'

'Huh! Early days yet.'

Then it come out that she hasn't even got her licence yet . . .

'I've sent off—won't that do?' she says.

Christ! I didn't let her drive no more after she said that. We'd seen that police car and all.

'Let's go for a walk,' I said to her. I mean she's a sight better at shagging than driving, but she said, 'What for? It's too cold,' so I said, 'I've always wanted to do it in the open air.'

'It's too wet—anyway, you get insects and things all over you.'

She's got a point there. Still, with her on the bottom it'd be like being on an air-bed.

Saw John and Cherylle down the pub tonight. He'd been round her place to see her and after she wouldn't speak to him for half an hour or so they got back together again and he told me he had it off with her on the spare room bed when her Mum was making the tea. Cherylle had on this engagement ring he got her which looked just like the one he give to Dawne, but course Cherylle don't know that and I'm not telling her—that would be a really dirty thing to do. Still, just for a giggle I says to him, 'I think I've seen one like that before,' but all he says is 'Where was that then?' Then later in the bogs he says, 'You had me really worried there for a minute, mate—that's the one Dawne had,' so I said, 'That so? Thought I'd seen it before.'

I shan't tell nobody, I promised him I wouldn't.

Tina and the other girls kept on looking at Cherylle's ring and then she had a little cry. John says she's a bit quiet and shy but she's really good in bed, she was pretty shy and nervous and that but now she's really keen and can't get enough. She's a sweet kid anyhow, I could fancy her myself.


17 March        Monday

Tina's old man was out again last night so when he got home his old woman cracked a saucepan over his head. Tina thought her Mum had killed him, his head was cut and when he gets up he smacks his wife round the mouth and knocks her half across the kitchen and would have done more if Tina hadn't picked up the bread-knife and her

Mum hadn't grabbed the kettle and threatened to chuck boiling water in his face. Tina's really fed up with the pair of them. Like a couple of kids she reckons.

Some stuff about our holiday come today.

'What's all that?' asks our Mum so I just said, 'Oh, only from the tour company.'

'I hope you and Tina will be in separate rooms.'

Well, I've got nothing against our Mum but she does poke her nose in sometimes.

'Well?'

'Well what?' Then she shut up.

'Let him get on with it,' says our old man, 'that's all kids are good for these days.'

'Well, I don't like it,' says Mum.

Straight, anybody would think she didn't know what life was about half the time.

'Weren't you never young?' I asked him and the old bugger goes and says, 'Not like you I weren't.' Christ! I remember Anna asking that time why they didn't start a family sooner and them saying they couldn't afford to and people were more responsible in those days. Then Anna used to keep on asking our Dad if he'd been a teddy boy. I guess he might have been—he's got these long sideburns in their wedding photos anyhow—but he'd never answer her. Who cares, eh?

18 March        Tuesday

Had to leave the car and walk home—bloody raining of course. It always fucking is round here.

'Where's your car?' says Anna.

'Bust.'

'Shame.'

'And I got to use it Friday and all.'

'Oh?' says Mum. 'What's happening on Friday?'

'Going to London.'

'You didn't say—with Tina, is it?'

'Course.'

'Oh. Whereabouts?'

'We're going to see Marilynne and Angelo.'

'To stay?'

'Yeah—any more questions?'

'Watch your mouth,' chimes in my old man.

Then we had it all over again when we sit down for our tea.

'Are you staying up there, Andrew?'

'That's right.'

'With Marilynne and Angela?'

'Angelo.'

'Oh.'

Course I could see what all this was leading up to so I just said nothing.

'What—the whole weekend?' says Mum.

'Yeah—longer if we feel like it.'

'But what about your work?'

'Dunno. Might chuck it in.'

'Oh Andrew! You don't mean it?'

I didn't, but I just kidded her on for a bit just for a giggle like, then she caught on in the end, but I wasn't letting on no more. I could see she wanted to ask about where we'd be sleeping and so on but she couldn't quite work out how to, then my old man does it for her.

'Going for a dirty weekend that's what he is.'

'Oh dear,' says Mum.

'Jealous?'

'Go,' says him. 'It's all little sods of your age think about anyhow.'

'Get—' I says to him. That's all, there's no point. We didn't get nothing else out of our Mum all through tea. Afterwards Anna says to me she reckons I ought to have a word with her, but I told her it wasn't none of her bloody business and she just tosses her eyebrows. It's all so bloody childish, they just try to bloody show you up all the fucking time.

Had Tina tonight—magic. From the back—she likes it like that so I let her have it that way once in a while, bit of what you fancy I reckon. It was great, really great. Course she didn't like me being without the car but I know how to get her in the mood. When we got to her place I said why didn't we sneak in and go up to her room, but her old woman was still up so we went in their garden shed. Well, we couldn't lie down in there, not in all the coal, so I bent her over the wheelbarrow and she grabbed hold of the handles. We'll have to nip in there again I reckon because it was so good, I don't know why but doing it in there made us both really randy—we made so much noise I thought her Mum would hear. The barrow was thumping around with Tina hanging on to it and she was saying stuff like 'Yes! Yes! Do it to me— fuck me! Harder!' and bucking and groaning, and course all that just made me even randier and my feet were sliding around in the coal and

I was hanging on to her tits and then when we finished we just fell down and the barrow tipped up. Then we had an hell of a job finding Tina's knickers because she'd whipped them off and hung them up on a nail, then we couldn't find them at all so she had to leave them till the morning because we was getting coaldust all over our hands. Bloody good job I didn't take my jeans off—I'd have looked a right pratt having to walk home bare-arsed. As it was I walked home with not a care in the world and feeling just great. Nice night too.

19 March          Wednesday

Got my car after work—Duane Trott reckoned he couldn't find nothing wrong with it. By now I'm stuck in the five o'clock traffic and next thing the bloody useless car's boiling over again so I just had to pull in. I'm getting so fucking sick of sitting in the car all the time, not going nowhere but just waiting for it to cool down. I wasn't far from the garage so I left the car and went back to see if Duane was still there—he wasn't course. Really pissed off today. One laugh though—Tina says she can't find her knickers in the shed and asked us if I'd taken them home by mistake, which I haven't. One thing, their Mum's going to get a surprise next time she goes out to get some coal in, though half the time she forgets and it goes out. We just about made it down to the pub and back tonight but it's no good having a bloody car you can only go two miles in, is it?

20 March          Thursday

Took my car into the garage first thing. Duane said he took the thermostat out yesterday so it must be the water pump and if it was then we were talking about a lot of money. I said there was no harm in talking about it. Then he said they didn't have one in stock but he could get me one in three weeks or so. I told him that was no bloody good at all, not with us going up to London tomorrow, and he said he wouldn't risk it with the water pump playing up. Went to work and rang up a few other places—one place had one but they couldn't do the job till next week, then in the end I found a place out on Wellington Road who are going to do it tomorrow.

Well, Tina's found her knickers—they turned up in the coal bucket last night and she managed to whip them out before her old man saw. Her Mum's not too good right now, walks about in a dream Tina says, so she must have shovelled them up without seeing them. All's well that ends well I guess, anyway Tina says it was her favourite pair and they've washed out OK so that's good—I'll stick them in my pocket next time.

Anyway, tonight was The Police concert—fantastic! Best concert I've ever been to by a mile. Some band! Really, really magic. Everybody was cheering and clapping their hands over their heads and jumping up and down and it was really terrifically hot in there but I didn't care, it really blew my mind. And Sting said at the end we were the best audience they'd had for any gig on the whole tour. *Must* buy their latest album—I've heard most of it and tonight they played a couple of tracks off of it. Really great!

Now I'm looking forward to tomorrow. It's been a great week so far and this weekend ought to be great and all. Hope to christ my car's going to be OK but it's not sure now we're going to take it. I told Tina about it and she reckoned even if it was repaired tomorrow how do we know it'd be OK all the way up there. We could go by train only it's so bloody dear these days, then John had a good idea for once, he said why not go up by coach. I reckoned Tina would be mad about the car but she wasn't, she said it'd be the best thing all round if the coach wasn't too expensive because it'd cost a bomb in petrol anyhow.

Too tired to write no more of this now. I've got to be up early to pack, we don't want to be hanging around for no longer than we can help after we leave work.


23 March          Sunday

That was some weekend! Magic, really magic! Anyway, to cut a long story short, I got the car fixed but we went on the coach, like Tina said we wanted to get there not spend two days on the side of the motorway.

'You ought to have took a couple of hours off like what I did,' Tina said when I got to the bus station. I was nearly late and all—my old man wouldn't give me a lift down cos he said he wasn't missing his tea and I didn't want to leave my car in the car-park all over the weekend because I wanted some wheels left on it when I got back. Luckily Anna's Dermot was just arriving when I was leaving and he offered us a lift which was really nice of him. Our old man really made me mad just sitting there saying I'd have to go on me two flat feet with that stupid look on his mug so I fixed him all right—I parked my car right across the driveway so's he couldn't get out and took the keys on with me to London. So that served him just right I reckon. Anyway, we get to Victoria Coach Station but no Marilynne . . . We looked all over the place, then we fell over some old dosser on the pavement and Tina broke his bottle of meths. He starts shouting, 'You'll have to pay for that—it's the law,' so Tina looks at him and says, 'Like fuck I will—you'll get a kick in the mouth in a minute.' That shut him up—Tina can get really ratty when she wants to and she wasn't standing any old nonsense from the likes of him and I give him a bollocking and all.

We waited round for more than half an hour with me starving by now cos I missed tea, then we phone Marilynne up and she says to Tina she forgot all about us coming up, and Tina gets a bit mad with her so Marilynne says she'll come round. Now I thought she said her and Angelo had a penthouse in Chelsea but she took us to somewhere near Paddington Station where they got a flat on the first floor in this old house.

'Thought you had a place in Chelsea,' I says.

'Oh we did—but the lease ran out so we've moved in here temporary while we look for something else,' says Marilynne.

Well, some of the furniture was OK and they had a stereo and a colour telly but the rest of it was a bit tatty to tell the honest truth, but she said most of their best stuff's in store. Angelo was having a meeting with some of his business associates so we all sat down and watched the telly, then he comes out.

'Hello—don't I know you from somewhere?' he says so we tell him who we are. Course he's only kidding and he says, 'Come up for the weekend, have yer?' and we say yes and then he asks Marilynne where the scotch is and goes out again.

'Aren't we going out?' I asked her.

'Eh?' says Marilynne. 'What for? You don't want to go out, do you?'

'Oh—he's hungry,' says Tina, 'missed his frigging tea,' and so Marilynne says, 'Oh ah?'

'Any chip shops open?' I says.

'Wouldn't advise it,' says Marilynne, 'not round here. It's all Pakis and you don't never know what you're eating. You're not hungry an' all, are you, Tina?'

'Well, I am a bit,' says Tina because she's a big girl and she eats more than I do any rate.

'Oh—well, we got some beans,' says Marilynne.

So we had some beans on toast and some coffee. Come half twelve Angelo's still in his meeting and the telly's shut down and we was a bit pissed off.

'Does Angelo have many meetings?' asks Tina.

'Oh, yes,' says Marilynne and she looks really uptight.

'Oh,' says Tina looking at her watch.

'You can go on to bed if you want.'

I reckoned that was a good idea, I was getting a bit knackered and I wanted a screw. Marilynne wasn't saying much and it looked like Angelo was never coming out, then all of a sudden he does—with these four other guys, real hard-looking blokes they was. Then he says to us, 'All right then?' and Marilynne says, 'We thought you was never going to finish, Ange. Want some coffee?' but he says, 'Not for me, love, I've got some paperwork to sort out, OK? G'night.' And that's the last we see of him.

'Best go to bed then,' says Tina.

'Suit yourself,' says Marilynne and Tina gives her a look.

Well, it wasn't bad but it was a bit cold—still, me and Tina soon warmed up, we were in that bed quicker than you can say knife and on the job right away. Tina said she reckoned Marilynne and Angelo were splitting up and it served her right.

That's the first time I spent a whole night in bed with Tina and it was really good lying up next to her—like a big hot-water bottle she is. She doesn't half kick in the night though and she wants more than her fair share of the bed . . . I screwed hell out of her, then we fell asleep in each other's arms with her hand down between my legs—at least that's the last thing I remember. It was so, so good. I knew then I really loved her.

Tina and Marilynne were in the kitchen when I got up Saturday and Marilynne said Angelo was out on business and they'd already had breakfast but I could have some if I wanted. Angelo works ever so hard at his business, she said if it was a question of a job then he'd go out any time.

'Hurry up,' said Marilynne giving me my breakfast after telling me she's sorry it's only cornflakes. 'We want to go out and do some shopping.'

That was a bit boring really and of course they didn't buy much. All women are the same, all they like to do is look in the windows and we went round all these big West End shops all crammed with people and into these boutiques and so on, then we went into a pub for our dinner and Marilynne pulls this blue top out of her bag.

'I didn't see you buy that,' I said to her and they giggle a bit.

'Who said I bought it?'

'You didn't nick it?'

'Right first time,' she laughs. 'He's quick he is.'
And then Tina pulls a slip and three pairs of knickers out of her bag.
'Suppose they catch you?'
'Course they won't,' says Marilynne, 'everybody does it.'
'It's a giggle,' says Tina and she laughs.

Sometimes I reckon she lets Marilynne lead her on a bit but Marilynne said all these big shops don't bother about stuff getting nicked because it's all allowed for in the price anyway, otherwise it wouldn't be so easy, and these Asian women do most of it even though they could pay if they wanted to but they're brought up to it.

'Hello then, young lovers,' says Angelo when we get back and he looks a sight more cheerful than last night.

'How'd it go, Ange?' says Marilynne and he nods his head and says, 'No problem, love, no problem.' Then he tells us how he's got us some pizza for our tea from the local Italian place where he used to go to school with the manager who's called Mario and is a really great guy. I was starving but I could have done with some chips to go with it.

I asked Angelo how his business interests were going and he says, 'Great, son, great. No trouble.'

'Are we eating out tonight?' says Tina after we'd had our tea.

And Marilynne gives her a look and says, 'You've just had your tea, Tina.'

'You don't want two big meals in a day, do you, lover?' says Angelo and then he pats Tina's arse. 'Don't wanna spoil your figure, eh?'

'No—all right then.'

'Yeah—you don't want to eat out, do you, Andy?'

'No, not if you don't reckon so, Angelo.'

'That's all right then—only you'd find it a bit expensive up here, mate, specially if you got any of the old cash-flow problems.'

'I got them all right.'

'You want to get yourself a good accountant, pal.'

'We can go down the pub,' says Marilynne and Tina says that'll be great.

'All right, darling,' says Angelo, 'down the boozer it is then.'

'What about your entertainments complex?' I say.

'Oh, I see enough of that place. Don't want to mix business and pleasure, old son, eh?'

We had a pretty good time down the pub. There was a couple of strippers and two comedians on in one corner of the bar, but Angelo reckoned they were tat and Marilynne said you could see better pairs of knockers in an old people's home than they had. Angelo said most

London pubs have some live entertainment these days even if it's only a good fight—there almost was one and all when these six skinheads come in with collecting tins and selling little flags.

One of them sticks his tin under my nose so I said, 'What's it for?' and he says, 'You want a nigger doing your job?'

'How you mean?'

'They got our jobs.'

'Eh? How's that?'

'Over here doing our fucking jobs.'

Then Angelo tells him to piss off out of it.

'You what? They got our jobs.'

'You heard. Go and polish your head and paint your dong black and white, then you can get a job as a belisha beacon.'

Then some spade guys come in and the skins cleared off rattling their tins. Come closing time we got some bottles in and went back to their place. Marilynne put some music on and then some other people turned up, Angelo got out some dope and passed around some joints and we had a bit of a party. One of their friends—this girl called Lianne—was really stoned out of her mind before she arrived and Angelo said she's into a really bad scene drugwise and it was an hell of a shame because she'd most likely be dead inside of a year. She must have been a really good-looking girl once too, her face was all thin but she was still nice in spite of it, I could have fancied her anyway. Angelo said that she'd go with anybody for the price of a fix and the other week she let these four Chinese have her on a building site and they'd really hurt her, the dirty little yellow fuckers, but Angelo was on the look-out for them. And the bastards never give her the money neither.

We danced a bit and drank a bit and smoked a bit and to tell the truth I don't know when I've ever felt so happy—except maybe after that first time I fucked Tina. Then Angelo danced with Tina and me with Marilynne and I could see him touching up Tina's bum so I told her to come and sit down.

'Aw, he's jealous,' says Marilynne, then gets me to dance with her again.

'Don't worry, Andy,' says Angelo, 'I ain't trying to steal your woman, mate.'

Well, I said course I didn't mean it like that but I don't reckon Tina believed me, not the way she looked. It was daft. I said I was sorry, then I danced away with big Marilynne—she's really something, I could feel those ginormous tits of hers up against me cos these were all slow records because everybody was tired and so they just held each other close and drifted round the room. Anyway, maybe I oughtn't to have done but I tried my hand at feeling Marilynne up, she lets me get so far then she whispers, 'Who's jealous now?' so I said, 'Not me,' then she says, 'Get your frigging hand out'—just like that. So I had to but I whispered back, 'Some other time maybe.' I could see Tina and Angelo and they were still dancing real close but he'd stopped feeling her bum, Tina was looking at me anyhow with her head over his shoulder and I could tell from the way she had her mouth open and from the look in her eyes she was really sexed-up. I looked straight at her but she didn't see me, then she does and she smiles her little far-away smile. That sure turned me on so when we sat down I told her I was knackered and why didn't we go on to bed, but she said she wasn't ready yet. Then she danced with some other guy. I had a job staying awake, then I guess I must have dropped off because I didn't see the other people go. Tina and Marilynne and Angelo were over in the corner laughing and giggling so I got up and went over—least I tried to but my legs didn't seem to want to.

'Go to bed,' says Tina, 'you're out on your feet.'

Her voice sounded all funny, like it was coming from miles away. I heard myself saying something like, 'I want you to come with me' and her saying, 'OK, OK—I'll be along in a minute. Marilynne's going to make some coffee. Do you want some?'

Then I said, 'No, I want you,' and they all laugh and Angelo says, 'You wait till you're married, mate.'

So I said, 'What? Who's getting married?'

'Well, you're engaged, int you?'

'I dunno,' I says, and next thing I'm sinking on to the floor and looking up at them. I could hear Marilynne saying, 'He's stoned out of his tiny mind,' and me saying, 'Shit! Who's stoned?' and they all laughed and shouted, 'You are!'

'Oh, I suppose I must be then. And my mind's not tiny—it's fucking big!'

Then I whispered to Tina, 'Come on, Tina—I really want it,' but instead of whispering I must have been shouting because they're all killing theirselves. Anyway, Tina gets up and her and Angelo help me to our room. Tina gets me on the bed and I get one hand up her skirt and the other on the zip of my jeans—I was right when I said how much she wanted it, she's saying things like 'Steady, Andy, steady,' and 'Yes! Oh! Hurry up,' and I was going to ask her to make up her fucking mind . . . Anyway, it must have been the state I'm in because no sooner do I get my prick out than I shoot my load all over the bed.

'Oh christ!' says Tina. 'You little sod.'

'I'm sorry, Tina,' I said but she breaks away.

'I'm going to have some coffee,' she says and goes out and leaves me on me tod.

Well, I reckon I'll be ready again in a half minute so I try to get up and go after her to tell her to hang on but it's no good—no legs—then I guess I dropped off, I could hear them all laughing and talking but I was well away. I don't know what time it was when Tina got back—all I can remember is she didn't have no clothes on.

'Hey! Hey!' I says. 'You come prepared then?'

'Go to sleep—I've just had a bath.'

'Come here,' I says. 'Mmm, you smell all nice.'

'Yeah—and you smell like a fucking brewery.'

'Come on, Tina,' and I got my hand up between her legs, then I go out like a light.

Woke up Sunday with one hell of an hangover, I was lying there next to Tina—funny how sometimes when I've had a skinful I wake up earlier than normal—and all of a sudden I thought of what Angelo said about us being engaged, least that's what I thought he said. Tina was half awake by now so I said to her, 'What did Angelo say last night about us being engaged?'

'He thinks we are.'

'Oh—yeah.'

Well now, I knew I loved her—I've thought about it a fair bit and I'm sure. So I said all of a sudden to her, 'What do you reckon, then?'

'About what?'

'Well . . . about us getting engaged,' I said—and I have to admit there was a lump in my throat when I said it.

'What about it?'

'Well, are we?' I say—and I could feel my heart pounding all the time—'Are we engaged?'

'Suppose so. Why not?'

'OK then.' I kissed her and ran my hand over her tits. 'I love you, Tina,' I said and she smiled at me and nods her head. 'It's OK—eh?' I said.

'Great. OK,' and we're there just smiling at each other. Magic! I felt really great. Well, I was ready for it but Tina reckoned there was no time.

'Just a quick one. It'll be OK now—look.'

I lifted up the blankets and let her have a look. Well, you can't tell me when she wants it, her cunt's nice and slippy and I'm giving her the old finger in and out nice and slow and she grunts, then it's legs open and in we go.

'Hang on,' she says.

Well, I wasn't waiting for her to change her mind so I stuck it in. 'Ooh!' she goes—that noise really turns me on. She was dying for it.

'I love you, Tina,' I says to her.

'I love you, Andy,' she says and she squeezes the cheeks of my arse and I really ram into her. Magic!

'We had some fun last night,' says Marilynne when we come out.

'Yeah,' says Tina and Angelo looks kind of confidential at me and says, 'Women, eh? What can you do with them?'

'Too right. Say no more.'

Then we told them we got engaged and they both said it was great and when was the big day, but we said we hadn't had time to work it all out yet.

Went down the pub after dinner but I was still feeling a bit queer. That's one of the worst hangovers I've ever had except when I got poisoned that time. I had a couple of pints but I didn't feel much better.

Angelo and Marilynne took us to the coach station and it was funny on the way back really, Tina and me wanted to talk about us getting engaged but neither of us knew how to start so we didn't say much for a bit except the odd chat, then I said to her, 'Well, what's it feel like to be engaged then?'

'Oh—it's great—you know.'

Well, then the ice was broken and we talked about this and about that with getting married and all.

'You reckon it's a good idea then?'

'Course I do,' says Tina and I felt really good, I didn't want her to think I'd never have asked her, I reckon I would have done sooner or later looking back on it now. Can't see myself doing the old down on my knees bit. Still, who does that anymore? I reckon it'll be OK with Tina—she's great.

'Think I'll have tomorrow off,' Tina said when we was almost home.

'Yeah, me too. I'm a bit knackered. I'll drop around tomorrow.'

Then I give her left tit a little squeeze.

'OK then?'

'Yeah—great.'

Magic!

So there we are—that's how me and Tina got engaged, and I reckon it's the best thing I ever done.

I was looking forward to telling our Mum and Dad but soon as I get in he starts sounding off at me about how he hasn't been able to go out all weekend because my car was in the way.

'Stuff you, mate,' I told him quick.

'You what, you little bugger?'

Honestly, he's really boring. So I ignored him.

'Did you have a nice time?' asks our Mum.

'Great, yeah. By the way—'

Then I stopped. When it come down to it, I didn't know what to say. I worked it all out and then I just dried up.

'Yes, love?' she says. So I just shot it out.

'We got engaged.'

'What? To Tina?'

'No, to the bloody Queen.'

There's no stopping our Mum, she's all over me like I'm a bloody kid or something, saying stuff like 'Oh!' and 'How lovely!' but 'Oh!' mostly, then she's got tears in her eyes. To tell the truth, I was a bit embarrassed—I just stood there, then my old man comes down off his high horse and grabs hold of my hand and says, 'Best wishes, son—Andy—best of luck.' Course then I had to tell them all about it, not that there was much to tell. My Mum wanted to know where I proposed but I didn't tell her we was in bed at the time, I said I couldn't remember and she laughed. Then Anna come back and I had to go over it all again. That was some weekend—I'm shagged out, I reckon I'll sleep for a week. Magic!

24 March          Monday

Took today off and had a good long sleep this morning, for once our Mum didn't wake me up, then I just lay there in bed thinking about the weekend and me being engaged to Tina. Had a good think about it all and I reckon it's a good thing. I'd been thinking of asking Tina sometime if maybe we could get a place together so as it is things couldn't have worked out better than they have. Come September it'll be a year since we started going out—we get on fine and sexwise things couldn't be better. I reckon it was on the cards we'd get engaged sometime. Yes, I reckon it's good, I'm really looking forward to it.

Saw Tina this afternoon. Her Mum was pleased, Tracie said she couldn't care frigging less so Tina give her a belt round the head and their old man was out. He's just lost his job—been made redundant. Still, sod him—Tina says he'll be lucky if he gets an invite.

Saw John and the rest of the crowd tonight down The Anchor—big celebration when we told them our news.

'Welcome to the club, mate,' says John. 'Nobody gets out alive.'

'Thanks.'

'We ought to have a double wedding. Be a laugh, eh?'

We got pissed and John and me ended up saying we'd be each other's best man. Cherylle kissed me on the cheek and then she cried a bit because she said she was so happy for us. Great evening. Really on top of the world. Magic!

25 March          Tuesday

Today John's told everybody at work about me and Tina, so when I open the door there they all are and they start singing 'For He's a Jolly Good Fellow' and all that stuff—made me feel a bit queer to tell the honest truth. Tina says they did the same to her in her office.

Course we was all laughing away there when in comes Moses wanting to know what all the noise is about.

'Andy's getting married,' John tells him.

'Oh—indeed? Well, Andrew, marriage is a very serious business—a very important step.'

'Right on,' I says.

'Come and see me later,' he says, then he goes out. Course soon as his back's turned everybody giggles and the girls all laugh.

I goes along to see him after our first coffee break. 'Congratulations, Andrew,' says him. 'I hope you'll be very happy.'

'Thanks a lot.'

'I've no need to tell you, I'm sure, how serious is the step which you are taking. I'm sure that you're going into it with your eyes open.'

'Hope so,' I tell him though I felt like going to sleep right then.

'Quite. Marriage is an institution, ordained of God that we may not be consumed utterly by our, ah, physical lusts to the detriment of our eternal souls.'

Well, he'd lost me so I just kept quiet, it's the best way.

'But marriage is far more,' he goes on. 'It is far more than mere physical—it is the joining together of a man and a woman in holy matrimony and as such is not to be taken lightly.'

'No,' I says, bored already. And still he hadn't finished.

'No doubt you are aware of the penalties for lust, that is to say, unbridled lust?'

'You mean for rape and stuff like that?'

'No, what I mean is the price one pays in one's soul if one gives in to the temptations of Satan with regard to, er, our carnal appetites.'

'You mean paying for it?' I said. I was getting bloody fed up with this by now.

'Um—paying for it?'

He'd lost me again.

'Yeah—you know.'

I was going to tell him it wasn't none of his business when he starts dishing out the books again—same old stuff and not a decent story in the lot.

'I have some pamphlets here,' he says and I think to myself here we go again, 'which I should like to give you.'

'Oh ah?' I thought he'd stopped all that. 'How much?' I said—he won't catch me a second time.

'Oh, no charge. Yes, they deal with our responsibilities in the marriage relationship and of course to our children. Do you intend to have children, Andy?'

'Dunno. We haven't thought about it. Early days, eh?'

'Ah yes, children are a blessing indeed.'

Well, by now I was pretty sick and tired of all this personal stuff, I felt like telling him where he could stick his fucking pamphlets.

'Is that all?' I said and got up to go.

'Please, take the pamphlets. They will guide you and help you. And if you want more advice then I as an older—'

I just grabbed them and said, 'I'll let you know,' then I walked out. I wasn't having no more of that old shit, no way. One more minute of it and I'd have told him where to get off, job or no job, and that's a fact.

'You should have laid one on him,' says John but I told him I handled it, no sweat.

All the pamphlets were about stuff like how you ought to reckon your body's a temple of the spirits and that and how you ought to look after it by not having it away too often and always do it in bed in case anybody calls round and anyway you're human beings after all and not the beasts in the fields. John and me weren't going to bother reading none of it to start with but we read the first page and it was so funny we had a squint at the rest. Neither him nor me'd ever seen nothing like it. It fair had us in stitches most of the time. Like John said I know what bodies are for—so does Tina. We specially liked the bit where it said a guy with the horn was not a pretty sight and you might frighten your wife if you ponce about the bedroom without your clothes on—I told Tina tonight and she reckoned it was all so much rubbish.

Wish I'd kept them for her to read, but when me and John had finished and showed them to a few other people I stuck them in the bin where Moses could see them.

'Next thing they'll want to make sex illegal,' says John.

He reckons now old Moses isn't getting it no more with his missis than once a month he's turned into a voyeur and gets his thrills by asking other people personal questions. Next thing he'll be down the bogs in the park with his Black and Decker John said and I roared.

Then after dinner Moses comes in with this envelope in his hand. We all made out that we hadn't seen him cos we reckoned it was more pamphlets.

'Can I have your attention please, everybody,' he says so we all looked up.

'I am sorry to say that shortly after dinner I found a certain magazine in the toilets.' Then he waved the envelope. 'I have thought a great deal about this,' he goes on and John and Marc and me grin at each other, 'and I am decided that it ought not to be pushed under the carpet.'

'Have a job reading it under there,' says John.

'What sort of magazine's that?' asks Marc.

'A magazine—of a certain nature—of an—indecent nature.'

'Let's have a look then,' says Marc and all the girls giggle.

'It is a magazine of an offensive and sexual kind.'

'Oh yeah? Sling it over here then,' says John.

'I think it might be best if it were not seen by young ladies.'

'Go on,' says Tanja.

'No, it would be best if it remained where it is.'

'Spoilsport,' laughs Sue. 'Bet it's nothing much.'

'It is no laughing matter, Sue. If you find the sight of people, men and women, in, er, amusing, then—'

'Depends what they're doing,' says she and they all giggled some more.

'Well, if you won't show us then we can't tell what all the fuss is about, can we?'

'I have been in touch with the police and they have assured me that they will make the utmost efforts to ascertain its origin.'

'Christ!' says Marc but Moses didn't hear him.

'They have told me the magazine is obscene under existing legislation and that they will find out if such things are being sold either openly or secretly in the town. I will take this'—and he waves the envelope again—'round to the police station after work for them to dispose of. However, if anyone here knows anything about how it came to be in the toilet, I would like to hear from them.'

'If we can't see it, we can't say,' says Marc.

'Most likely fell out of somebody's pocket when they was pulling up—' says John and then stops because Moses is looking daggers at him. 'The seat,' he says with a straight face.

'Very well, you can have a look at the cover—but not the girls.'

'Are there girls in it then?' says Marc but Moses don't answer him. We all had a quick look then Sue leans over and grabs it before Moses can stop her.

'Please—please give it to me, Sue.'

'Ooh!' she goes and we all laugh and John looks at me and says, 'Told you so,' but her and the others have a look.

'Oh, I've seen worse than that,' she says passing it on.

'I sincerely hope you're joking, young lady,' says Moses putting it back in the envelope and Sue makes a face at him when he's not looking.

'So. Nobody knows anything about it?' Moses says and nobody did, then John says, 'Why? Do you want to know where you can get hold of some more?' And Moses gives him such a look! Even John went red—and that don't happen very often.

'What do you reckon to things like that then, Mr Collins?' says Sue.

'Well, of course there's nothing wrong with sex in its rightful place, Sue,' he says to her. And she looks all serious at him.

'Right on,' says Marc and he gets a look too.

'Sorry,' says Marc and he grins.

'But all this sort of thing'—and he taps the envelope—'well, I find them rather amusing to tell the truth.'

'Oh yeah?' says John.

'Yes—don't you think so?'

'Oh yeah—course,' says John, 'bundle of laughs.'

'Oh yes, sex is the most natural thing in the world, but I think one has to feel sorry for the people who buy this sort of thing. But it's when it falls into the hands of children and those of weaker minds . . .'

'Yeah,' says Marc, 'who knows who might have found it in the bogs, eh?' We all kill ourselves laughing and Moses just says, 'That's quite right—you never know.' Then he pushed off.

'Reckon that's why he always goes in the bog after his dinner,' says Marc.

'Must be his lucky day,' says John.

When I got home our Mum was on the phone and my old man said she'd spent the best part of the last three hours ringing up relations telling them about Tina and me getting engaged.

'Don't know what my bloody bill's going to be,' he says and Mum looks up and tells him out of the side of her mouth to stop moaning all the bleeding time.

'Auntie Dor wants to know what date the wedding is,' says Mum to me but I didn't have the faintest idea.

'Oh, they don't know yet but we'll fix it up and let you know.'

I liked that bit—the bit about 'we', I mean. When she's made about ten more calls and our tea was late she says, 'Now, Andrew—about June would be nice, wouldn't it?'

'What for?'

'Well, the wedding of course.'

'Oh—we'll see.'

'Little bugger's having second thoughts, I expect,' says our old man.

'Quiet, Brian.'

Well, I wasn't taking that sort of bullshit from the likes of him so I says to him straight, 'You stuff that sort of talk.'

'You what?'

Then Mum quieted him down. He really pisses me off these days.

'He doesn't mean it,' she says to me later. 'It's his back.'

'Yeah—likely story.'

Then in comes Anna and says oh, you can't get married in July cos that's when her and Dermot might be off to Greece.

'Oh yeah? Whose bloody wedding is this anyhow?'

'Well, yours,' says Mum, 'but there are so many people to be considered.'

Saw Tina tonight.

'What do you reckon then, Tina?' I said.

'What about?'

'Well, when shall us get married?'

'Oh, I dunno—in the summer I suppose.'

'What about the holiday?'

'Better make it the honeymoon—and you'd better get me a bleeding ring and all.'

Our holidays are booked for the last week in August and the first in September so it looks like we'll be getting married in August. Lots of things to work out before then I guess.

'Don't fuss,' says Tina.

'Who's fussing?' says I and slipped my hand up. Nice one.

26 March        Wednesday

Bloody car packed up again today. Took it to the garage and they said it needed a new engine. Well, that's the last straw and I'll be buggered if I'm going to that expense. I told them to do what they could—picked it up tonight and they'd put in a new dynamo. Seems OK now but they said the water pump's near to going. Christ! I don't know—I told them they only put the bleeding water pump in the other day and they said it might have been a rogue one and you could never tell till you'd been running it but the first one's guaranteed.

It's expense all the way, went out with Tina at dinnertime to look at rings . . . course the crafty sods put the prices on in titchy little numbers you can't read so you got to go in and ask.

'I like that one,' says Tina outside so in we go and tell the bloke we'd like to have a squint at this ring in the window. Out it comes—fits Tina a treat too.

'How much?' I ask him.

Five hundred and fifty quid! You could have knocked me down with a feather.

'What else have you got?' I say and he brings out this tray of other ones—and not one of them under a hundred and fifty quid.

'This one's nice,' says Tina.

'Oh yes,' he says, 'that's only a hundred and seventy-five pounds, that one. What price range did you have in mind, sir?'

'Oh—about twenty,' says I.

When we got outside Tina says, 'You didn't have to say that.' So I said, 'What ought I to have said then? We can't afford rings at five hundred and fifty quid.'

'Oh yeah? *You're* supposed to get the ring.'

'You'll have a ring, Tina.' And so she will and all. I said she ought to try and be more practical but she just turned off funny after that so I didn't keep on at her, you don't get nowhere that way.

We went in another shop and they had some at seventy-five quid but she didn't like none of them. Typical. Still, her family's got to fork out for the wedding, that's what our Mum said—least her old man's supposed to but Tina says he's skint because he spends all his money on that barmaid he's having it off with and anyway come August he'll probably have cleared out more than likely. This afternoon John and me were talking and he had a good idea—he said why not get her one of those rings they got on offer in the paper sometimes? They're only about fifty quid he says. Sounds like a good idea.

My birthday the week after next—Tina reckons we can have a joint engagement and birthday party. Our Mum says you're only twenty-one once in your life, which is right I guess, but I'm not having the sort of do she wants, like I had for my eighteenth when she went and invited all those relations. That was really painful. I can still remember it, all my friends in one room and all the rest in the other complaining about the noise, then trust our old man to go and find a couple in one of the bedrooms—I reckon he did it on purpose—anyway, he caused one hell of a scene and I felt really shown up so I'm buggered if I'm going to go through all that hassle again. Then Nan got drunk and all, right after he's been going on about the 'youth of today' as he calls it, and she staggers in and asks him what time the sodding moon comes up. Everybody kept telling her not to keep knocking it back so but she wouldn't listen. I'm not going to remember no more of that night, it was really awful.

Three phone calls from relations teatime, all wanting to give us congratulations, didn't know what to say to them so I just said, 'Oh ah—ta very much,' then our Mum took over. What she finds to say to them all the time I'll never know. I said if any more of them rang up they ought to say I wasn't in. If you ask me though, Anna's being the most sensible of them about it. She just said, 'You're lucky to be moving out. Where are you going to live?' Well, I can't say Tina and me have talked about it much—guess we'll have to work something out but there's plenty of time.

'Dermot's got a friend who's an estate agent—I can get him to introduce you if you want,' says Anna which was really nice of her.

Anyway, to be honest I was a bit pissed off with Tina today what with all that about the ring, then tonight when I really fancied some sex she says she don't feel like it.

'Well,' I says to her, 'We're engaged now.'

'So what? If I don't feel like it, I don't feel like it.'

That's women for you. We didn't have a row or nothing about it though, I guess I can wait a day or two for her to come round.

27 March        Thursday

Course John has to go and say to Moses, 'What are the police doing about that magazine, Mr Collins?'

'Oh—they're making investigations and pursuing enquiries.'

'Could be an international gang,' says John just for a giggle but Moses only says, 'Yes, it could be, they say it's an increasing problem in the south-west,' then he goes out. He never had much of a sense of humour.

Still, the police did raid Bob's newsagents on Monday so I heard—bust in the door with axes at half one in the morning and just about scared poor old Bob to death by all accounts, but that was before Moses found the mag. I was talking to John about it and how when we were at school we used to go in Bob's dinnertimes and if you were lucky then he'd take you out the back and let you have a look at the stuff he kept for special customers . . . He's a bit weird, old Bob—I remember that time he says to me, 'Do you like my special books, young man?' in ever such a funny voice and I got the wind up proper because I reckoned he was going to have a grab at me any minute, but he never did. I never heard he touched anybody up—they say he just likes kids, talking to them and that, because he was an orphan. And sometimes he'd give you barley sugars and tell you when you grew up you'd be doing what the people in the nice pictures were doing.

There was a letter from Moses in the paper last week saying that shops who sold indecent material were a strain on the fabric of society and ought to be closed down.

Tina got her ears pierced today so when she comes back she's got those little plug things in her ears to keep the holes open. This big bloke with tattoos all up his arms and all over his chest did it to her and she said he had these funny eyes which looked right into her and she felt her legs go to jelly.

'It was like he was hypnotising me, like he could do anything he wanted to with me,' she says so I asked her if this guy tried anything on with her.

'Course not—don't be daft. But it was sort of nice all the same.'

She gives a little smile and I could see she was joking. John reckons all women have got this thing about being dominated by a man. Deep down he says they all dream of being slaves but most of them don't never get around to doing nothing about it and he says he wishes he could find one who did.

Anyway, hope she hasn't gone and messed up her ears. She said they really hurt tonight, then some bright spark goes and says you can get blood poisoning that way, so then Tina wants to know what blood poisoning felt like if you had it but nobody knew. Her mate Eve had one of her tits tattooed last summer with a little snake curled around the nipple.

Told her what John said about rings and she said she'd think about it.

Our Mum told me to tell Tina to tell her parents they ought to all get together sometime for a chat. If you ask me, they're trying to run this wedding—our Mum's already written out a list of the guests, I told her straight it was me and Tina what was getting married and we'd invite who we wanted to, then she got uptight and Dad said, 'Ungrateful little buggers,' which is about what you'd expect off him.


28 March          Friday

Tonight me and Tina started planning our party for the 8th.

'What about your house?' I said knowing what my old man'd say about having it round our place, but that's out anyway because of last time and I'm not going through that again . . .

'No way,' says Tina. 'Me Mum's close to a breakdown right now what with Tracie going off again.'

'What? Has she cleared off again then?'

'Best thing for her—I don't never want to see her again.'

The social work people are hopping mad—so are all the coppers. Tina's old man's got the shits because he's scared they'll be after him for murder again and Tina's Mum's taken to her bed with what she reckons is nervous exhaustion.

'It's like living in a bleeding hospital,' said Tina to me. 'Roll on August.'

'Sure—it'll be great.'

'Have to have the party at your place then.'

'Nope—I've had some of that, and you know what my old man's like.'

'Huh! What's that matter?'

I told her about my eighteenth and she got a bit snappy, then John come along and said why don't we hire The Griffon for the night. He said you could get it for only a tenner and then you didn't have no hassle with people busting up your house and having trouble getting drinks—be well worth it he said.

'What about music?' asks Tina.

'Todd Westlake'll do a disco for you,' says John, 'or you can do it yourself.'

'How much?'

Well, John says he'll ask him for us but he reckons about a tenner. We thought about it for a bit and Tina said, 'C'mon, we can afford it, you mean sod,' so I said yeah OK then and John said he'd get Todd to give me a ring. So that's that settled—we'll go round and book it up tomorrow.

Wanted Tina tonight but she said her ears were hurting her. I said I hadn't heard that one before and she said if I didn't believe her then I could do the other thing. I said that it was just a joke but then she told me to grow up in that voice of hers—well, I couldn't be fussed to row with her so I just said I was sorry she couldn't take a joke, that's all. Bit pissed off tonight.

## 29 March          Saturday

She was in a better mood tonight. We went on down to The Griffon about half eight but we didn't stay, it's really dead down there, mostly all the older people from the office and their wives sitting around drinking halves and talking shop. They don't like the juke box on neither. So we just nipped in and booked up the big room for the 8th.

Well, the weather's turned mild just now. Our Dad got the mower out but it wouldn't work—still, he wasn't moaning for once.

'Bet you wish it was always busted,' I said to him and he says, 'You ought to do it by rights.'

'Stroll on.'

Anyway, when we come out from booking the room, Tina looks at me and says, 'Nice night,' and she's got that little smile on her face and there's all the little stars twinkling away like fuck.

'Yeah.'

'Like my perfume? I only got it today.'

So I took a sniff.

'Lovely,' I says to her up close. 'What's it called then?'

'It's called Feedijoy Body Spray.'

'Nice.'

'You spray it on all over.' She looks really sexy when she does that little smile.

'Oh ah? Everywhere like?'

'Yeah—I put some on me boobs.'

'Great! Come here. We can hop in the field.'

'I don't want green all over me bum,' says Tina but it was lucky I'd remembered to put that old anorak in the car in case of rain so I sat her down on that and we was well away.

'Ooh!' she says. 'Me bum's all cold!' We had a good laugh about that and she said she reckoned I must be the randiest little bugger in the town.

'Who's arguing?' says I. Magic!

There was those sheep making funny noises and she says she reckoned it were me! Great time tonight.

## 30 March          Sunday

As the weather's so fine last night John said why don't him and Cherylle and me and Tina all go out somewhere this afternoon. Sounded like a good idea so Tina and me said why not.

'I fancy going to the seaside,' said Cherylle.

'Right, my love, the sea it is then.'

'Make a change from watching my old man eating Branston Pickle,' says I.

We thought about Minehead first off but John says there's shit all over the beach so in the end we went up to Lilstock. I'm having to cut down on expenses right now and I don't trust my car anyhow at the present moment in time, not for longer trips anyway. If it fails the MOT next week I don't know what I'll do. You have to have a car—I don't know what I'd do without one. Suppose I could get Tina to go halves on one but then we'd have all this learning to drive stuff again and before you knew where you were the car'd be a wreck and so would my nerves. Then she'd only keep on wanting to lend it all the time. So John offered to drive and he goes like the clappers as usual—he even scares the shit out of me sometimes. His cousin tuned it for him last week and got him one of those black steering wheels with all holes in it cost price. Tina reckons he got him a head to match. Cherylle really goes for fast cars and fast driving—she sits up front with John and keeps telling him to go faster all the time, she used to go out with a guy in the Rally Club who had a tuned Escort and she reckons he once did a ton ten on the Bishops Lydeard bypass. He smashed himself up pretty bad last year and they reckon he'll be lucky if he drives again.

It's a nice place, is Lilstock. I like the sea. We got down on the beach and John and me wanted to go and have a look at the sea but the girls didn't so we split up, them going along under the cliff and me and John walking out to where the sea was.

'When do you think you and Cherylle'll get married then, John?' I said to him.

'Dunno—gonna be a long engagement I reckon. The longer the better, eh?' says him with a grin. 'Reckon we'll find a flat first.'

We walked on a bit and it was really nice, we had the beach to ourselves.

'You and Tina fixed on August then?'

'Yeah.'

'Reckon you'll be all right there, mate, do you?'

'I reckon so—we got things pretty well sorted, you know.'

'Get it right from the start, no trouble.'

'Yeah, I reckon we got it worked out.'

'Still, no great problem if it don't work out—so long as you don't have no kids to worry about.'

'Couldn't afford none.'

'What's Tina reckon? She want kids?'

'Dunno—don't reckon she likes them.'

'Best keep it that way.'

I told John I wouldn't mind having a kid one of these fine days.

'Load of trouble—never worth it.'

By now we'd reached the sea almost and the mud was getting on our feet, so we took off our shoes and rolled up our jeans and had a paddle.

'Sex life OK, is it?' asks John.

'No trouble—couldn't be better. How about yourself?'

'Great, man,' he says with a little smile. 'Cracking. What do you want to get married for?'

'Just do I guess.'

'Ah—don't do any harm to have a place of your own. She's all right, your Tina.'

'What about Cherylle? She keen on settling down?'

'Probably. Women are funny, eh?'

'Sure are, John.'

Then he tells me he had this other girl last week—one-night stand he said.

'Jammy sod.'

'Well,' says him with that grin on his face, 'if it's there then I don't like to say no.'

'What about Cherylle?'

'What about her? What she don't know won't hurt her, eh?'

'What if she had other blokes then, John?' I asked him and he pulls a face.

'No way, Andy—no way.'

Well, by now our feet was getting cold and the girls was waving at us so we went on back.

'What you two been talking about?' says Tina.

'Swapping partners,' says John with a smile and the girls giggle.

'You ain't having me,' she says. Too right.

'What was you waving at?' I asks her.

'You, dummy—there was this bloke looking at us.'

'Oh yeah? What did he want?'

'What do you think?' says Cherylle and her and Tina laugh.

'What was he like then?' says John.

'Couldn't see,' says Tina, 'except he had on a grey coat and he had this huge dog with him.'

'Reckon you can handle yourselves, girls,' says John.

'I can handle you,' says Cherylle and she bursts out laughing.

'All the same,' says John to me. 'They don't think of nothing else.'

'I'm bored,' says Cherylle.

'Anyway, he's gone now,' says Tina, 'and my bleeding ears are getting cold stood here.'

Her Mum give her a pair of her earrings. 'My days for jewellery are over,' she'd said at the time, then went off crying in her room. Tina's proper fed up with her.

Still no sign of Tracie so their Mum's practically up the wall and their old man's gone into hiding with this barmaid called Beryl. Tina says she's a right slag and her old man couldn't find nobody else who'd have him and he really ponces himself up with Brut and everything when he goes down there and he looks a right pratt with his hair over his ears and his paisley shirt on. And he's taken up badminton. She feels sorry for him she says, but she hates him for walking out on her Mum so she don't hardly speak to him.

Great day today. I really enjoyed it—the air made us all tired, I don't know why it does that but it always does, and we went to this little country pub for the night, one of those real ale places with blokes like Dermot in there and MGs all over the car-park. All that real ale tastes the same to me. Gnat's piss like John says. Great time today.


31 March          Monday

Short week this week because it's Easter and we get the Thursday off as well as the Friday. Tina told me Tracie's been found in Bristol, she'd got a lift up the motorway with this lorry driver and stayed with him over the weekend, then his wife come back and found Tracie in bed with her old man so she took the carving knife to the pair of them. She punctured one of his lungs and slashed Tracie's leg before Tracie managed to nip out of the window. Course all that brought the police in. They reckon Tracie'll be put in care now because her folks can't look after her proper no more.

1 April       Tuesday

Todd come round and he can do us a disco no trouble or he can get us a live band. He said he couldn't go no lower than twelve quid for the disco so that's that fixed up.

I'd been turning out my drawer today and found that tube of Superglue I'd got from Boots and didn't take home in case our old man got hold of it and stuck his hands together or worse.

'Here,' says John when he sees it, 'we could have a laugh with that. You know what day it is?'

'April Fools—but no putting it on anybody's chair or nothing like that, John.'

'No, course not—you know me.'

'Yeah, that's right.'

'Here, I know what we can do—got 50p?'

'What for?'

'Give us it here then, you tight bastard.'

'Piss off—I'm skint.'

'10p then.'

Anyway he got 10p off Marc and goes out into the corridor with it and takes the glue as well and then he sticks the 10p to the floor.

'What the fuck are you doing with my 10p?' says Marc.

'Hang on—you'll see.'

Then he gets us all behind the door so we can look out but nobody can see us and tells us to wait till somebody comes along—course now we can see what he's up to. Sure enough, along comes Kika from Accounts and right away she spots this 10p lying on the floor, so down she goes to pick it up thinking it's her lucky day. Just picture her there trying to pick it up and then trying to work out why she can't! Then she pulls a face and says to herself, 'Fucking hell!' and goes off. Well, next one along is old Moses and he's tight as a duck's arsehole so straight off he's down on his knees—John reckons he was praying—and trying to get it up with his car keys. Then we must have laughed too loud cos he looks up all red in the face and we dash back to our seats. We must have seen about two dozen people try to get that 10p up before the word got round . . .

Next thing John goes a bit wild and stuck a file to a table in the next office. Then when Marc's in the bog, John nipped in and stuck one of his drawers shut.

'All right, you bleeding A-rabs,' says Marc when he gets back, 'who did it then?'

In the end he got the drawer open with the fire axe and split the wood right across the top. Moses said as it was an accident he'd just put in for a new one as you couldn't use it like it was in case you got splinters. He wasn't too pleased when he found out about the file though—he said it'd just have to stay stuck there till the glue wore off. But Justin Shattock—it was his table it was stuck to—was really good about it and instead of dropping John in the shit he just said to Moses it got spilled by accident. We ran out of glue after that and stuck the tube to the side of the wastepaper bin to give the cleaner something to think about. All in all, we had some good laughs today.

2 April          Wednesday

That 10p still stuck to the floor today. Ratty note left by the cleaner about the waste bin.

Had Tina in the usual place after the disco.

'I love you, Teen,' I told her.

'Yeah—course,' she says.

I whispered in her ear, 'I love you, Tina' all soft like, and she wriggled a bit under me and says right back, 'I love you, Andy' which made me feel really great. Then I got on with the job. Magic!

When we'd finished I said to her, 'I can't wait till we're married, love.'

'No,' she says, all dreamy, 'it'll be really great, yeah.'

I really like her when she's like that—it really turns me on. She's got some stuff about rings from a mate of hers that she's going to show me tomorrow. But somehow when we were there it seemed like everything and that had stopped. It's hard to say what I mean but it was like—well, I don't know, it was great anyway, that's all I can say.

The social people have put Tracie out at the Juvenile Assessment Centre out Monksilver for the time being. Tina says Tracie bit the warden's hand when she got there so they stripped her down and stuck her in a padded cell. Serves her right says Tina.

3 April          Thursday

No work today or till Tuesday because it's Easter Monday. Thank christ for that—I could sure do with a rest. We thought about going off for a day at the weekend but in the end we reckoned we couldn't afford it and my MOT's due on the Saturday anyway.

Tina brought all that stuff about rings—they look OK to me and you can get one with a diamond in it for forty quid. Tina likes it so then we had to measure her finger in these little cardboard holes—I sent off for it tonight.

Our Mum keeping on at me today about the wedding and all the plans and so on. 'You ought to get it sorted out,' she tells me and I told her there was plenty of time, just relax.

'All the same, it pays to get it worked out—and you haven't got long.'

She's a worrier like that—if she ever goes anywhere she worries about it for a week or more before and then she's ready about six hours early. I remember when we used to go on our holidays when I was a kid she'd have the cases packed the day before so if we wanted anything we'd have to unpack it out of the cases again.

'Don't keep on.'

'I'm not keeping on, Andrew.'

'No—don't sound like it.'

Then she gets on the phone to Tina's Mum and asks her round to tea tomorrow to talk about 'it all'—all what I'd like to know.

'You won't get no sense out of her.'

'Oh? Why not?'

'Tina says she's gone off her head.'

'Don't talk so daft—she sounded OK to me.'

Well, that's that. You can't tell them nothing.

4 April        Good Friday

Bit of a pain Easter, but it's a whole lot better than going to work, isn't it? Had a skinful last night so didn't get up till one o'clock, then went round to Tina's.

'Aren't you going to be here when Mrs Butler comes round?' says our Mum.

'No fear,' I told her and I hopped off quick.

Anna's gone away for Easter with Dermot to a mate of his house in Wales. So she got a lecture from Mum about not letting herself get 'carried away' and Anna looked right through her, but Mum reckons the sun shines out of Dermot's arse so she trusts him with Anna she says. He's such a gent of course that he don't want to screw Anna at all—who's she think she's kidding? Then our Mum goes on all the time about what a perfect gentleman he is just because he knows how to butter her up a bit with all his 'How are you, Mrs Baker?' jazz.

Anyway, when I got round to Tina's I met her old man coming out the front door with a suitcase.

'Hello,' I said. 'Going on holiday?'

'You take my advice, son. Break it off before it's too late. Screw the bitches but never marry 'em.'

'Oh ah?' I said and he mutters something about you'll learn, then Mrs Butler pokes her head out the window, chucks his pipe at him and shouts, 'And don't bother coming back, you bastard!'

'Don't you worry, you fucking cow, I bloody won't!' he shouts back. He picks up his pipe and looks at me with his eyes popping out and says, 'Bitch has bust me fucking pipe now. Well, you just watch this!' And he gets this stone and slings it straight through the front window! I was just stood there with my mouth open, then Tina comes out and screams at him to piss off or she'll get the police, so off he goes.

'And what the fuck are you gaping at then?' she says to me.

'Oh—nothing . . . Hope we don't end up like that, Teen.'

'Huh! I wouldn't let no man treat me like he's treated our Mum, the bastard.'

That social worker was there yesterday again, she come round to talk to them about Tracie and like me she'd walked right into the middle of Tina's Mum and Dad going for each other hammer and tongs.

'And you can keep out of it, missy,' says Mr Butler to her.

'I'm not here to take sides, Mr Butler—there's no hassle on my part. Perhaps we could all try to be reasonable?'

Well, Mr Butler wasn't feeling reasonable, he never does.

Tina and me went on out and left Mrs Butler to sweep up the glass.

Got home and Mum said Mrs Butler never turned up. Big surprise.


5 April        Saturday

My MOT today—passed! And I nearly passed out—I'd been fair dreading it but somehow the bloody thing got through. They reckon the water pump's about to go and it's been running pretty hot lately so they're getting one for next week. They said it'll be OK till then if I keep topping up the rad. No charge, thank christ.

Talked about the wedding with Tina and in the end we fixed on August 23rd, that's a Saturday.

'Why Saturday?' I said.

'Because you always get married on a Saturday.'

'Oh yeah? Who says?'

'Course—everybody knows that.'

Then I said were we going to have a church do then? And she said we were.

'What for?'

'Because.'

'Because what?'

'Because I want to.'

'You don't never go to church.'

'So what? You don't have to go to church to get married in one.'

'Which one then?'

'I don't know—we'll have to look around I suppose.'

Well, I said I didn't fancy spending too much time looking round a load of old churches and she said, 'Don't be daft.'

'What's wrong with the registry office?'

'I want a church wedding—like our Mum.'

'Look what happened to your Mum,' I says but she wasn't having any. Later on I told our Mum.

'Well, of course all girls want a proper wedding,' she says. 'Quite right.'

'What for?' I said and she gives us a bloody lecture about it being the most important day of your life and all that.

'Men!' she says. 'You're all the same, no romance in you. Every girl loves a white wedding.'

'Oh yeah? Why white?'

'Well, because . . . because that's the tradition, that's why.'

So there we are. Looks like being a church do. Our Mum reckoned St Jude's was a lovely little church but it's very popular so we'd have to hurry up and go and see the vicar to book early. I don't fancy going to see some old vicar, I don't know what to say, but she says it's the proper thing to do and so does Anna.

'Where you going to live?' says Dad.

'Dunno—we'll find somewhere.'

'Well, you'll have to get a bloody move on, my boy, that's all I can say.'

'Thanks a bunch.'

And that was that.

6 April        Easter Sunday

Our Mum kept on so I rang up that vicar tonight about half six but nobody was there.

Bloody drag tonight. Didn't see Tina and our Nan and Auntie Beryl come round. Spent most of the time up in my room listening to records. Bought the new Police album when I was in town yesterday—magic!

'Congratulations,' says Auntie Beryl to me.

'Thanks.'

'What?' says Nan—she sounds like a frigging parrot when she says that—'What's he done?'

'He's going to be married, Nan,' says Auntie Beryl opening her mouth like a fish and speaking very slowly.

'When did he get married?'

'No, no, you silly old—He's *getting* married.'

'Who to?'

'Tina!' I shouts and Nan jumps a mile.

'When's it due?' she says. I ask you!

7 April        Monday

Had a good think yesterday—well, there wasn't much else to do round our place. Couldn't watch the telly, they didn't want it on and anyway you got to have the sound turned right up or else Nan can't hear it. They had on 'Songs of Praise' for her cos she likes that and I could hardly hear myself think for the noise, what with her singing along and all. Anyway, I had a really good think about everything, where we're going to live and all that. Don't know if we can afford a house—it would mean getting a mortgage unless they've started giving houses away. A flat would be nice. I'll have to talk to Tina about it all, see what she thinks. I'm not sure how much money she's got—she's got her savings account anyhow, I know that. It's a good thing I've got my building society account because Mum reckons they have to give you a mortgage if you've got an account with them. She opened it for me when she started working there because she said it looked better if you did, so she opened one for Anna and one for her and the old man too, 'for a rainy day' like she says. Well, I reckon it's raining all right. Mind you, I haven't got much in mine—about two hundred and fifty quid, which isn't much. Mum says she'll have a word with her boss but I'm not having her running about after me all the time so I soon told her that I'd do it myself. She's fussing about all the time now, I don't know what she'll be like on the day—well, I've got a fair idea I guess.

Saw Tina tonight—she didn't fancy it though. We just kissed a bit, that's all, and I asked her how much money she'd got and she said she couldn't remember so she's going to check up but don't bank on her having none.

Ought to be a good crowd at our party tomorrow—better turn in now I suppose, but I'm not really very sleepy. It's funny, I'd like to be with Tina all the time. I wonder to myself what she's doing and what she's thinking and is she thinking about me and her taking her clothes off and having a bath and all kinds of stuff like that. Every time I leave her at her place I think of her going in the door and going up to bed and I try to see her doing all that in my mind—and sometimes I just don't want to leave her. Well, that's just because I love her I guess, still, we'll be married soon and then we can be together all the time. I keep thinking about that too. You know, what it'll be like to have a place of our own and all that. It'll be great I know but you keep on thinking of just how it'll be, don't you? Makes me feel really good—I wish I was with her right now, I know that, all snuggled up next to each other like we was that time in London, that was great. I could do with a quick one.

'Bout time you had that bloody light out!'

Well, that's our old man, just like usual, sounding off like a bloody foghorn. I don't answer him these days. He's a pain, that's what he is. Anybody'd think I was a fucking kid or something.

8 April       Tuesday

My birthday.

We had to have Anna's trip to Wales all the way through breakfast. She kept on saying it was super and how they used to go for long walks up in these perishing mountains and then sit round the huge log fire in the evening making fondue and bouillabaisse and singing folksongs and playing some Chinese game like chess only much better, then I suppose it was in the sack with old Dermot only we didn't get to hear about that bit. Sounds bloody great, if you ask me she don't know shit from sugar. Our Mum said she went to Wales once when she was a kid, but Anna said oh, tourists never go to where she was so it's just like getting back to nature. Dermot's given her a new shawl made of some Welsh sheeps' wool, knitted by some little old women somewhere who don't speak English. That's a good one.

Anna give me the new Police album and to tell the truth I didn't have the nerve to tell her I'd already got it. My Mum and Dad give me a kettle—'It's for your house,' says Mum and she sniffs a bit.

'Great.' Well, I was going to say it was what I always wanted but I didn't. I ask you—a frigging kettle, it's really incredible.

Most people give me money though—Nan and all those—and they
had a whip-round at work and got me a couple of albums and a *Men
Only* calendar. Tina give me the best thing of all, it's this great silver
chain necklace with a silver A on it. Said I'd wear it all the time.

Great party tonight! Toni Napper offered to stand by in case of any
aggro, but luckily there wasn't none. There was a few gatecrashers as
usual but nobody minds that, everybody just had a great time.

Course then John has to get up on that table and do a little speech
about me and Tina getting engaged and all that. 'Tina and Andy have
decided to make it legal,' he says, 'and you're all invited to the
wedding,' so everybody gives a great huge cheer and drink our
healths. Got smashed and had a really good screw with Tina tonight.
Usually it's not much good if I've had a skinful but she got really
horny which turned me on like crazy, then she stuck her hand down
the front of my jeans and said if I didn't fuck her bloody quick then
she'd look elsewhere—course she was only joking, anyway I let her
have it hot and strong. I said to her, 'I don't know about Tony
Napper, but I reckon you've got the best pair of bouncers round here,
Tina,' and she laughs so much I thought she'd wet herself. Magic!

I'm writing this tomorrow—what I mean is today only I was too far
gone yesterday when I got home so today is yesterday, at least I think
so. Fact is I've got an hangover today and stayed home from work but
I get a bit bored stuck home all day. This diary's getting too big,
what's more. Our Mum come in just now when I was writing it and
asks, 'What's that?' so I says, 'Nosey,' and she says not to be rude so I
just said I was doing the list of the guests for the wedding.

'Don't forget Auntie Trixie,' she says. Well, we haven't seen her for
ten years at least. She'll be wanting to dig up Gramps next.

11 May        Sunday

Have missed out a fair bit in this diary just lately. Honestly, I don't
know where the time's gone. Looks like I'll have to write a bit every
now and then if I'm not to stop for good, I mean it's not as if there's
nothing to write about.

To cut a long story short, we've been looking for somewhere to live
after we've been married, but what with prices the way they are it
looks like the only thing Tina and me can afford is a tent—and then
only a titchy one.

We went to see those estate agents—well, that was a good laugh for

a start, all smarmy they was till we told them how much we could
afford if we got a mortgage. Then we went in to see the deputy
assistant manager at the building society.

'We'd like a mortgage,' I says to him.

'Doesn't everybody?' says he.

'Well—how about it?'

'No chance.'

'But I've got an account here.'

'Oh yes, I know that. I don't know what we'd do without you.'

'Well—can we have one?' I asks the cheeky bugger.

'Hmm. Think you can cope with the interest?'

'Don't know.'

Then he asks what sort of house we were after.

'Nothing too big,' I says, and he nods his head.

'Well, we'd like at least ten per cent down. Can you do that?'

'Down where?'

Well, the short answer was no, we couldn't. Then he got out his
pocket calculator and works out the cost for us. No, we still couldn't
afford it—whichever way you looked at it.

'Thought about a flat?'

'Good idea.'

'Far better. We really don't like turning people out—it gets us a bad
name.'

So there we are—no house. We're looking for a flat now.

'If you didn't drink and smoke so much, you'd be able to afford an
house,' says our old man.

'Turn it up.'

'I'm just telling you for your own good, son. Kids these days don't
know how to handle money.'

'Stuff it,' I tell him. Then he starts getting stroppy as usual.

Well, the estate agents didn't have many flats, only ones costing a
hundred quid a week with a view over the park. Stuff the park, it's full
of courting couples anyhow.

Went to see that vicar the other week too, only a young guy—Tina
reckons he looks like a poof. Anyway, he's all friendly like, right away
it's 'Tina' and 'Andy' and 'Call me Steve' but I didn't like to.

'I take it you've thought it out?' he says.

'Yeah.'

'There's no hassle there then. Do you go to church by the way,
Andy?'

'Well, not a lot, no.'

'You believe in God?'

'I suppose so.' Can't really say I'd thought about it much. Ought to have told him I know Moses.

'Tina?'

'Suppose so.' Well, that's not what she told me.

'That's all right then. Marriage is a serious affair. And you're both decided on a church wedding?'

'Oh, yeah—you know.'

'Good. No trouble. When were you thinking of taking the plunge?'

'August 23rd—that's a Saturday.'

'Sorry,' he says looking in his diary, 'I'm fully booked then. One wedding, two christenings and I've got a funeral pencilled in.'

'But we've booked the honeymoon,' says Tina.

'Oh dear. I can do you on August 2nd. That's a Saturday.'

We didn't get no further than that. We went back to the travel agents and tried to get the honeymoon changed but they didn't seem too hopeful. They said to call in again Tuesday. And Tina's getting really ratty because the engagement ring still hasn't come.

'You sure you wrote off?' she says.

'Course. What you think?'

'Well, it ought to have been here by now.'

'Who's arguing?'

'I look a right pratt, telling people we're engaged and having no ring.'

So tonight I wrote off saying if they didn't hurry up and send the ring then I'd want my money back.


14 May          Wednesday

Went in to the travel agents yesterday and managed to change the honeymoon for the last two weeks in July—that's from the 13th to the 26th—it's either that or nothing. So we said we'd have to see the vicar again first so the manageress says she could hold everything till Friday as a special favour cos she knows Tina but no longer. Dashed round to the vicar's after work but his wife said he was called out to an emergency funeral, said I'd call back tomorrow. Things moving at one hell of a pace right now. Still no ring.


15 May          Thursday

Said to the vicar, 'It has to be 12th July.'

'Oh dear,' he says looking in his diary, 'I've got two baptisms then.'

'Shit!'

'Granted—what about July 10th? That's the Thursday.'

'Done!' says I quick, in case we missed that and all.

'Now, what sort of a service do you want?'

'Well—a marriage one.'

'Yes, but do you want the old one or the new one?'

'What's the difference?' asks Tina.

Then he said in the old one you got a load of stuff like old-fashioned words nobody can understand no more and the girl can say she'll obey her old man and all, but the new one doesn't have all that jazz.

'Do you wish to take the vow of obedience, Tina?'

'No fear.'

'Well, then may I suggest you go for the new service?'

'Whichever you reckon,' I say.

'Yes . . . I think that the revised service has more relevance to today's world, don't you?'

'Right on—we'll have one of them then.' Don't ask me what he was on about.

'Fine. No trouble. Now—no second thoughts?'

'Nope.'

'Good. Then you work out all your guests and best man and so on, then get back to me and we'll fix up the rehearsal.'

'Right. No problem.'

'Then there's the bands,' he says.

'What bands?'

'Oh, that's when notice of your wedding is given—I'll see to it.'

'Right ho—do we have to be there?'

'Oh no, not if you can't make it.'

'Don't think we'll be able to.'

'No hassle then, Andy—see you.'

Then we pushed off. For a minute there I thought we'd never get married . . . And if it hadn't been for a last-minute cancellation we wouldn't have got the honeymoon either. So we're going straight round to the travel agents tomorrow first thing—it's the same holiday only in a different hotel, but Tina's friend said it was a better one because the hotel we're going to now has two saunas whereby the old one only had one.

16 May    Friday

Booked up our honeymoon, thank christ!

Now we've got to find somewhere to live . . . Still no fucking ring.

## 18 May        Sunday

Great party last night at Donna Mitchell's. Had Tina in the garden shed out the back cos all the bedrooms were in use and we couldn't wait. Got not a little pissed—that's John's new saying, he says it all the time. Magic!

## 19 May        Monday

Still no ring. Rang them up from work but got no answer, tried six times, then that woman come on who says she's the cleaner.
'Where's everybody gone to?' I asked her.
'Don't ask me, man, I don't understand foreigners.'
'Who's foreigners?'
'Well, they is—Greeks or something.'
'I sent off for a ring.'
'Oh dear. I should stop your cheque, love.'
Then she told me she'd got no more wages after tomorrow so she wouldn't be there much longer herself and I hung up. Phoned the bank and they said the cheque was cashed weeks ago. Shit! Tried ringing again after dinner, no answer. Then I wrote off saying they'd better send me the ring or else my money back or else I'd get a solicitor after them. Then I had to tell Tina tonight.
'You fucking berk,' she says.
'Thanks.'
'Ooh—honestly!'
'What do you reckon we ought to do?'
'Huh! You ought to dry behind your ears, you did.' Then she walks off. Well, I wasn't having that sort of shit from her so I went after her and grabbed her arm. 'Let me go,' she snaps.
'Here, it's not my fault,' I says, but she wouldn't listen, wouldn't speak even. I left her alone, it's the best way with her when she gets like that.

## 20 May        Tuesday

Tried ringing those people again but no answer, then John said a mate of his could do me a ring no problem—ask no questions, you know, and I wasn't feeling like asking any right then.

'I'll fix a meet if you want,' says John. So he gets hold of this Patrick and he says he'll drop by after dinner.

'Come round to our office two o'clock and you can have a ring,' says I to Tina dinnertime.

'It's not Christmas is it?'

'Just be there, Tina,' I told her and she gives us one of her looks. Anyway, she turned up at two on the dot or almost, pity that bleeding Patrick didn't. Come half two and she says, 'You having me on?' Patrick got there at half three.

'Hello, darling,' he says to Tina. 'Want a ring then, do yer?'

'That's the general idea,' she says. Nice one!

He puts his attache case on the table and opens it up—there's all these rings in there all jumbled up. He waves his hand.

'Take your pick, my love.'

'You got a shop?' I asks him while she's looking over them but he just taps the side of his nose and grins.

'Oh, I moves about.' Yeah, I bet he does—and a bloody sight quicker when the coppers are coming and all.

Still, Tina found one she wanted and—magic!—it fits her . . .

'Forty-six quid—say forty to you, my love.'

'Right. Is it a diamond?' I asks him.

'Is it a diamond? Is it a diamond? That's better than a diamond that is—last a lifetime that will, matey. Cut glass like butter that will. Now—want a wedding ring an' all, do yer?'

'Guess we do, don't we, Teen?'

'No, I'll use a washer.'

'Then I can do you, cock,' says Patrick and he opens up another bit of his case and there's all these wedding rings and watches in there.

'Don't want a watch, guvnor? Nice these are, Swiss. Or a nice lighter?'

I said I didn't—getting married is costing me enough as it is.

'Here,' says Tina, 'this one's got "To Kathy, all my love from Frank" written on it.'

'Has it? Oh—well, some of them come ready done, see. Here you are, my love, try this one—all twenty-nine carats, they are—thirty quid to you.'

'Fine—take a cheque?'

'Ah—well, if it's all the same to you, son, cash'd be favourite.'

So then I had to go like the clappers round to the bank before they shut and cash a cheque.

'Thanks,' says Patrick, 'and the best o' luck to yer in your years of wedded bliss now.'

So now we've got Tina a ring and I hope she'll bloody shut up about it—and I'm seventy quid down. When John's showing Patrick out she gives us a kiss. 'Now I feel engaged,' she says. Christ, I come over so randy I could have fucked her there and then but as it happens old Moses had to come in when I'm snogging with her and he coughs a bit.

'Who was that shady character I've just seen with John?' he says.

'Dunno.'

'Well, you mustn't let anybody and everybody just wander in off the street, Andrew.'

'Right ho.'

Then he looks at us and Tina says she'd better be going. Then Moses says, 'Beware of the lure of the flesh, Andrew.'

'Eh?'

'Temptation,' he says and he shuffles about a bit.

'I'll keep an eye out and let you know if I see any.'

1 June        Sunday

Fallen behind with this diary again but today's Sunday and I'm not seeing Tina so I've got some time to myself. She's been better since we got the rings. I never did hear no more about the one I sent off for—don't reckon I ever will now. I rang up again and that guy said the firm had gone bust and they'd all gone back to Hong Kong. Suppose I ought to have seen a solicitor but I don't reckon to it. Ronny Trump from the Legal Dept said there'd be no point—just throwing good money after bad. It really pisses me off.

We've been looking everywhere for a flat—even in Wellington and Bridgwater—but no luck yet. That pisses me off and all—nobody wants to let to young people, they reckon it's all late-night parties and drugs and writing on the walls and all that so they'd sooner let to old folks or middle-aged people with families. Course we can't afford to buy one. We could have that place the other day but it was really grotty and we didn't fancy it. It's driving me spare. Most every day now we go round the estate agents and there's enough of them but they only got places to buy or else rent at prices we can't afford. Then we're looking in the papers and ringing up all over the place, no wonder I hardly got time to turn round.

'Ooh, you look tired,' our Mum keeps on saying—little bleeding wonder, I must walk about ten miles a day. And the car's playing up again, they put that new waterpump in for me but now they reckon the radiator's on the blink.

'Why don't you get a new car?' says Tina to me the other day.

'Cos they don't take beans,' I says and she shut up after that.

Wasted yesterday night going over to Wellington to look at that flat—took us about two hours to find it, then they said it had gone the day before the advert went in.

The council said we could go on the list after we was married but then we'd have to wait for about three or four years unless we wanted to buy one off them. Little cunt we saw too—I says to him where was we supposed to go for four years so he looks at me and says that weren't none of his business, so I told him to get knotted and he told me not to be so rude to a public official or else he'd smack me in the mouth.

Still, everything's good with Tina at the present moment in time. She says whatever happens she's not staying at home much longer— her old man's still with the barmaid, Tracie's out at the home—she spends most of her time in the old padded cell—and her Mum's really let the house go. Tina says if her old lady does go off her head we could always move in there, that's if the house isn't sold first because the bills are piling up and Mrs Butler's lost her job due to the state she's in and hasn't got around to seeing a lawyer yet about screwing some money out of her old man.

But like our Mum always says, what matters isn't if you get on OK when times are good but if you can stick together when the going gets rough. We fuck round Tina's place pretty often now because we was getting pissed off with the car all the time and when her Mum's had a few and her pills she wouldn't know if the house fell down—she's in a dream most of the time, it's great.


4 June          Wednesday

Tina spent the dinner hour buying stuff for the honeymoon—too much stuff, if you ask me, all clothes and make-up and that.

Still no flat, but in one way maybe it's just as well we haven't got nowhere to live yet, cos then we'd have to buy furniture.

'You can take your bed,' says our Mum.

'Oh yeah? And where's Tina going to go then?' and then she goes red when Anna giggles and says, 'On top of course.'

The other day we tried it a different way she'd heard about from one of her mates but either she heard it wrong or else my legs aren't long enough . . . Give us a laugh though.

**6 June          Friday**

Got the wedding licence today. More bleeding expense!

'I want a wedding licence, please,' says I to that little guy down the registry place.

'Don't they all?'

'You what?'

'What you done then—put her up the spout, is it?'

'Look, mate, I don't want any cracks like that off you,' I tell him straight. And I wasn't joking neither.

'OK—just a joke.' He gives us a sick grin, then he gets up and goes over the room and I can see that he's only got one leg on him.

'Oh—sorry, mate,' I says.

'What for?'

'Um . . . bout your leg.' I felt a right pratt.

'I don't want your sodding sympathy.'

John says he's like that to everybody and if it's a death certificate they want then he asks them how they did it.

Tina's old man reckons he's skint so he's not paying for nothing. Well, we didn't know what to do and in the end we reckoned the only thing was to have a whip-round among everybody in both families—it was either that or hold a flag-day like John said. Fuck knows where the reception'll be—things are getting out of hand. Still no flat. Then there's the invites, and Tina's dress and my clothes and and and . . . shit! Things *are* out of hand. Must stop now, no time left . . . do some thinking . . .


**10 June          Tuesday**

Found a flat at last! I can't hardly believe it . . . Thought we'd never find one—anyway, we have. It's a fantastic bit of luck. Over the weekend Tina's mate Patti said she knew this flat which was going down Herbert Street—this couple she knew had the bottom half of this house and they were looking for someone to let the upstairs. Well, we had the address off her double quick and went round there first thing next morning—it's one of those big old semis with a cellar and everything. We saw Jon and Mij, the couple who own it and live downstairs, and they showed us over. It's not half bad neither. We got a kitchen, bog with bath, living-room and two bedrooms—well, one and a half really because the spare's a bit small. Still, it's all we need like they said. The decor's OK but they said we can do it out if we want, then we can have it how we like and we can share the phone if we want.

Jon's an art teacher out the Tech—he knows Anna a bit—and Mij works in that little craft shop down Bath Place. They've got one kid called Samuel and they're really nice people.

'We don't mind who you have in here,' says Jon. 'Only no trouble with the pigs if you can help it—and if you use grass then we don't know nothing about it. Keep it in the cistern so you can get rid of it quick.'

Seems fair to me, Tina thought so too. She was talking to that kid of theirs and he was trying to touch her up and saying 'big boobs' all the time, but Mij said that was OK, he was just at a crucial age and coming to terms with life. Tina said after he was just like me—all hands—and we had a good laugh about it.

So there we are—somewhere to live at last. That sure is one hell of a weight off my mind. We said we'd take it there and then signed the agreement to run from now. We had to, it seems a waste as we won't be living there just yet but it was the only thing to do. Anyway, it means we can use it and do some decorating and so on so it'll be all ready for us after we're married. Moneywise it'll be a bit tight though. Had a good talk to Tina about it, told her she'll have to cut down on expenses, which she will and no mistake, but that's how it goes.

I didn't have time to put it down before now but we've got two other important things sorted out—that's the list of presents and the guest list. Our Mum's been keeping on about getting them done. Keeping on—I reckoned her bloody needle was stuck.

'You're leaving it too late,' she says.

'Everybody knows when the wedding is.'

'People like to know in advance.'

'They do—everybody does.'

'Not the family. What if they can't come?'

'So what? All our friends are coming.'

Straight, anybody'd think her relations was getting married.

'We want a list. Then there's the reception. Where's that going to be?'

'We reckoned on The Anchor—or The Griffon.'

'Not a pub!'

'OK—The Griffon then, unless you'll pay for The Castle.'

'And what about the catering?'

'I dunno.'

'No idea, no idea at all!' says our old man. Going on at breakfast all this was.

'You've left it very late,' she keeps on. That's her trouble—always fussing and worrying when there's no need.

'You'll be lucky to find anyone. I'll look into it for you both, shall I?'

I said, 'OK—go on then,' cos I reckoned she was scared of getting left out of things and she wanted to do something, maybe she won't keep on so then.

We did the present list in twenty minutes, Tina and me—we just put down everything we could think of.

'What about sheets?' says our Mum.

'Well, what about them? Who wants sheets?'

'Honestly, our Andrew, I don't know . . . You'll want sheets, won't you?'

'Suppose so, yeah.'

Then she reads a bit more.

'You can't put "money" down.'

'Why not? We need some.'

'Yes I know—but you can't.'

'If we had money, we could buy things.'

'Don't be silly—you've got to have things.'

That list isn't half long, we got it photocopied in the office and started handing it round.

'What's this, mate?' says John. 'You've not forgotten much, have you? Don't you want a new car then?'

'I can just about manage a couple of forks,' says Marc.

'You fork off,' I told him.

'You tell us what you'll give,' says Tina, 'then we can cross it off.'

'Ah—wouldn't want half a dozen fridges, would you?' says John.

Then we did the guest list, that was easy—Tina and me did all our friends, her Mum did their relations and our Mum did ours. Then we put them all together.

'You can't have a hundred and fifty people,' says Mum.

'Why not?'

'Well, look at the expense—'

'We can't have a hundred and fifty people,' I said. Too right, it'd cost a fortune.

'No, we'll just have to go through and cross some off.'

'We're not crossing off none of ours,' said Tina.

Anyway, we went off and left the Mums to it.

'When's the big day then?' says Slim when we get down The Anchor. We'd forgotten him—one more for the list. In the end we got the list down to sixty somehow or other.

'Sixty-one,' I said. 'We forgot Slim.'

'Who's he?'

'The barman down The Anchor.'

'Oh!' sighs our Mum. 'What's his other name?'

'Dunno.'

'Well, how well do you know him?'

Not all that well, but I've had quite a few drinks after closing time thanks to old Slim and anyway I'd promised him he could come ages ago.

'Oh,' says Mrs Butler after a bit, 'I forgot Uncle Henry from Crediton.'

'Christ! He's been dead for a twelve month,' says Tina.

We got the invites from Boots next day—more expense. Well, I've decided not to put down in this diary what anything costs if I can help it because then I'd go and add it all up and I don't want to cry—if we're going to go bankrupt then I'd rather not know about it. Anyway, they just say that Blank requests the pleasure of Blank at the wedding of their daughter Blank to Mr Blank, the son of Mr and Mrs Ditto, at Blank on Blank and RSVP—John reckoned that meant bring your own sherry but Anna said it meant you got to send an answer to the invite. We shot in the blanks and sent them all off.

'You really going through with it then?' says John when he gets his.

'Sure. You want to get a move on yourself.' And he grins at us like he does.

It's a lot of fuss I know, and most of it is driving me up the fucking wall, what with trying to remember it all, but I don't know, in a way it's a bit of a laugh—now we got the flat sorted out I'm quite enjoying the rest of it. I never thought I would but like I say it's a bit of a laugh. Course I don't take it so serious as our Mum but, well, you don't get married every day like she says. Guess I'm a bit nervous about the wedding. It's the honeymoon I'm looking forward to, Tina as well. It'll be great, really great.


12 June        Thursday

Our Mum's fixed up the reception—I'd asked Tina if she could get on with it and she reckoned that'd be a good idea.

'Do you want a sit-down or a buffet?' says Mum.

'Dunno.'

Anyway, we're having a buffet so's everybody can grab what they want—and it's cheaper. She's getting some friends of a friend of hers to do it because all the hotels and people cost too much, and the baker said he'd do the cake cost price because he's married to one of our cousins though we haven't seen him for ages and Mum likes the bread up Tesco's. Tina's Mum wanted to make the cake but like Tina said to her, we want a cake people can eat, not one that'll put them in hospital. So now the baker's coming to the wedding and all—that's sixty-three with his wife. Then there's the vicar, he'll have to come and all—that's sixty-four. Next thing we'll be back to a hundred and fifty again. The rehearsal's tomorrow night at 6.00p.m. and I'll need a few pints after that one.

Then I had a row with Tina. She wants to invite that Janette and I said no way, so she turns off.

'Jesus,' I said, 'what's it matter? Stick her down.'

OK, maybe I ought to have put my foot down but it's too late now.

## 15 June          Sunday

Tina all in a panic now because we haven't got our clothes yet. We'll be bankrupt soon. Then our Mum reckons we ought to go to church a couple of times before next month.

'I'm not going to no bloody church,' says our old man—good for him.

'Brian! You'll have to go on the 10th.'

'And when they bury him,' says Anna. Then he goes purple and starts shouting. Mum goes very quiet and says to her, 'Really, Anna, that wasn't in very good taste.'

'Good taste or not, it's true.'

Then she left, which all in all was a good thing because Dad was getting so steamed up it looked like he was going to have an heart attack and we'd be burying the old bugger sooner than he expected.

'Bloody kids want me dead!' he shouts. 'Bring the buggers into the world and they can't bloody wait to see the back of you.'

'Calm down, Bri,' says Mum looking like she's seen a ghost. 'She didn't mean it.'

Saw the vicar at the rehearsal on Friday of course and asked him if we had to go to church—or our Mum did because she wouldn't believe what we'd told her he'd said to us.

'Oh, only if you want to,' he says. 'Pop in if you're passing.'

'Don't think we can make it,' I said quick.

'No hassle then, Andy. Just be here on the 10th!'

'Oh yes, vicar,' says our Mum smiling at him.

She puts it on sometimes, like when Dermot's around. And he's coming and all because he's got this mate of his who's going to do the photos for us cheap. He's number sixty-five.

The rehearsal didn't go too bad really, our Mum kept asking bloody daft questions and showing us up and then Tina's old lady'd ask the same questions all over again because she'd been too busy trying to stare her old man out and so she hadn't heard the first time.

'Marriage is made in Heaven,' says the vicar and Tina's old man says, 'Ours bloody weren't.'

Both Mums started crying and that just about finished it, what they're going to be like on the day I just don't know. Even my old man looks all solemn and poker-faced and keeps saying, 'Best of luck, son, best of luck.' Then we had to work out who was going to sit where, and John asks where the coffin's going to go and he gets a look from my old man for his trouble. Tina's got three bridesmaids—Marilynne, Tracie, who's getting let out for the day and Tina says she'll kill her if she don't behave, and her cousin Charmaine from Yeovil. Then we've got John as best man, and for ushers there's Uncle Stan and Tina's Uncle Fred who's Charmaine's Dad, then there's her little cousin Shaun who's only four and he's supposed to be pageboy, whatever that is, not forgetting me and Tina of course—though I reckon sometimes if we didn't bother to turn up they all wouldn't notice and my old man'd probably end up getting married to the vicar.

'It'll be OK on the day, you just see, no hassle. You're not the first and you won't be the last,' says the vicar.

I sure hope so. Told John if he *does* lose the ring then I'll kill him—very slowly.

'Just one thing,' says the vicar when we're all piling out—I somehow got the idea that he wanted paying.

'And if you don't mind,' he goes on while he's counting the money, 'please, please, no confetti in the churchyard—or use rice if you must because then the birds can eat it. Only the sexton's said he'll go on strike if he has to sweep up any more confetti before Advent.'

'Use bird seed,' says John. 'Bleeding poofter.'

All that meant we missed those catering women but they come round again yesterday. Mrs Peese and Mrs Moore they're called and they do all the catering for the WI and the Conservative Club and stuff like that. To cut a long story short, we're having a cold do though some of it'll be hot—little biscuits and cheese and sandwiches and Mr Kipling's cakes and vol-au-vents and jelly and trifle and ham and salad and cold roast turkey (two of them) and veal-and-ham pies—some with eggs in them, some with no eggs—and flans and pickles and fruit tart and Battenburg cake and chocolate fingers and sausage rolls and Ritz biscuits and crisps and nuts and wedding cake and roast spuds and christ knows what else. There's Asti Spumanti and cider and orange squash and coffee and beer and lager and shorts to drink— Tina and me said we'd take care of that, I mean we don't want to be stuck with just wine and a couple of pale ales. We'll get Slim to give us an hand with all that.

'Port and lemon's nice,' says our Mum, 'lots of people like that.'

So we said we'd get some. I reckon people ought to bring their own by rights. They totted it all up on their pocket calculator . . . I refuse to write it down . . . Like I said before I don't want to cry. *Must* get our finances organised—Mum said go and see the bank manager but I don't want to have to invite him along. Tina says it's no good seeing her bank manager, she had a row with him last Xmas. Shit, am I tired, I've never felt so knackered. I'm worn out all the time right now— soon as my head touches the pillow I'm asleep. Must stop now, I'm dropping.

22 June        Sunday

Funny thing is, it seems a long time since last week but on the other hand the time's going so fast I hardly got time to turn around. Still, I reckon we got most things sorted out now, except the furniture and we're working on that. I keep thinking the day'll come and then we'll have forgotten something . . .

We've had some presents and a lot of people say they're coming. Auntie Sadie died last year so we're back to sixty-four, that's a saving I guess. It's really incredible how much there is to work out and organise when it comes down to it. We had all that fuss about finding somewhere to live and I thought to myself there wasn't much else, but course I was wrong . . .

We're still looking for furniture. The main thing last week though was to book the cars and to see about the clothes. Daimler limos we liked the look of—two, one for each bunch—but they was too dear and like Tina said it looked like we'd end up going in frigging bubble-cars, but then they said they could do us a couple of Granadas for half the price of the Daimlers and they'd throw in a bit of white tape to stick on the bonnets, so that was that.

Then there was the clothes. Well, getting our old man into a suit is like trying to get into the Bank of England after closing and getting him to try one on is even worse. In the end Mum said she'd take Dad into town to get him a suit as there's no telling what he'd end up else if he went on his own—boiler suit I shouldn't wonder. He said what was wrong with the best suit he already had—I ask you, it's at least twenty years old, Anna reckons it's his demob suit and told him he'd look good in one with little arrows all over it . . .

'Dermot's got a morning suit,' she says.

'Oh ah?' I said to her. 'Only wears it in the mornings, does he?' So she stuck her nose in the air which is just what I knew she'd do.

Mum got herself this dress with flowers all over it and Anna said it was horrible but Mum wouldn't listen, and a bloody great white hat and she made Dad get himself a suit—he looks a picture she says though he wouldn't show it me. She even made himself get some Brylcream to put on his hair, what he's got left of it. Then Anna's got this 'gown'—strapless with a great split half-way up the side in powdery blue—and she's got herself that daft little hat with a black veil down over the front, and gloves. Our old man reckoned she looked like tarts used to look back in the fifties and she said he ought to know.

I left all ours to Tina. Marilynne come home for a couple of days and they worked it all out together and told me afterwards. In the end what they decided on was a white dress of chiffon and lace for Tina with a juliet cap and orange and pink long dresses for the bridesmaids with some stuff on their heads and all, and the lot of them carrying bouquets of mauve roses and some other flowers I can't remember. They've ordered all that anyway—and the buttonholes (red roses). Tina's Auntie'll do the dresses which'll save a bomb.

'Suppose I'll have to wear a suit,' I said.

'Velvet's nice,' says Marilynne.

'Yeah!' says Tina. 'That's great.'

'What colour?' I asked hoping they weren't going to say pink.

Blue—there was one in Pfaffs' window. Forty quid. Not a suit—just the jacket. I snapped it up quick and got a pair of light grey trousers to go with it. I had to buy a mauve shirt and tie as well, but my new brown shoes will go OK with that lot, so I saved there as well. Then I have to put it all on to show our Mum . . . christ! I shouldn't encourage her really. And our old man said velvet was only for poofters so I told him to get knotted.

I feel as if we've bought up the whole town. Tina's got a whole load more stuff for the honeymoon and I got a pair of swimming-trunks.

That just about does it for this week—it just about does for me and all. I had a word with my bank manager after all and he's let me have an overdraft for a couple of hundred quid. If it weren't for that I don't know what we'd have done, as it is we'll just about get by—I hope . . . No furniture, but we'll just about make it. Still, Tina's old man's paying for some of the cost after all—our Dad went round to have a chat with him about it, he says he told him to cough up like a man or else which I don't believe for one minute, but least he managed to screw something out of the old cunt which I guess is good of him when all's said and done. But Mr Butler said he couldn't pay it all no way so we're making up the rest. My old man says he's skint too and there's no point in saving for his old age now. I ask you . . . Now I'm going to have a rest—and I've earned it, what's more . . .

24 June          Tuesday

I reckon we got it all sorted at last, except the furniture. It's all so expensive. Anna says what we want is Habitat furniture but there isn't a shop round here.

We've been spending a fair bit of time round at the flat tidying up and so on. Me and Tina tried a bit of decorating—course it all takes a hell of a time and what with everything else and being out at work all day we've only managed to strip the paper off in the sitting-room so far. Usually when we go round I strip the clothes off Tina and we hop into bed, which don't help the decorating none but it's a bloody sight more fun.

The plaster's terrible underneath—we'll have to do something about it but right now we got used to it and we don't notice.

Our Mum and Dad come round to see the place just after we got it. He wants to do the sitting-room for us but I've seen some of his decorating—our house is full of it. Better get in there first, so Tina and me reckon on doing it next weekend. We can't afford to go out anyway. We was talking, Tina and me, about the decorating and our old man wanting to do it and she says to me, 'Let him do it if he wants. Why not?'

'You don't know what he's like,' I told her.

'Oh, he couldn't be no worse than you.'

'Shit,' I said. 'Thanks a bunch.'

We got the bed though. It's the one out the spare room at Tina's place and her old lady let her have it for ten quid. Still, it's OK and like I say it's getting a good bit of use at the present moment in time. We've been to look at other furniture but the trouble is it's all so bloody expensive so we reckon we might get a bit on the HP. Jon and Mij threw in the carpets and the kitchen curtains—they're a bit tatty though and Tina's Auntie who's doing her dress, she's giving us the rest of the curtains.

We've had a good think and we can't think of nothing we've forgot to book, least I hope not. Seems a bit funny now everything's fixed up. Our Mum said, 'I was sure you'd not do it all in time,' but then you'd expect that off of her. She's put a lot into it though—more than Tina's Mum anyhow—and you've got to give her credit, she's a good Mum when it comes down to it even though she does go on a bit sometimes.

We got Todd to do a disco at the reception and he said as we was old customers and on account of it being a special occasion and as he's just formed a new band, then they'd play for us at no extra charge—that is twenty quid plus drinks. That was really nice of him I reckon. He says they've already done one gig so we're lucky to get them so cheap but they just happened to be free that night.

Weather's hot right now—not so hot as it'll be in Spain I hope, but it's nice so we went down to the baths for a swim tonight. Had Tina in the changing room when she was all wet and that—Magic!

26 June          Thursday

My old man had to change his new suit today because he reckoned it was too tight in the crutch. Typical.

'Why ever did you buy it then?' says Mum. 'You said it was all right in the shop.'

'Trust him,' said Anna. More hassle—too tight round the frigging neck if you ask me, or not tight enough, whichever way you look at it.

Tina's had a word with Marilynne and she said Angelo's probably got to go away on business and she'll most likely go with him so we can stay at their place till the Sunday. They've just got this new place down by the river and Marilynne said she'll let us have the key on the day of the wedding and we can go straight up then if we like. Tina says it sounds really nice. So we reckoned it'd be best if we leave before the reception's over, then we can drive up through the night and have a good sleep for most of Friday, that way we'll be nice and fresh for the honeymoon. Everything seems to be working out really OK—it's all been a bit of a rush I know, what with altering the honeymoon, but everything seems all right now. And it's not long to go now neither. I'm really looking forward to it, so's Tina.

Weather still hot. Her next-door was out sunbathing in the nude again today, she's really something.

29 June        Sunday

Tina's got her dress now—her Auntie must be the world's fastest dressmaker. Course I'm not allowed to see it. I told her she couldn't see my jacket in that case but she's already seen it.

Really looking forward to getting married to Tina. I reckon she's the girl for me all right, we get on really well. I knew I'd get married one day of course but you never know who to, only you do sometimes wonder about it, except now looking back on it and all I reckon Tina and me were made for each other. It's funny that—everything seems just right about it but you can't never put your finger on exactly when you started feeling it, can you? No, you just sort of know, but you can't say when and how you first knew, it's not like that. I'm glad it's happened anyway, I know that much.

Mum was crying in the kitchen the other day. I saw her turn away when I come in so I says to her, 'What's up with you then?'

'Oh—nothing, it's all right. I was just thinking, that's all.'

'What about?' I said but she wouldn't tell us. Then she says right out of the blue she reckons Tina'll make me 'a good little wife' and that she's a lovely girl. Christ!

Tina says one of her Aunties wants to get a new fridge so she's going to get her to sell us the old one. Tina sent off a load of stuff about new fridges to her so's she won't change her mind. Our flat's filling up now. Not long to go, anyhow. We got this swivel chair off of Brad Tottle yesterday for only a tenner. It don't swivel no more but other than that it's OK.

'How can it be a swivel chair if it don't bleeding well swivel?' says Tina.

'Well, it's a chair and we're having it,' I told her.

'You fucking sit in it then.'

'I fucking will, don't worry.'

She'll just have to be more practical, that's all.

1 July        Tuesday

Tina's birthday. We couldn't afford another party so we just had drinks down The Anchor, then went back to the flat for a fuck—at least that's still free.

Couldn't really afford to get Tina a present at all but I had to give her something more than just the screw, after all she can get that anytime she wants, so in the end I got her a Boots gift token and she got herself a bikini and some Ambre Solaire suntan stuff. Anna reckons that's the best you can get.

Our wedding presents are piling up now so it's not all paying out—stuff like sheets and plates and knives and forks which will all come in useful, and some things which will come in bloody useless like that God-awful vase from Auntie Dor. We got a toaster and a clock, Anna and Dermot give us some fancy saucepans and our Mum and Dad are giving us a cooker—not a new one, they couldn't afford that, but a good second-hand one. Tina's Mum's going to give us a chair if she can remember to buy it, and we haven't had nothing from her old man yet. The girls at work had a whip-round for Tina and give her some perfume costing fifteen quid a bottle—very sexy and all. The people at work are having another collection for our wedding present instead of giving us lots of little things and Moses give me a book called *Christian Marriage* costing 70p. Trust him. John says his wife fancies this priest bloke who's old enough to be her father but he's playing hard to get.

Course we can't do without a telly but we reckoned we'd hire one. We *must* get down to some decorating. Tina says she can't do without a washing machine neither so we've got to have one of them, but they're bloody expensive and we'll probably have to get one on the HP.

6 July          Sunday

We'd put a washing machine on the list but nobody give us one so we went down to Currys on Wednesday and got one on the HP and they come to fix it yesterday. Spent the afternoon in the flat and tried it with Tina on top—she's a bit of a weight but least she did most of the work. Christ, she was really randy, bouncing up and down on my cock like she was on fire and groaning and pinching all the time, and I felt really good under her and I gave her tits a really good going over—man, they looked good swinging around, just like melons they are. It was really good and it was nice after too, we just lay there holding each other. Then Mij come up and wanted to know if we'd like a cup of tea and to come on down if we did.

'I'm just having a wash,' I shouted through the door and I could hear her laugh a bit on the other side.

'Oh—well, come down when you've finished.'

They're really nice her and Jon, we've got to know them quite well now. We heard them at it a couple of times, always makes me and Tina really randy. The ceiling's not as thick as all that and anyway he makes so much noise when he's on the job I reckon you could hear him out in the garden.

'Yes, yes, my darling!' Mij shouts like someone was killing her—it sure as hell turned me and Tina on anyhow, so we hopped in the sack and tried to see if we could come off at the same time as they did but they just beat us to it. Mij told Tina Jon's a real horny bastard most of the time, but specially at the full moon, and sometimes he comes home from the Tech dinnertime if she's going to be there just for a quick bang to see him through the afternoon, and half the time he'll just pull her skirt up and have her on the kitchen table or bend over the sink.

Anyway, we get on with Jon and Mij really well and though he's clever he's not stuck-up or nothing like some of them. He's written this book on the sex life of the natives out in South America—he lent us it but it's not up to much. Their flat's really great, all those thick rugs and carvings on the walls, Jon's lived for a bit in South America and he picked them up cheap in Rio when he went there to study the local art. One of them's this little black bloke with horns and a massive cock—it's a fertility symbol and if you rub your hand up and down his prick and say some magic words then you'll never go short. Both me and Tina did it just to be on the safe side. Had some of Jon's home-made onion wine and they even give us a wedding present of some glass balls on wire to hang up by the window and then they make noises in the wind. Well, course we didn't expect a present from them so it was real nice. We invited them to come along to the wedding and they said they'd love to. He's been to LA too and he reckons it's the greatest place in the whole world and one of these days he's going back.

We're not too bad off for furniture now. We got the fridge from Tina's Auntie for forty quid and we're going to hire a telly. Jon said don't bother with chairs if we don't want to but just have big cushions on the floor. Auntie Amy give us a picture for the sitting-room of this woman with a green face and black hair and huge tits walking in this river, our Mum said she reckoned it weren't in very good taste but Anna said it was Art. My old man had a good squint at it anyway, but he don't know nothing about Art.

Less than a week to go now . . . Tina's fussing about her hair and spots and her dress and so on. Pretty much what you'd expect I guess.

John's given us a frying pan and a tube of Giant Erection Creme he got down the new sex shop.

'You keep it, mate,' I said to him.

'Don't need it, mate. Thought it might come in handy on your honeymoon.'

We had a good laugh about it.


8 July        Tuesday

Tomorrow me and my mates have got me stag party and Tina and her mates got her hen party and I don't reckon I'll be in a fit state to write nothing after that, next day's the wedding and then it's up to London and on to the honeymoon so I don't know when I'll be able to do this diary next.

'Just think,' says Tina to me tonight in bed round the flat, 'we'll be living here soon.'

'Great—I really love you, Tina.'

'Do you, Andy?'

'Yeah, course I do—what you think?'

And she gives a little sigh and a smile. Magic!


12 July        Saturday

Everything's fine. We're up in London and Tina's popped out so I've got time to write a few lines. We never did get round to doing that decorating, we left the key of the flat with our Mum and she said she'd pop in and clean the place up for us, which is nice because it'll save us the trouble when we get back, but right now I'm not thinking about going back . . .

To start at the beginning, Wednesday night was my stag night so a whole crowd of us started off in The Anchor and then went round all the pubs seeing how many we could get in before closing time—and we didn't miss out many neither. Trouble was we kept on bumping into Tina and all her mates doing the same! Ended up taking everybody back to the flat and took along some bottles. Got not a little pissed. Don't know how I got home—leastways it was gone three when I did get back and our Mum's waiting up for me looking all worried with a face as long as her arm.

'Wherever have you been, Andrew?' she says but I just belched and said, 'On my stag night course.'

Then my old man comes out. 'Oh,' he says, 'back at last, is he?'

'What's it to you?' I says to him but the words didn't seem to come out right.

'You're getting bloody married in the morning.'

'Am I? Who says?' Then I started singing, 'I'm Getting Married in the Morning.'

'Sssh! You'll wake all the neighbours,' says Mum.

'Why?' says I feeling chipper and not tired one bit. 'Aren't they getting married and all?'

'He'll not be in a fit state to get married,' says Dad. 'Just look at the little bugger.'

'Brian!'

'Have to cancel it, that's all.'

'On your bike,' I tell him. 'I'll be all right—just wake me up at dinnertime.'

'Dinnertime? You're bloody well getting married at eleven o'clock.'

'Am I? What are you keeping me up all night for then?'

Anyway, felt really shitty next morning. Our Mum woke us up hours too early of course and said I had to be sure to eat a good breakfast. 'It's going to be a disaster, I know it is,' she says.

'Perhaps *this*'ll stop him drinking,' says my old man.

I never did have that breakfast—and my guts rumbled all the way through the service.

'The car's late,' says Mum. There we was all dressed up and sitting in the front room with her looking at the clock every two minutes.

'No it isn't—don't fuss so,' says Anna.

'Have a sherry, dear,' says Dad to Mum.

'Yes please, duckie,' says John and our old man gives him a look and John looks at Anna's legs and she looks right through him.

'Is my hat all right, Anna?' says Mum.

'Jesus!' says Anna. 'That's the fourth time!'

'Well, Andy—big day, eh?' says Dermot and he shakes my hand.

'Yeah.'

'Best of luck.'

'Ta very much.'

Don't suppose he's too bad anyhow. Our Mum asks him if he's seen the car.

'No, Mrs Baker, I didn't.'

'There! What did I say? It's all going wrong.' She gives a cry—I could tell she was going to start sooner or later. Our Dad looks out of the window. Honestly, I never seen such a carry-on. My old man looked like he'd just been given six months to live.

Tina told me they'd been in the same state round her house and her

Mum got through half a bottle of valiums before they left and wouldn't let their old man in the house so he kept on shouting through the letter-box.

It's funny but it seemed like we was sitting for hours in our front room—like when we buried our Gramps then everything went so fast after that it was like it only lasted five minutes, the wedding, the reception, everything. Tina says the same.

We was all sat in the church and I could feel all these eyes on me, then John gives us a poke and says, 'What if she don't come?' Well, I set to wondering what if Tina didn't show and all that. It's queer how you worry about things and for a minute I went all hot and cold, next thing the organ starts up with 'Here Comes the Bride' and everybody turns round to have a look. Tina looked really lovely, she looked a picture, I'll say—she's got her little hat on her head and her tits are pushing her dress out like anything and she took up a bit of her dress in her fingers so's she could walk, then she just sort of glides down up the middle like she was a queen or something. She made me feel really proud of her. After, she said she was so scared her knees were knocking and she could hardly walk straight because everybody was looking at her. But she didn't have a thing to worry about looking like that. Her old man was next to her holding her arm and then at the back was big Marilynne and Tracie and Charmaine all done up like dogs' dinners.

Course my Mum and her Mum and Cherylle and our Nan and most of the Aunties start crying. I took a look at my old man—he was fingering his collar in and out and looking all solemn and I reckoned he was going to cry and all. John gives us another poke and says, 'Cheer up, mate—here we go, unless you've changed your mind. Thought you'd shit yourself there for a minute.'

It's funny but looking back I don't reckon I was half so nervy as I reckoned I'd be, it all just seemed so right and natural I didn't seem to think about it. Tina says I looked all serious and when we got next to each other and the vicar started off I give her hand a little squeeze and she whispered to me, 'Hello, love.' Guess I enjoyed the whole thing—maybe it's all a bit of a fuss but then I guess it is something special. It's got a sort of atmosphere I mean. I reckoned my voice'd crack when I had to say my piece but it was OK, then when Tina's turn come, she said it so quiet I could hardly hear her, I could hear our Mum sniffing more than I could hear Tina . . . We had a hymn or two and some folksongs—Steve said have folksongs when we didn't know any hymns. He said we could have what we wanted except my old man

wanted 'Abide with Me' but he got told he couldn't so we had
'Morning Has Broken' and Pete Creed played guitar which was really
good.

Then I had to kiss her and she pokes her little tongue in my mouth,
John says, 'Steady on, young lovers,' and the vicar's grinning, my old
man's saying, 'Best of luck, Andrew, er, Andy, best of luck to you
both,' and it's off out into the sun after we've signed the register. Nice
day too. Few showers of rice from all our friends, Tina chucks her
bouquet to Cherylle and John groans, then we're all lined up for the
photos.

Next thing I can remember, we're at the reception, our Mum says
she never felt so happy in all her life, then bursts into tears and Dad
tells her to shut it then he goes red.

'Where's the drinks to?' says Tina's old man. 'As I'm paying I
might as well have me fucking money's worth.'

He sure did. Ate a lot too but then so did everybody, they were on
that table quick as lightning, the bloody gannets. And that vicar can
sure pack it away too—I reckon if he has a couple of blow-outs like
that a week he never needs to eat at home. It was like D Day.

'Hello then,' says John to me through a huge mouthful of turkey,
'look who's here.'

I looked. It was Kev and Trev. Well, we didn't invite them nor their
women.

'Hello, matey,' says Trev, 'thought we'd just look in. This is Rita.'

'Lovely ham,' says this Rita. She ought to know, had enough of it
on her frigging plate.

They hadn't been out of stir all that long and as they said they
hadn't had a good meal for months we said they could stay.

Neither Tina nor me felt like eating much though everybody said it
was all really nice.

'Here, what about the cake?' says my old man, then we found
they'd already eaten the top layer so he grabs up the rest that Uncle
Ken's just about to bite on and brings it over to Tina and I to cut it.

'Er, ladies and gentlemen,' he sings out, 'can we have your kind
attention for the cake?'

'Why—what's it going to do?' says John.

Tina and me held the knife together—that was a laugh—and we cut
the cake and everybody cheered.

One bit I wasn't looking forward to though and that was the
speeches. Well, course it was OK for John—he just told jokes for ten
minutes and I didn't think he'd never stop. Some of them were what

my Mum called 'a bit blue' but most people laughed including her.

He read out a couple of telegrams—one from Auntie Queenie telling us to name the baby after her so John says, and one from my cousin in Australia wishing us all the best and to drop in anytime we was passing.

'I suppose he thinks he's funny,' says our old man—then it was my go.

'Well,' says I when I'm on my feet, 'thank you all for coming . . .'

'Here! Here!' says John.

'Thank you, John,' I says to him. 'Well, here we are—Tina and me's married and . . . we'd like to thank you all for coming . . . and thanks for all the nice presents.'

I didn't say much more, I forgot everything I was going to say.

'Well done, mate,' says Angelo, giving me a clout in the back. 'Best of luck to you. Now, me and Marilynne got some business so here's the keys of the flat. There's some booze in the cocktail cabinet and the place is all yours. Leave the keys with the caretaker.'

Then we had the band and dancing and Shaun spewed up and our Nan got pissed again, didn't she.

'She's got impossible,' says Auntie Beryl. 'Heaving her guts up out there she is.'

'Oh dear,' says Mum. 'Too much port and not enough lemon.'

'I told her not to mix it but she never listens. It's no good, she'll just have to go into a home.'

Tina's old man got pissed and all, then he had a row with his old woman.

'You're a disgrace,' she tells him.

'Yeah? And you're an old cow.' Then she chucked a glass at him and it as near as fuck knocked the vicar's head off for him.

'Come on, come on,' says my old man, 'remember where you are now.'

'Huh!' says Mr B. and goes off for another drink.

'He's a pig, that man,' says Tina's Mum.

'Yes, yes,' says our Dad. 'Come and have a nice bit of trifle, Mrs Butler.'

The Pubes were good—sort of heavy-metallish and that stuff which I don't like that much but good really. They played 'Don't Cry For Me Argentina' for our Mum and Crispin Holly did a drum solo in the middle. Everybody danced, Angelo danced with Nan, then she had to go out the back again, the vicar danced with Marilynne and told her he liked her dress so she told him she liked the one he was wearing in church and all. Angelo gives us a nudge and says we'll have to watch out or else the chaplain'd be running off with our women but I told him he didn't have nothing to worry about, then I danced with Tracie and she told me to mind where I put me bleeding hands and then Tina danced with Angelo for a bit.

'You've got yourself a good woman there, Andy,' he says to me, then he told me about his wife who was a Greek or something and when him and her split up all her brothers come round with flick knives saying they was going to do him up good and proper, but he knew a few guys who'd look out for him so in the end they never tried nothing.

We got away about half one. Somebody'd tied a load of cans and old shoes on the back of the car and written stuff all over it—guess who? But we didn't mind, we was just happy to be together.

'Now, you will send us a postcard to let us know you've got there?' says Mum crying all over again.

'Yeah, course we will.'

'Look after yourself, son,' says Dad, 'and look after Tina.'

'Yeah—I will.'

'Oh dear!' says Mum and cries again and Dad puts his arm round her.

'All right, Andy—I'll look after her. You two get along now.'

'Don't do anything I haven't thought of,' shouts John and Cherylle pokes him. Tina's old lady won't stop crying so Marilynne took charge of her and bawls out their old man and their old man says to me, 'She's her mother's daughter, you know.' 'Oh ah?' I said. Then we left.

'It's all like a dream, innit?' says I to Tina as we get out on the motorway.

'What is?'

'All this—you and me. Getting married.'

'Yeah, suppose so—still, nice dream, innit?'

'Yeah,' I says and strokes her leg.

'Spain here we come,' I said and she gives us a feel and all.

So there we are—Tina and me's married.

We had a hell of a job finding Marilynne and Angelo's flat. We got to London OK then we got lost. By the river Marilynne said but her map was hard to follow and it's a big river but somehow we got here in the end, it's not a bad place—in Wapping it is—and when we got in, there was this parcel on the kitchen table all done up in fancy paper with a big red bow and a card saying 'Have fun, from M. and A.' and when she opens it it turns out to be this bloody great vibrator! 'Christ!' says I. 'It's massive. Who'd ever have one that size?'

It's called a Supakong and it's sure lifelike, with a terrific head on it and balls you can fill up with milk or something and squeeze and it all shoots out . . .

'You won't need it,' I told Tina and we had a good giggle and she said she'd keep it for a spare, then we put some water in it later on and had a laugh squirting it at each other, but I was right, she didn't need it . . .

Here we are then, married almost two days already, funny thing is it seems longer—I can hear Tina coming so I'll have to stop now . . .

12 July          Saturday (again)

Tina's in the bath. We just had the police round looking for Angelo.

'Sorry,' I told them. 'He's not here.'

'Who are you then, squire?'

'Just a friend.'

'Oh yeah? Mind if we come in, friend?' and he pushes the door open.

'Well—'

'Look, son, we're the law,' says the other one and flashes his ID at me.

They asked us loads of questions like who we were and what we was doing there and where was Angelo and how well did we know him and that, then they asked us for our ID.

'You don't know where he is then?'

'No—sorry.'

'Yeah, I bet. How long you two going to be here?'

'Till Sunday morning.'

'OK. You tell Angelo we'll be round.'

Well, I said what did they want and what were all the questions in aid of but they just said *that* was none of *my* business and if I didn't want to cooperate then they could always take us down to the nick but it might delay the honeymoon a bit.

'What's he done anyhow?' I said to Tina.

'I don't know. Whatever he's done, you don't want the pigs to get him, do you?'

'No, I guess not—but suppose we land in trouble?'

'He's a mate, isn't he?'

'Well, course.'

'Well then.'

Then we had a word with the caretaker—and a right seedy-looking little cunt he was and all.

'How can we contact Angelo?' says Tina to him.

'Oh well, I don't know about that—well, I—I never done no contacting before, you know.'

'Look,' says Tina, getting a bit ratty with him, 'where's he gone to?'

'Search me.'

'No chance.' says Tina. Nice one!

We found an address book upstairs but it only had the numbers and then 'M' or 'B' and like that next to them. Tina rang up a few.

'Is Angelo there, please?' she says but no he wasn't and one of them put the phone down on her. Then one guy says, 'Who wants him?'

'I'm a friend.'

'Oh yeah? What's it about?'

'Do you know where he is, please?'

'Maybe I do, maybe I don't.'

'Well, the police are looking for him—can you tell him?'

'When was that, love?' So Tina tells him.

'OK, love, I'll see he gets the message. Whom shall I say phoned?'

'Oh—it's Tina.'

'Right then, Tina—ta very much.'

Wonder what the cops want Angelo for? Anyway, about half an hour ago somebody rang up and asked to speak to Tina but it wasn't Angelo. He wouldn't give his name—all he said was don't leave the key with the caretaker cos he couldn't be trusted no more but to stick it in an envelope and post it to the address of Angelo's nightclub when we left. I was a bit worried in case the police would be after us but like Tina said we wasn't doing nothing wrong. Angelo's been good to us and we ought to stick by him. Must stop now, she's coming . . .


28 July        Monday

Home again. Time flies—it don't seem five minutes since we left and now it's all over. Come to that, we almost didn't leave—we got stopped by the coppers at Luton Airport asking a load of questions about Angelo all over again.

'Wonder who they're looking for?' says I to Tina about those two coppers waiting up by the desk having a good squint at all the passengers. Well, we didn't have long to wait, when we got to the desk it's 'Would you just go with this officer?' and this old bag behind us in the line says to her old man, 'They're terrorists they are, you mark my words,' and he says, 'Oh yes—no doubt, Hilda.'

So then we had all this 'Where's Angelo?' and 'You going to meet him in Spain?' lark again till we was sick of it. We said no to the lot, then one copper takes us on one side and says, 'Look, son, you do us a favour and we'll see they go easy on you.'

'Eh? What is all this?'

'Look, son, don't mess us about. You look like a decent kid—you don't wanna get mixed up in all this now, do yer?'

'All what? And I'm no kid—we just got married.'

They let us go after we'd been searched and that was no fun neither. Tina has to go off with these women coppers and then I have to strip bollock naked in front of these blokes. Bloody disgusting that was, even looked up my arse. Fucking liberty.

'You got no right,' I told them.

'No?' says this copper. 'You wanna make something of it? Get 'em off.'

Then they searched our cases—and found that bloody vibrator.

'Hello!' says one of them to Tina. 'What's this then, love? Your old man let you down already, has he? Or does it belong to him?'

'Piss off,' says Tina to him but he just laughs. I told him I'd put in a complaint.

'You can try, mate,' says one of them, 'but I'd keep me nose clean if I was you and think yourselves fucking lucky we're letting you leave the country.'

'Yeah,' says another, 'see how long you can stay out there, eh?'

That all put us in a right good mood. Tina said those women pigs were a couple of lesbians the way they kept on handling her and she told them to lay off or she'd kick them where it hurts. I reckon she would have done and all. Then when we do get on the bloody plane everybody's staring at us and whispering so Tina looks straight at the old bag who was behind us in the queue and says to her, 'Seen enough, have you?' and the woman has to look away. You've got to hand it to Tina, she won't take that sort of shit from nobody. We reckoned they'd be waiting for us when we got back on Saturday but they weren't, thank christ.

The hotel was great, all modern—our room as well. Not too big, but it had a balcony and a nice view all out over the sea. We got our duty-frees on the plane and spent most of the first day in bed, then went down to the beach after tea and saw Elvira who was our courier, she's half Spanish, a right little cracker and all . . . She spent a fair bit of time with us on the beach or round the pool with her boyfriend who's the assistant hotel manager which was handy because he kept coming out with bottles of wine he got from the bar, he said they can take what they want, it's part of the job. I wouldn't mind a job like that anyway—it beats sitting in the office any day. All Elvira did most of the time was go on the beach or go water skiing cos it was her job to be available to the people all the time. Both me and Tina tried water skiing—both of us kept falling off and never did get the hang of it. They had surf boards too but the surf's not much good so nobody bothered. We got pretty friendly with Elvira and Manuel—they said if we want to go again just to get in touch with them direct and they could fix us up much cheaper than with the tour company. Manuel's going to be manager of the hotel soon when he's old enough, he once did a year as a waiter in Paignton and he knows the West Country well, specially Devon.

Drink's really incredibly cheap out there and the pubs stay open all day too so we'd start off in the hotel, then nip into town to one or other of the discos, getting back when we felt like it and sometimes we'd go for a midnight swim just to cool off. You couldn't get decent lager—only bottled stuff—so we drank wine and vodka and this Spanish brandy mostly. We had tequila pretty often too—you've got to put salt on the back of your hand and then have a drink of tequila, a lick of the salt and then suck a bit of lemon. It's really strong stuff. Most times we ended up smashed out of our minds so going for a swim was a good idea.

Then we got to know a couple from London on our trip called Loretta and Ken and went out drinking and dancing with them to start with, but they was older than us, he was about thirty I guess. Loretta was really nice and she's got really nice tits. Not as big as Tina's though. I could see she had nice ones because course her bikini didn't cover much, then on the second day we went down with Elvira and met Ken and Loretta and soon as Elvira sits down she strips her bikini top off—Nice!

'Everybody does it,' she says, then Loretta whips hers off and all.

'What about you, Tina?' says Loretta. 'You going to join us?'

Well, Tina's never been behind in coming forward so right away she spills them out. I could see Ken eyeing her up, then he says, 'You don't go short, Tina,' and she giggles and her boobs start bouncing up and down. Made me really proud that she was mine I can tell you. I could tell Ken really fancied her and Loretta keeps looking at me and giving me little smiles and every time she can she leans over in my direction and once her tits touch my arm—that sent shivers down my back so I come to wondering . . .

'What about us men?' says I for something to say. 'We haven't got no tops to take off.' Wished I hadn't fucking said it afterwards.

'Ooh,' says Loretta, 'you want to go up to the other end of the beach, you can take everything off up there.'

'That a fact?'

'Try it,' she says, 'it's lovely.'

'Yeah, that's right,' says Ken, 'get a proper suntan that way.'

'Great, yeah.'

'We'll be going up there tomorrow,' says Ken and he looks straight at Tina. Well, a joke's a joke and I like jokes but there was something about the way he looked at her I didn't like. I reckoned I'd keep my eye on him. He didn't say no more and he didn't do nothing but—I don't know, I felt a bit out of it somehow, I don't know why.

Tina's quite a sight in her bikini but I reckoned she didn't ought to have got one that small. Loads of blokes were giving her the eye, specially when she took her top off. The bottom really bit into her and her arse and guts stick out a bit. Course she knew they was looking at her.

Trouble was, we stayed in the sun too long that day and got burned—me more than Tina. She had her oil stuff and didn't have enough for me, then that Ken offers to do her back for her—so I did it instead and she gives us a look, but I wasn't having him touching her up. Anyway, me getting burned means I couldn't go up to the nudist beach next day.

'You're scared,' says Tina to me.

'No I'm not—I just don't fancy it, that's all.'

What's more, I didn't want her to go—I didn't say as much but I reckon she knew. Anyway, she did go and I got pissed off. She said they had a really great time and swimming in the nude was so sexy it was incredible and that Ken had a fantastic body which I reckoned must mean the bit of it she hadn't seen already because his trunks didn't go over much. Yeah, he looked pretty well hung all right. Makes me puke.

Still, he couldn't have tried nothing on the beach. I reckoned if he did try anything with Tina I'd have to hit him, never mind if he was a big guy and that. Don't know if Tina would have gone with him—I hope she wouldn't have.

I don't know why but I kept worrying about it. I'm sure she didn't go with him though. Well, I wasn't going to stand by and let that smooth bastard screw my wife like she was there for the taking, was I? OK, so she might have fancied him but I just don't want to think about Tina doing it with some other guy and that goes for all this group stuff too. It could have come to that I reckon—well, it almost did. Tina told me Loretta told her how nice she reckoned I was and why didn't we all take a bottle or two back to their room and have some fun—and I guess I know what she was on about all right. I could have had her anytime no trouble, but I just don't fancy that group scene, that's all.

All the time she was up the other beach with them I was getting madder and madder and my sunburn hurt me like fuck too so I jacked it in and went on back to the hotel. Course that was wrong because Tina didn't know where I was, then we had a row—our first row I suppose I ought to say, our first married row anyway. I was mad about her going off up there and she was mad because I'd gone back to the hotel instead of staying on the beach like a good little boy. It was all so bloody daft really and we made it up in the morning.

We didn't see Ken and Loretta that much, we'd just see them every so often and they were always nice and friendly but I didn't like them—well, I liked her I suppose, I fancied her anyway, but it seemed to me like they was making fun of us. There was something in the way they carried on I didn't like, that's all. Course Tina said they were very nice and I was talking daft. Then they got to know this couple from Manchester and they'd go up to the nudist beach most days. Tina kept on about us joining them but I put my foot down and she sulked for a bit but she didn't go up there again.

I don't reckon she could have done nothing with that Ken—course I didn't watch her all the time but I don't reckon she would have done anyway, and like I said we didn't see much of them after they got together with that other couple.

Next night I got so pissed I fell over on the beach. Felt really awful. Tina said she wasn't half worried for a minute and that cheered me up a bit—she said she thought I'd get drowned when the tide come in. She was worried too, I could tell by her face. I told her I was OK and we kissed a bit. Then a couple of nights we had it off in the water and it was really lovely.

Got bitten by things and remembered about that girl in Morocco. Then after we'd been there a few days our shit turned black. It always happens—must be the bloody food. We didn't eat all that local muck but we reckoned they even put garlic in the chips, so on the Wednesday my shit turned black, then I couldn't go at all so we had to find a chemist in a hurry.

'Shits,' I tell him but he looks a daft bugger, he's too busy eyeing Tina anyway.

'Eh? You have the shits?'

'No, no—I can't go.'

'Go? Go where, señor?'

'Gawd! Forget it, you daft fucker.'

You'd think they'd learn to speak English, wouldn't you? In the end got some stuff off Elvira which cured my trouble.

'Drink plenty of wine,' she says—as if we need telling! I got quite a taste for it.

The weather was great—I like it hot, so does Tina. Like me it makes her feel really randy. We did it so many times in that two weeks I lost count. Christ, she's got some staying power, I'll say that for her. It's OK for the woman but I need a rest every now and then. She's full of ideas too—we tried it every which fucking way, then one night she says she fancies her big bum slapped. Well, I just tapped her up a bit. 'No, not like that,' she says. 'Harder.' Then she says, 'Let me do it to you.' I felt a bit daft to tell the truth but I just rolled over and she spanked my arse—it bloody hurt and all. Then one time she says, 'Put your fingers in me bum'—that really turns her on as well. And she give the old vibrator a go too, she filled it up with tequila that time and then had to jump in the bath quick to cool off!

Her arse was really red when I'd finished with it and I had one hell of a hard on so then I just pulled her legs open and stuck it into her—man, that was good . . . She's the best girl I've had by a mile. Then she gets me to take down the curtain rail in the bog and dust her arse with that. It was made of this bendy plastic and was about four foot long and no way was I going to have her cutting that across my arse, but I did it to her and she loved it. Personally I felt a bit daft hitting her with that but she just said to shut up and get on with it so I did—thought it might hurt her but it didn't seem to. I like it straight—a good fuck, that's what I go for, not all this spanking jazz, it don't do that much for me.

We had a great time out there though. Most of the daytimes we'd spend on the beach—both of us come back with great tans, ever so brown but a bit sore. We'd get up round eleven or so, then we'd have a bit of an early dinner in the hotel, then go down to the beach till the evening. Saw a film with Elvira and Manuel one night—*The Sweeney*, in Spanish of all things. They had some daytrips organised but mostly we didn't bother and saved our money because it was extra. We went on one of them round the town but it was a bit boring, all these old churches and stuff. There was another one to this castle place with a load of old pictures in it but we didn't go and hardly nobody did. I mean who wants to go to Spain to see a lot of old pictures and that?

Some of the clubs are good though, with Spanish dancers and singers, and strippers in some of them too. Then they used to ask all the people to have a go at this Spanish dancing and everybody was too pissed to care so we all got up and jumped around stamping our feet and trying to do those castanet things and shouting 'Olé!' Then we all sang 'Viva Espana' and something else I can't remember about this guy called O'Hara.

Out there the blokes hang around in bunches with their hair combed back and shades on gawping at all the English girls, so I had to keep my eye open in case any of the greasy little cunts tried it on. Elvira's Manuel said that Spanish men always fancy English girls and Swedes most, specially blondes. They go down the discos and if they find a girl who's willing then it's out into the alley the lot of them and if she don't fancy it then that's too bad—it's one for all and all for one with them. We heard a story when we were out there of how this girl from Bideford went down the lane with six of them and ended up a nervous wreck.

Trouble was, it all went too quick. Seems no sooner we got unpacked then it was time to come home and we had to dash round at the last minute buying presents for everybody. What with that and our duty-frees coming back we're skint but we reckon it was worth it. Got our Mum and Dad one of those queer things they drink out of— it's got a point at one end where the drink comes out and you fill it up at the top. In the club these guys did a demonstration how to do it and then they got people to have a go—course nobody could and got wine all over their faces, including yours truly . . . Got Tina's Mum one of them and all and John and Cherylle this big toy donkey. I didn't reckon that was much good but Tina said Cherylle wanted one— looked around for some trick present for John but they only had dirty postcards and you can get them anywhere. The Spanish don't seem to have much of a sense of humour anyhow, old Manuel never understood one joke I told him so in the end I give up.

Apart from that one row me and Tina got on fine, and you can't expect marriage to be a garden of roses as that song says so I reckon it was a good start. She likes to have her own way course, I could see that before, but it's just a question of pulling together, that's all. When she could see I didn't want her going around with that Ken and Loretta all the time she didn't and we didn't see that much of them after though we promised to write—we won't though. I couldn't see how to get out of giving them our address so we did, Tina did anyhow. They said they'd drop in if they was ever down our way and we'd be welcome to do the same if we was up in London but I don't reckon we'll do that neither.

Great time—best holiday I've ever had, that's for sure. Seven hour wait on our flight getting back—typical. You hear about it and everything you hear is true. One right joker said he's just been outside and a wing had dropped off and did anybody have a screwdriver, so about ten people dash over to the window trying to see which wing had come off . . . Some people'll believe anything, they really will. We never did find out what the delay was in aid of. They sent round two cheese sandwiches each to make up but it was that Spanish cheese and nobody could eat it except the seagulls.

We were shagged out when we got back. Some fucker's scratched my car door and all so I told the bloke in charge of the car-park but he only said, 'What d'you expect me to do about it?' I was pretty stroppy by then so I told him where he could go and the best way to get there and he threatened to call the cops so we went off quick.

Both of us stopped home from work today—too shagged out to go in. Our Mum kept on ringing up yesterday to see if we was back so then we had to go round to see them in the night. This is the first time I've had a chance to write anything down—Tina's gone round to see her Mum and get some stuff.

Our Mum's cleaned up the flat a treat and my old man's slapped some paint on the walls, Jon says he spent four days on it and shouted a lot and he says my old man's 'quite a character'. I'll say. But I don't suppose he's made too bad a job of it—as good as I could have done but I guess that's not saying much. The daft bugger's gone and painted the light switches, hasn't he.

Raining when we got back. I don't know why, but when you come back from holiday it's always raining. Feels cold too after Spain. Looks green and all—everything's brown out there.

Mum kept a pile of *Gazettes* for us with the bit about our wedding in it and there's our wedding photos and all—not bad, except the ones in the paper, they're all blurry and our faces are so dark you can't see who we are. Somehow it all seems a long time ago. Spain seems a long time ago too—reckon I'm glad to be back now. Tina says she wishes we could have stayed forever, but like I say—and I don't know why—in a way I'm glad to be back, it's funny that. Oh well. Coming back from holiday always makes you pissed off, Tina says the same.

Back to work tomorrow, worse luck. Still, all good things come to an end I guess, and it was a great time.


3 Aug          Sunday

Got our holiday snaps back from Boots yesterday—pity about the ones that haven't come out. There's some good ones though, plus one or two they said they wouldn't do because the young lady didn't appear to have any clothes on. All the little shop girls were giggling away when the assistant manager comes out and says, 'If you take *that* sort of pictures you can go elsewhere for developing,' so I said to him, 'Oh yeah—got the negatives, have you?' and he says, 'Here you are' in that shitty bloody way, sticks them in my hand and walks off with his nose in the air.

'Hard luck,' says this girl assistant to me. 'He's a Mormon, that's why.' She was a bit of all right and all and we had a good laugh about it. She said he's always like it.

If you hold the negs up to the light you can see all right—don't know if I'll fuss to have them done now. I don't know why but it set me wondering if that Ken's come out. Fact is, Tina let it slip he took some when they went up the beach that time but she wouldn't say what ones and course then I had to keep on wondering what they were like and all that. I guess I ought to have put my foot down about the whole thing but it's no good to keep on thinking about it now—best just try to forget it I reckon because she'd only get stroppy or something. She didn't go with him anyway, I know that.

My old man's birthday tomorrow—got him a record token, don't reckon he can do much harm with that.

It's hot right now, not so hot as Spain but anyway we went for a swim down Lyme with John and Cherylle—it's not the same though. Course Tina's seen this advert in the paper for nudist swimming down the baths and she said why don't we go along. Stuff that for a lark.


4 Aug          Monday

Bit of a laugh at work today—Marc's gone and caught VD! He was really narked when John asked him about it. 'Hear you got a dose,' says John. Good one that.

'Who fucking told you that?' says Marc.

'Oh—isn't it true then?'

'It might be.'

'Everybody knows,' John tells him which was helpful, considering.

'You tell 'em, Davis?' snaps Marc and he gets really stroppy.

'No, course not—you know me, Marc.'

'Yeah—I do. That's why I'm asking,' says Marc but John says he heard it off somebody and they heard it off somebody else and so on—you know.

'All right, it's true.'

'Wish I bleeding well knew who it was,' he keeps on saying. 'I'll kill the little cow.'

Well, it's a tricky subject—you don't like to ask too many questions even if you are dying to know all about it. That bloke I knew at school got a dose just after he left off of this Chinese girl who worked in her old man's chip shop in Frome but he's cured all right now. Some of his mates and him went round and chucked bricks through the chippie's windows and all these Chinks come pouring out waving these bloody great hatchets and chased them half-way to Radstock.

'Who do you reckon it was then?' says John.

'Dunno. But when I find out I'll kill her. They told me down the hospital I gotta lay off sex.'

How John and me stopped laughing I'll never know—I was pinching myself under the table. Then Marc says, 'Don't spread it around, eh?'

'We won't if you won't,' says John laughing his head off, then he has to make a dash for the door cos he sees Marc coming. It was something to watch but John's pretty quick on his feet, specially when there's a bloke Marc's size after him.

Anyway, everybody knows about it, old Moses and all—he said it was 'most regrettable, but only to be expected in the circumstances'. A judgement from above he reckons it is.


6 Aug.        Wednesday

Seems a long time since our honeymoon—I could do with another holiday. We got about seven or eight days of our holidays left but we can't afford to go nowhere. Just think—me and Tina'll have been married for a month in a day or two. It's working out really well too— right from the beginning we decided to share all the cooking and stuff like that, Tina said she weren't going to be tied to the sink, not that she can cook very good anyway. So we muck in with the cooking and we have some good laughs and all too.

I found an old table-tennis bat the other day and every time Tina

fancies a bit on the arse I use that on her—well, she likes it but I don't
like it on my arse, I don't mind doing it to her I guess, I feel a bit daft
though it's no good telling her. She keeps on at me to let her do it to me
but it hurts too much. I told her to think herself lucky I'd do it to her
let alone her doing it to me and she shut up after that, and I gave her
bum a good leathering for her and she lapped it up, don't ask me why,
it don't do nothing for me. Give her a real good screwing after—great.


8 Aug.        Friday

Shit, shit, shit—everything's gone wrong. The fact is Tina and me
had one almighty row and she's gone back home to her old lady.
Christ, it makes me puke. And all over nothing really—well, it seems
nothing now.

The car's playing up again so neither of us was in a very good mood
when we got home, then we find a letter there from that Ken and
Loretta and it's got some pictures of Tina in it—her in the nude, the
cunt must have took them when they went up the other beach that
time. Well, I don't know but it just made me mad. I mean the ones
with just her in them were OK I guess but he was in some of them and
I didn't like that one bit, like she was his woman or something with his
fucking arm round her and both of them in the nude. I tried to tell
Tina I didn't mind the ones with just her in them but oh no, she wasn't
having none of that, she sticks her nose in the air and tells me it's none
of my fucking business.

'You're my wife, Tina,' I said to her straight.
'Huh! You don't own me, Andy.'
'I'm not saying I do.'
'Yes you are.'
'No I'm not.'
'Well, *I* liked Ken.'
'Oh yeah—I can see that.'
'Oh? And what's that supposed to mean?'
'You know—the bastard's touching you up.' Well, it looked like it,
but it hurt me even to have to say it. There's her with everything
showing and him and all, the pair of them with grins on their faces
like—
'I didn't sleep with him if that's what you're on about.'
'Good.'
'What's that mean?'
'We're married now, Tina, that's what it means.'

'Oh—married, is it?' she says and she sticks her chin out at me. 'And what's married mean? You think you own me?'

No, I tell her, that's not what I mean but by now she's really worked up and nothing I say's right, just nothing. I've never seen her like that, that's all.

'You ought to grow up, Tina,' I told her, then she gives me such a look—I thought she was going to do something really stupid but she just goes all calm and says to me, 'Piss off, little boy,' and goes out. I didn't know what to say.

'Tina! Where are you going?' I said but by now she's locked the door.

'Let's talk it over—come on out,' I said but no, she's too stubborn. Next thing I know out she comes with her case.

'What's that for?' I asks her.

'What are cases usually for, dumbo?'

'Where you going to?'

'Never you mind.'

'Oh?' says I. 'Going to see that Ken, are you?' I still don't know why I said that last bit, it was daft but it's too late now.

'If I want, least he's not boring.' Then she's off.

'And don't fucking come back,' I shouted after her. Don't know why I said that neither.

'I fucking well won't, so don't worry,' says she.

So there we are. She's gone now. And all over a few daft bloody photos. But she had no right to go off like that, no right. And she had no right to let that bastard take those photos neither, that's another thing for sure. I feel sick, really sick—I miss her like hell already but if I've told myself once then I've told myself a million times it's not up to me to go crawling to her, which don't make it no better and don't bring her back. I don't know what I'm going to do so I haven't done nothing, just hung around and waited for her to come back but she hasn't. When John and Cherylle come round just now course they asked where Tina was so I told them. Wish I hadn't, it'll be all round the bleeding office now.

'Gone back to her mother's I expect, mate,' John says. 'They usually do.' Though what the fuck he knows about . . . I told him to turn it up and Cherylle tells him to shut it and offered to ring up Tina's old lady as if she didn't know nothing about it. So that's where Tina is—that's something, least she's not with that Ken guy, I didn't really think she would be I suppose. I've been sitting here ever since. Made some beans for my tea but I wasn't hungry, then Jon come up. I told him Tina was out but I don't reckon he believed me, then I wrote to that Ken—don't suppose I ought to have done that neither but I was mad and it's posted now. I sent him back his pictures and wrote on the back, 'Keep your prick to yourself and leave my wife alone.' Bloody nerve the bloke had—he started the letter off 'Dear Tina', then 'Hope you can come up soon and we'll try to recapture the mood of those hot nights in Spain.' Fucking nerve. Still, it don't do to write about it too much I reckon. My head's spinning as it is, and thinking's bad enough . . . Reckon it's time to stop this bloody daft diary too, high time.


9 Aug.          Saturday

Tina didn't come back last night. I reckon it's finished now. If she'd have come back I'd have given her a second chance but she didn't so there we go. I thought she would, I really did. I stayed up till about two, didn't think I'd ever sleep again—woke up in a cold sweat at half five and she wasn't there. Shit.

Then Anna dropped in to ask us to come to her birthday party. Amazing how everything happens at once.

'Oh, where's Tina?' she says straight off.

'Gone.'

'Oh? Gone shopping?'

'Nope—just gone.'

'What? You don't mean—?'

I'll say this for Anna, she looked shocked. 'No!' she says, which was a bloody daft thing to say, then I told her—she'd have to know sooner or later I suppose.

'Why,' she says but I just said we'd had a row.

'Stupid little pratt!' she says. 'Will you have her back?'

'Dunno—suppose so.' I was feeling too low to think about it much, there didn't seem much chance anyway. I thought about it a bit since Anna left. I guess I'd have Tina back, hell, course I bloody would—I love her, don't I? If only she'd see some sense—that's all I want—then everything'd be fine. Can't be bothered to write no more now. Tina hasn't come back so I reckon she don't want to now or else she'd have come. Worst night of my life.


10 Aug.          Sunday

Tina and me got back together today—thanks to Anna, it's all thanks to Anna. Last night I drank a bottle of tequila and ended up spewing in the bath, thought I was going to die I felt so bad—didn't want to but I couldn't think of much to live for anyhow. Felt really bad this morning and I had the shits something awful. Then Anna come dinnertime and says she's been round to see Tina and Tina wanted to come back. Our Mum cried all night about it Anna says and my old man kept saying 'Stupid little buggers' like he does. That made me smile a bit but I wasn't feeling too much like smiling what with everything.

'She told you she wanted to come back to me?' I says to Anna.

'Well—not quite. But you can go round.'

'I'm not going round there. She walked out on me.'

'Don't be daft, Andy. She wants to see you.'

'Then tell her she can come back—if she wants to.'

'She doesn't like to.'

'What? What the fuck's that mean?'

'Oh I don't know, it's just who makes the first move, that's all.'

'Well, I'm not making it,' I said and neither was I.

'Come round and talk to her—her Mum's gone in hospital to have her nerves done and she's all on her own. She looks really pissed off, Andy.'

Anyway, in the end Anna got us to go but I didn't much want to till she said Tina told her she was sorry.

'Oh,' says Tina when we get round there, 'hello.'

'Hello.'

'I'll make us all a coffee,' says Anna.

Well, Tina and me just looked at each other. Suppose maybe I ought to have waited for her to say something but anyway I just said, 'Well, how are you?' which was daft, but she just said, 'Oh—OK. How's the flat?'

'Oh, fine. Fine. OK. You know.'

Then we had another bit of looking at each other.

'You go out last night?' she says.

'No—you?'

'No.'

'John and Cherylle looked in.'

'Yeah, I know. Cherylle rang us.'

'Yeah.'

Funny that, here we were—my wife, and I couldn't think of a bleeding word to say to her. 'You coming back then?' I said all of a sudden.

'OK.'

'Right then.'

Then Anna brought the coffee in.

'Well!' says she. 'All settled then, is it?'

'Guess so,' I said.

'Yeah,' says Tina.

That's it then. I didn't tell Tina about what I done with the pictures. I put my arm round her when we got back and I don't know why but I felt a bit weepy. It's bloody daft I know but it's good to have Tina back—hell, it's good, course it is. I really think she's learned a bit of a lesson though I'm not going to rub it in. Then we had it off and she was different somehow—normally she's moving about a lot and that but this time it was all sort of gentle and quiet like, and I fingered her arsehole cos I know she likes that. We kissed and cuddled a lot and then just lay quiet together afterwards and I stroked her hair and she just lay there with her eyes closed. It made me feel different somehow but I liked it like that and Tina said she did too.

I can't say how grateful I am to Anna—she's really come up trumps. If it wasn't for her . . . well, I don't want to think about it, that's all.

## 12 Aug.         Tuesday

Everything's fine with Tina now—we haven't rowed once since she come back. She never asked about those photos and I reckon she must know what I done with them and she's not going to say no more about it. I won't say nothing else neither, it's best forgotten.

John said to me, 'Glad you're back with Tina, mate.'

'Yeah—thanks, mate.'

'Still,' he says and shrugs his shoulders, 'you're bound to have a few rows now and then, int you?'

'Yeah, yeah.'

That's true I guess, but you don't need to go over old wounds. Neither me nor Tina said nothing and I reckon neither of us will now—she's sorry, I can tell that, and we'll just leave it there. And I don't reckon to hear from that Ken again neither—leastways if we do then he'd better bloody watch out. Tina was a bit quiet yesterday and I reckoned one time she was going to get stroppy again but she's OK today, just like she used to be, so everything's fine.

## 14 Aug.         Thursday

John and Cherylle went off to Corfu for their holiday yesterday. It'll be a bit quiet without John around for two weeks.

Tina's learning to drive now. She's having a few lessons from the brother of a friend of hers who's a driving instructor and he said he'd do it on the side for half price. Still pretty expensive though and like I told her we got to watch our pennies right now . . . We've not got too many expenses though, it's just a question of getting over all the cost of getting married and that, when we've been settled for a few months we ought to be OK, no trouble. Tina's out right now on her first driving lesson. Nothing much else to write about really.

15 Aug.      Friday

Had the washing machine people round today—Tina hasn't paid the instalments. Had to pay them on the spot and they didn't really want to take a cheque but I was out of ready cash. Tina says she forgot and can't remember what she did with the money. Well, sure we could have had a row about it but she gets that look in her eyes and I reckoned well, what's a quid or two. Then I thought they don't come round and try to take your bleeding washing machine on account of you missing just one payment . . .

'What you looking at?' she says to us.

'Oh—nothing.'

'Yeah,' she says and she's got that look on again. Well, some guys'd belt her and no mistake, they'd just grab her hold and knock the fucking shit out of her—christ, well that's what some bastards'd do.

'Piss off,' she says to me.

'Oh, fucking get stuffed, Tina.'

That was it. Leave it there, mate, I reckoned. Went on down The Anchor. Got pissed.

17 Aug.      Sunday

Our Mum said we had to come round today for dinner—it was good and all. Tina can't cook a joint and anyway we don't get up till dinnertime of a Sunday so we just have a big breakfast.

Nan got gravy all down her front, then started crying. Dad says she's gone a bit senile and Auntie Beryl said Nan's a real handful these days and wets the bed. They made her go and lie down in the afternoon so's they could all talk about putting her in a home and hope she wasn't up there wetting our bed right now. Me and Tina went for a walk and when we got back they were still at it. My old man said it'd cost a packet and Auntie Beryl said well, *she* wasn't putting up with it

for much longer and anyway the council had places for old people.
Tina wanted to come home but I wanted to stay for tea. Boring day.

18 Aug.        Monday

Very hot so some of the girls went out sunbathing on the grass but
Moses wasn't having none of that, was he, and went down to clear
them off, but they told him what they did in the dinnertime was up to
them so then he goes and complains to the Dept Head.

Course Tina has to go and tell them she'd been sunbathing in the
nude out in Spain which they all said was great and one of them said to
me, 'You as well, Andy?' and before I could say Tina butts in with,
'Oh no, he was too shy,' so I said, 'It was only for one afternoon
anyway,' and she gives us a look and I give her one and all the girls
look at each other and grin.

'What were you shy about?' says one but I made out I didn't hear
her. Tina don't half go on sometimes. Then I went down The Anchor
and saw Roy Vicary and he says, 'Hello, Andy, how's married life
suiting you then, eh?'

'Oh—great, Roy—great. You know.'

'Not cramping your style?'

'No, no trouble.'

'That's right—you got your rights.'

He said when him and his wife split up she told him she was
expecting. 'How do I know whose it is?' he said to her.

'Whose else would it be?'

'Ah,' says Roy, 'but we can't be sure, can us?' Then she chucked his
dinner at him.

He said it was just a dodge to get maintenance out of him but he
wasn't having none so she had an abortion and went to live with a
fishmonger.

'And there ain't many of them left neither so she's fucking lucky.'

'What—abortions?'

'No—fishmongers.'

We had a good laugh about it. Tina's still taking the tablets—not
that we can afford to start a family right now so it's just as well. Thank
christ for science like John always says—that and rubber planters.
Anyway, Tina says she don't want kids. I've said all along that I
wouldn't mind a family one day but she don't fancy the idea.

Tracie's birthday was the other day so they had to let her out. She
kicked the warden in the balls when she left but still he couldn't keep

her, then she dropped in home to collect her stuff and went off up
north again. She's got to report to somebody every so often but Tina
don't reckon she will.

Got a dirty postcard from John and Cherylle what said, 'Weather's
great, wine's great—glad you're not here.'


22 Aug.          Friday

Had a few words with Tina today. I happened to say the flat could do
with cleaning and she snaps at me, 'You're standing around doing sod
all—why don't you do it?'

'I thought we agreed to share it'—which we did.

'I got a driving lesson.'

'OK. No need to row about it. We can do some when you get back.'
That seemed fair to me.

'Huh—you can.'

That's another thing—I don't like the look of that driving bloke.
The other day he calls for Tina and I answered the door cos she was
still getting ready.

'Hello, mate,' he says. 'Is Tina in?'

'Yeah.'

'Who are you by the way?' says the cheeky cunt.

'I live here.'

'Oh,' says he with a little look, 'What? With Tina, is it?'

'That's right. I'm her husband.'

'Oh—nice to meet yer.' Just like that.

So when Tina got back I offered to give her a driving lesson but she
said, 'Oh, that's OK. I don't want you shouting at me all the time.'

'Don't Whatsit shout at you?'

'No,' she says with that little turn of her head. 'He really knows
what he's doing. And his name's Mick.'

Then before I could get another word in she goes in the bedroom
and she comes out in that new top she'd bought and says, 'Well, aren't
we going out tonight then?'

'What about the cleaning?'

'Don't be boring. Sod the cleaning, I want to go out.'

So we went out. Drinking beats cleaning any day of the week as far
as I'm concerned and she was OK for the rest of tonight. She looked a
bit vacant some of the time but that's nothing new. Everything's fine
really.

23 Aug.        Saturday

Got up late and took a look round and the place was a bit like a pigsty so me and Tina cleaned it up this afternoon, then we reckoned as how we done enough for one day so we jacked it in and had a screw instead. Tina didn't feel like the old table-tennis bat today, she said she couldn't be bothered so I just shoved it in. It was good too—there's something about screwing in the afternoon that's really good.

Went to the disco tonight. That Mick was there, more's the pity, hanging round the bar looking smooth.

'Sorry about the other day, Andy,' he says to me. 'We hadn't been introduced.'

'I reckon I know you now,' I told him and I wasn't bloody joking neither. I kept my eye on him after that. We had a pretty good time.

25 Aug.        Monday

August Bank Holiday.

Went round Tina's Mum's for dinner which wasn't much good cos she'd forgotten to do the spuds, then Marilynne phoned up and said the pigs had arrested Angelo in Coventry where he'd been hiding with a mate of his who'd grassed on him. Next thing Angelo knew the police bust down the door at four in the morning and haul him out of bed. He's been done for some porno and forging racket Marilynne said, but it's all a frame-up and he's got a sharp lawyer who'll get him off. The word's gone round on that mate of his who grassed on him and Marilynne reckons he's going to get done up good and proper which serves him right. And that caretaker bloke's going to get taken care of and all. Sounds bad—poor old Angelo.

28 Aug.        Thursday

As time goes on I can't seem to find so much to write about in this diary. Life goes on like always and I'm pretty used to being married and having our own place and all that. It's fine. As for me and Tina— well, we're OK I guess. We don't row much and we get on as well as most but, I don't know, there's been something about us, I don't know what it is . . . I know I'm not very good at putting things into words but well, maybe Tina and I aren't so close as we was a while back. Yesterday I said to her, 'Anything wrong, Tina?' and she said, 'Course not—why d'you say that?'

'Dunno—I only wondered. You're not ill?'

'No, course not. Don't keep on so.'

But—well, I don't know. I'll have to think about it some more I guess.

Anyway, John and Cherylle are back from Corfu with lovely tans just like we had. They had a great time—and John told me he had this Italian girl on the side when Cherylle wasn't looking a couple of times but not to tell Cherylle, which of course I won't. Mind you, I reckon he's going to land in the shit one of these fine days and no mistake. They brought us back one of those things you drink out of which we got for our people.

We've reckoned it's high time we had our housewarming—we'd forgotten all about it—so it's this Saturday and everybody's invited.


31 Aug.          Sunday

Yesterday was our housewarming and me and Tina had another row.

Everything was OK till that fucking Mick turns up, just barges in like he owns the bloody place he does.

'Tina can't go out for a lesson tonight,' I says to him.

'Oh, that's all right, mate—she invited us to the party.'

Stone me! Soon as I could I got Tina on one side and asked her about it.

'Yeah, what's wrong?' she says. 'I can invite who I want.'

'Why him?'

'Why not?' she says, then she goes off leaving me looking like a pratt.

Anyway, that Mick's after her all right. I couldn't enjoy myself one bit because of having to keep an eye on him all the time—and her. And course she noticed.

'What are you following me about for?' says she.

'I'm not.'

'Yes you are. It looks frigging daft.'

'Suit yourself.'

'Oh, just grow up, Andy.'

'Oh yeah? What about you?'

'What about me?'

'You fancy him, do you?'

'Oh grow up,' she says again—I'm getting sick of that.

'Well, do you?'

'What if I do? He's very attractive.'

'Oh, is he?'

'Yeah—and he's not boring neither.'

That was that. We didn't speak a lot after that. She went out of her way to dance with him and I danced with Zandra a couple of times.

I don't know . . . If she reckons it's me what's boring, well, she's not so fucking brilliant herself.

Then we had another row today—the same one really. I could tell she was stroppy, the look she had on her face. She goes all sulky and won't say no more than yes or no.

'You still mad?' I said to her.

'No.'

'Thought you was.'

'No.'

'If it's about last night . . .'

'What about it?'

'We oughtn't to go on like this.'

'Like what?'

'Well, rowing all the time.'

'You start it.'

'No I don't.

'Bollocks.'

'You're never in the wrong then?' I said and she didn't answer.

Sat around for a few hours, then I put my arm round her and said, 'Look, let's forget it.' She didn't answer.

'Sorry if I lost my cool,' I said.

'OK.'

'Yeah.'

'You just get too heavy sometimes, you know?'

'OK. Just remember that I love you—right?'

'Right.'

So that's that sorted out. Somehow it looked like it was all my fault and I agreed to it, whereby it's not. I don't go round making eyes at other women—well, not like that anyhow. OK, so I don't own Tina, I've never said I do and neither of us goes for all that till death do us part stuff. I mean if it doesn't work then you don't hang around poking the ashes, do you? But if we're together then—well, what I'm trying to say is I won't stand for Tina having other guys, no way. Thing is—and that's what's worrying me—I'm not sure if—I mean I don't reckon she'd cheat on me, not when I think about it. I don't reckon she'd stop fancying other guys just because she's married to me, but all the same. I mean I fancy other women—take that Zandra last night, I could go for her in a big way and I know full well she's

anybody's after a few drinks but I didn't do nothing about it, did I?
Well, I mean who wouldn't if they was offered? But I didn't. Anyway,
it's different with Tina, she's my wife after all, isn't she? I don't want
them talking about my wife being an easy lay behind my back—course
some husbands don't mind, I'm not daft, well that's their problem I
guess. Like I say, I don't really reckon Tina would go with another
bloke but that don't stop me from worrying, do it? I mean to say if I
can't trust her then—No, I don't reckon she would, I'll just have to
ease off a bit, that's all. Sexwise, everything's great. We'll be OK I
reckon. It's just fucking daft, that's all.


3 Sept.        Wednesday

When Tina tells me today she's got another driving lesson after tea I
just said, 'Oh ah? That's nice, yeah.'
  'About half six. OK?'
  'Yeah, sure—OK.' And I can see that she wants to say something
else but she can't think of nothing.
  'Right. We'll have to have our tea a bit early.'
  'Fine,' I said. 'How's it going then?'
  'Oh, OK. You know.'
  So she went off for her lesson and I said I'd go down the pub. Well,
that was fine till I gets down there and somebody says straight off
'Where's Tina?' and I tell them, then they says oh, you wanna watch
that Mick, he's had more married women than he's had hot dinners.
Mick the Prick they call him, the bastard. I just grinned a bit and said
there's no problem like that and Tina can handle herself but it set me
off thinking again. Well, if he tries it on with my wife then I'll get him
for it—even if I have to get a few mates to help me—and that's for
certain. Anyway, later on I said to her, 'You want to watch that Mick
by the way, Teen.'
  'What for?'
  'They say he's after anything in a skirt.'
  So she gives me that queer look and says straight out, 'We're not
having it off, if that's what's eating you.'
  'I didn't mean that.'
  'Yes you did—you're just worried out of your tiny mind that I'm
sleeping with him, aren't you?'
  'No I'm not.'
  'Jesus!' she goes.
  Straight, I didn't know what to say so I said the wrong thing.

'If he bothers you then I'll deal with him,' I said.

'Huh! You reckon I can't put a guy in his place without asking *you* for help?'

I felt really stupid. Course I could see she never even thought of having it away with that Mick so I must have hurt her I reckon.

'Sorry.'

'Forget it,' she says, but I couldn't.

'It's not . . . It's only what I heard, that's all, Tina. I mean . . .'

'Oh?' says she with her eyebrows going up.

'Um—yeah—I mean—'

'You're still worried, aren't you?'

'Oh—no, no way. I trust you, Tina.'

'Oh yeah? Look, Andy, we're married, right?'

'Yeah—sure. Least I hope so. Anyway—'

'But you want to own me.'

'No I don't.'

'Look how you went on about those bloody photos.' Trust her to drag that up again.

'It was just his nerve, that's all. He—'

'What? Ought to have asked you? Why?'

'Well, because . . .'

'Because what?'

'Because you're my fucking wife, that's why!'

'Oh christ! For christ's sake stop going on about me being your goddam wife, Andy.'

'Well, you are.'

'Sure I am but . . .'

'Yeah but—those photos . . .'

'So what? I didn't mind,' she says, like she's proud of it or something.

'No—well, it's . . .'

'It's what?'

I didn't know what to say. Everything I did say just sounded daft so I kept my trap shut.

'When you married me, we agreed—'

'We didn't agree on you having other blokes,' I told her straight.

'Christ!' she says just like that and I can't get another word out of the daft bitch. Really pissed off, I feel really sick.

7 Sept.        Sunday

'I'm not going round your bleeding Mum's every week either,' says Tina.

'All right, all right.'

There we are sat in front of our sodding sausages and she's got a look on her face like she's just been given a month to live.

'What's wrong, Teen?' I says to her.

'Nothing.'

And then that Samuel kid starts bawling his bleeding head off again, he's shouting out 'arseholes'—and he can shout and all.

'Jesus!' says Tina. 'Just listen to it.'

'Coming to terms with life,' says I and we laughed a bit and it looked to me as if she wants to spew or something.

'Any pudding?' I asked her.

No—no pudding, it's arseholes, arseholes and no fucking pudding. In the end I had a banana and we talked about work for a bit. Well, work's still the same—boring—but there we go. Moses is on his summer holidays right now, him and his missus have gone to that summer camp for lay preachers in the Cotswolds. Best of bleeding luck to him. Our Mum and Dad have gone on their holidays and all— to Tenerife, bet he's moaning all the time. Had a postcard from them yesterday saying they've been up a mountain and he's gone and burnt his head in the sun. Anna's in Greece with Dermot and they're due back in a day or two. Before they went Mum asked Dermot if his villas had separate rooms and he looked a bit puzzled and says to her, 'Oh yes, Mrs Baker, the rooms are quite separate. Open plan's out right now.'

'That's fine then,' she says. And he looks puzzled again and Anna's there smiling to herself. Separate rooms! Best of luck to them and all. I've got more important things to think about. It's funny how all them and their troubles and what have you seem so far away now—not just that they're all abroad and that, but they just seem sodding boring, that's all.

Said I'd keep an eye on the house for them while they was gone but I'm blowed if I'm going to do the garden like my old man wanted us to.

9 Sept.        Tuesday

I don't know, I just can't think of nothing to write about these days. Anyway, we're OK now. I give Tina a driving lesson yesterday, she's not bad. Bloody near killed that kid on the crossing but it was his fault for being there in the first place like she told his Mum.

When I think about it now, I can see that maybe I was making too much hassle. I mean she's not having it off with other guys every day of the week, is she? Well christ, I reckon I'd know if she was.

And we're OK—I make sure the sex is good and just how she likes it. Money's a bit short and she doesn't like that but we got our autumn payrise coming up and I'm thinking of putting in for some higher-scale jobs next year but I'm a bit young yet. What we've got together is good, I'm sure of that much.

12 Sept.        Friday

All our family back from their holidays now and we've got two more of those drinking things, reckon we ought to open a shop. My old man says the gnats and flies out there went for him like dive-bombers and says he hasn't stopped scratching for a fortnight—nor complaining if I know him. He's covered in huge red lumps and Anna reckons he's got the Black Death. Mum told him that's because he would scratch himself but he wouldn't listen and said, 'What was I supposed to do then? I wouldn't have scratched meself if I hadn't have got bitten by the buggers, would I?' which is him all over.

Big news though—Anna's leaving home to go and live with Dermot.

Our Mum's not too chuffed about it. Well, she was at first cos she said, 'Oh! You're getting married?'

No, they're not—that got her. She didn't know what to say and our old man sat there with his gob open and she said, 'Oh I see.' Anna's ever so thrilled about it. They're getting this posh new flat and then they're off out to Greece again. She did a bit of modelling out there and Dermot says she's going to be on the cover of the brochure for these villas him and his mate are flogging. Reckon she'll be OK with that Dermot. She's landed on her feet I reckon. She said if me and Tina wanted to nip out for a week she'd fix us up—really nice of her that was I reckon.

14 Sept.        Sunday

Went over to our Mum's today for her birthday. Tina's fine. Everything's OK, we know where we stand now and that's good. It's not that I don't trust Tina or didn't never trust her—that's not what

I'm trying to say, what I mean is all that following her about at our party that time and everything was a bit daft, I see that now, but it's all water under the bridge. I mean I even thought of following her on her driving lessons, now that would have been crazy. If she had found out she would have really blown her top. Anyway, Tina's OK here lately, we have a lot of laughs. Yesterday we went up to Weston with John and Cherylle, there's not much of the hot weather left so we made a day of it and took a few bottles and some rolls and stuff for our dinner.

I asked John when him and Cherylle was going to get married themselves.

'No hurry,' says he. 'Plenty of time yet, eh?'

He said they'd probably get a flat first.

'How's you then?' he asks me when we were having a walk up the beach looking at the talent. 'Here, look at the bum on that.'

'Very nice'—and it was and all.

'Getting on OK then, are yer?'

'Oh—great. Yeah.'

'Well, if it don't work out it's not the end of the world you know, Andy.'

Sometimes he can go too far, that's all. One of these fine days he's going to get his head kicked in.

'No it's no problem—you don't own each other,' he goes on.

'Shut it, John.'

'Oh—sorry, mate, I wasn't meaning . . .'

Yeah, yeah, sure he wasn't and I haven't seen a fucking flying pig yet.

21 Sept.     Sunday

I don't know why but I don't seem to be able to do this diary like I used to, seems a bit of a waste of time. There don't seem to be much point in putting down everything like I used to. Nothing much seems to be happening anyhow.

John let off that rocket in the office Friday, bit of a giggle that was. Made a hell of a mark on the wall, then he went and told Moses it had been a thunderbolt from heaven. Went to a party last night. I don't know. Got some jeans yesterday. Tina got herself a skirt. She's put on a bit of weight since we got back from Spain.

30 Sept.     Tuesday

Our Mum keeps on about us going round of a Sunday but it's a dead bore even though the food's always good, so last Sunday we didn't bother. Mum knows Tina can't cook so she keeps on saying why don't she come round with stuff. Then she gives us a cake every time we go round there which gets Tina mad and she won't eat none of it, then Mum said she'd teach Tina to cook if she wanted which she don't and I said it wasn't on, but least that was better than having Tina shout at her which is what she said she'd do if my bleeding Mum didn't shut up about her frigging cakes all the time.

I reckon Tina could have shown a bit more of an interest instead of just looking vacant. The other day she says to me my Mum fusses too much and she must have always spoiled me or else I'd be more independent today. I just took no notice. If anybody fusses then it's her old lady not our Mum.

'Your old lady had her head transplant yet?' I asks her and she tells me to get fucking stuffed. Shit, I was only joking.

Anna's gone to live with Dermot now and Mum keeps saying they're engaged, so it's all right—they're not but she won't listen. She tells everybody it's only a 'temporary arrangement'. Depends what you mean by temporary. Our Mum keeps saying this new flat's ever so nice—bit flash but it's not bad I guess.

Then she says stuff to me like 'Is Tina looking after you?' and I have to say it's not like that, then she says, 'What about your washing?' so I just say we chuck it all in the machine once a week and that's that. Then she reckons I've lost weight—there's no end to it. To tell the truth, it's a right drag going round there these days and Tina hates it, she looks bored out of her mind all the time.

Nan's gone into a home so Auntie Beryl's got the house to herself and now she moans about having to live on her own. Dad keeps telling her she's lucky the rest of them let her stay on there because by rights the place ought to be sold and shared out now Nan's gone, then Auntie Beryl says, 'Oh, I know you're only waiting for me to die.' Cheerful buggers! If you ask me Nan's the happiest one of them—she's with people her own age and most of them are as mad as her and she just sits round trying to do jigsaws and make baskets all the time. They go to see her every so often and row all the way there and all the way back. I went once—Tina didn't want to go so I went—and the doctors said Nan's ever so happy and most likely'll go on for years yet, though course she don't know the time of bleeding day.

'Hello, Nan,' I says to her and she says, 'Give us a fag.' Well, she hasn't smoked for years but I give her one all the same. There was a whole room full of the old dears, about thirty of them, all looking as spare as Nan and half the time they'd as soon stick their food up their noses as in their gobs.

2 Oct.        Thursday

Had a row with Tina today. And yesterday. She wants a couple of those Parker Knoll swivel chairs. Well, we already got that swivel chair except it don't swivel. Anyway, I said we can't afford it and neither can we. Tina says when people come round they've got nowhere to sit—that's true but we still can't afford none. They cost a packet those chairs, specially the ones she wants. So then she said I was mean.

'Oh yeah?' I said. 'What about you?'

'What about me?'

I told her she didn't ought to spend so much on clothes and make-up. She's always buying stuff to stick on her face and none of it makes her look no fucking better.

'You're a right bore these days,' she says to me.

'Oh yeah? What you marry me for then?'

'Gawd knows,' she says—just like that, then she goes out. I can't stand it when she does that.

'Where you going?' I asked her when she'd gone and she shouts back at me, 'Never you mind.'

I thought she went into the bedroom but she'd gone out and she didn't come back all last night. I sat around till half eight, then I went out, ended up looking for her and got in a right state cos I couldn't find her nowhere. Saw John and Cherylle and they asked us to their housewarming but I didn't stay long. I was sick—and mad. Come two and she still wasn't back so I just said to myself 'Fuck her' and went on to bed and locked the door from the inside and all. I was buggered if I was going to sit up all night waiting for the daft little bitch.

Back she come this morning.

'Where you been?' I asked her. 'I was worried fucking sick.'

'It's none of your business.'

'You been seeing that Mick?' That was the first thing that come into my mind.

'Oh sod off,' she says like she's talking to a bleeding kid or something.

'Have you?' I said and grabbed her hold. You know, there was something about the way she was stood there with her eyes looking at me and her mouth sort of on one side like she was laughing at me that really turned me on, I don't know why. I know one thing though and that's not two—I really wanted her right then.

'Let me go,' she says. So I did. Ought to have belted her, I know that now—most men would have done too so she's lucky. I just looked at her and she looks right through me. I went on to work on my own. If she wants to play silly buggers then so can I. Thought about it this morning—it was daft to drag that Mick up again and I don't know why I did, she most likely went back to her old lady's again, that's what I reckon.

She come round going-home time and we come on home without saying nothing, then when we was having tea she says, 'We going to get those chairs?'

'You gotta see, Tina, we haven't got the cash,' I said but she didn't answer. Next thing I know she's got ready to go out.

'Where are we going?' I says to her.

'I'm going out,' she says, making me feel like a pratt. All I could think of saying was 'Oh', then I said 'Where to?'

'Out.' That made me mad too, I could see she was going out, couldn't I?

'Where to?'

'Just out.'

'Look, Tina, where you going?'

But still she wouldn't tell me, just says I'm boring her—that's a bloody good one.

'I can go out anytime I want,' she says.

'Sure. Why can't we go together?'

'Because,' she says. Fucking brilliant that was. 'If you want to go out on your own I'm not stopping you,' she says.

'Look, Tina, I just don't want you going out on your own.'

'Oh yeah? What you going to do then?'

I could have followed her but what's the bloody use? It's not that I don't trust Tina, it's just I'd sooner we went out together, that's all—least if we go out for the night or like that. I wanted to know where she went but I'm not going to bust a gut about it, am I? Half of it is she's just acting bloody daft about those chairs she wants and there's no way we can get them, so she might as well shut up about it.

I went on down The Anchor, didn't see why I should stay in. Had a good time too—bit like the old days really. Noticed how many guys there were down there without their women, course most of them was home looking after the kids or doing something in the house like that as far as I could tell. I mean that wouldn't worry me, it was just not

knowing where Tina was, that's all. She can go out on her own if she
wants to. But I can't stop thinking that she's maybe with some guy. If
she's got another bloke I reckon I'll kill her.


7 Oct.　　　Tuesday

I don't know—sometimes it's like it's dead between us.
　'Let's talk about it then,' I say to her.
　'Huh! With you?'
　'Yeah.'
　And there's that fucking look on her face again.
　'Who is it then?' I says.
　'Nobody.'
　'Come on, Tina, you don't want me no more.'
　'Yes.'
　'What? Who is he?'
　'Look, you daft cunt, I don't want other guys.'
　'Oh no?'
　'Jesus!' And up she gets so I touched her shoulder, then we sort of
held each other and it looked to me just like she wanted to cry.
　'Tina, for christ's sake . . .'
　Then we went to bed. Shit.


9 Oct.　　　Thursday

It's OK now, it'll be all right. Just give it time, mate, it'll be fine.


19 Oct.　　　Sunday

It's no good—it's not working, it's just not fucking working, is it?
Something's gone wrong between me and Tina. We really seem to
have drifted apart here lately. We don't row much, it's just we don't
seem to have nothing much to say to each other no more. I remember
what Glyn Dudderidge used to say—him and his wife only used to say
about ten words to each other in a week after they got married and
most of them was yes and no, but that's his business and his old
woman hated him anyway. No, this is different. The sex is OK, she
still wants it, so do I, but maybe even that isn't quite what it was. I
don't know how to put it—what I'm trying to say is I can't remember
what it used to be like, just it was good and it seemed like it was good
all the time, though I don't suppose it could have been good all the

time, not that it isn't good now. I mean sometimes it's bloody good—fuck me, I just don't know *what* I'm trying to say, that's what it boils down to. I don't know, I just don't know. She goes out on her own sometimes and christ knows what she does then. She sees that fucking Janette sometimes, I know that much. Then I followed her that time and it was dead embarrassing cos when I went round the corner there she's waiting for me and I have to make out I was posting a letter. 'Oh yeah?' she says. 'What letter?' so I just stuck this bank statement into the box before she could see, then we just stood looking at each other and I felt so shown up I just told her to have a nice time and I come on home. So I can't follow her now. Wished afterwards I'd clouted her one there and then for the way she was looking at me. I remember I screwed her when she got back—I was really rough and she liked it and kept calling me 'Tiger' and I got really turned on the way she was acting, I don't know.

We had a bit of a talk about her going out on her own and she said that if we had an open marriage then neither of us could complain if one of us went out on their own if they wanted to.

'What's an open marriage then?' I says.

'You not keeping on all the time.'

'I don't.'

'Yes you do—it's a proper drag.'

I told her that was OK but I didn't much like going out without her and she just said, 'Too bad.' And she reckoned *I'm* boring—shit, it's her what's boring—and childish if you ask me. She can be really catty when she wants. Anyway, it's got really daft not knowing where your wife is half the time when anybody asks you and you have to make up something, then somebody comes up to you and says, 'Oh, I saw Tina here' or 'I saw Tina there' and 'Where was you to?'.

Saw that Janette the other day and she gives me the glad eye—just what you'd expect off her. I should have had her, the little cow. Ought to have said something to Tina but I don't know what. I reckon it's over between us. I wish I knew why. Course I haven't told nobody, I can't, I've been feeling really awful lately, not that she fucking cares. Told her yesterday I had a guts ache and she just says, 'Oh—sorry,' just like that. Well, she can go and stuff herself, that's how I feel about it. John and Cherylle are having their housewarming on Friday and if Tina don't want to go then she needn't bother to.

I screwed hell out her last night. You know, when it's as good as that I want to stay with her for ever and ever, it's just the rest of the sodding time. Last night it was just like it used to be when we'd have it off in the car—really good it was. I don't know, if only it could be like that all the time then we'd be all right. Mostly this life is just driving me up the fucking wall. I keep wondering if she's got somebody else, it's fair making me ill. Anna reckons I'm getting an ulcer and I ought to eat plenty of oats or some crap.


22 Oct.        Wednesday

Well, it's happened. I knew it would. Tina says to me when we're having our breakfast bold as brass she's clearing out.

'What?'

'You heard, Andy,' she says but she's not snappy about it or nothing, it's just like she's tired or something.

'Why? What for?'

'Cos I'm bored that's why,' she says, then she looks and says sort of sweetly, 'It's no good, Andy—it's just no good. I can't take no more.'

'Aren't you coming back?'

'I dunno. We'll see. I'll see how it goes.'

'What is it, Teen—is it me?' I said like a pratt.

'No, it's not that. It's just . . . well, it's different, innit?'

'What is?'

Straight, I reckon she's got no idea.

'Well—you know . . . everything and that.'

'It's not—well, sex or nothing then?'

You see, I reckoned she'd got somebody else.

'No. I mean I do like you, Andy.'

Yeah, yeah, I reckoned, pull the other one.

'Well, and I like you and all,' I said.

'Yeah.'

Straight, I felt like I'd shit myself.

'Where you going to live then?'

'Back to me Mum's for a bit.'

Funny thing, I thought we'd have another row but no, she's all quiet and calm, just said it wasn't working out, that it wasn't my fault, we'd just see how it went for a bit. So that's that. I felt like I was dying.

It hasn't been right lately—I know that, I'm not a fool, but I thought it might work out. What I mean is I hoped it wouldn't happen.

'Is there somebody else then?' I said.

'No.'

'Oh yeah?'

'There's not. It's just—oh christ, just shut up. OK?'

I keep on thinking we ought to have been shouting or chucking things around or something, but we weren't. I said would it be OK if I come round to see how she felt about it and she said all right but leave it for a day or two.

Couldn't be bothered to go into work today. I just lay down, then I must have dropped off. I don't know, it churns me up just to think about it, I'm just glad we didn't part in a row or nothing. And she said she'd think about coming back. I mean if there's nobody else then it's no life for her at her old lady's is it? She'd soon get bored there all right.

I feel like I'm ill or just been ill but of course I'm not ill, I haven't even had a cold for months, not since last winter. I don't know—keep thinking maybe there's another guy, then I tell myself that it don't fucking matter now if there is or not and why don't I just go out and find a girl and bang her up for the night. But I don't know . . .

23 Oct.        Thursday

Had a flaming row at work today. Tina and me splitting up got round and old Moses heard about it so when I get in he asks to see me. I didn't know what he wanted and when I get in his office he comes right out with 'I hear you and Tina have split up.'

Well, that really got me, coming out with it like that so I snapped at him, 'That's none of your business.'

'Sorry, Andrew. I'm so very sorry, but have you fully considered your actions?'

'You mind your own fucking marriage,' I says to him straight. 'From what I hear you got your hands full without poking your bloody nose into other people's business.'

Nosey bastard! Then he goes bright red, calls me a fucking little son of a bitch and screams at me to get out, really screams at me he does, like a bleeding woman or something.

'Oh yeah,' I said to him—and I opened the door so's everybody could hear—'Got that out of your bloody religious books, did you?' Then I slammed the door on him.

Later on I got sent for by the Dept Head who says, 'I hear you've been abusing Mr, er, Collins,' but I soon put him straight about one or two things and in the end he says he'll say no more about it if I say I'm sorry to Moses, but I wasn't having none of that jazz so I said I'd have a word with Douglas about it and see what the union thought about old

Moses poking his nose into people's personal affairs. And then he
climbed down and said the incident was closed. Yeah, yeah. I just
walked out on him. He could have sacked me I suppose, but I showed
him I wasn't going to be messed about. Everybody cheered when I got
back and old Moses had to stay in his room. John said he'd been going
to have a word with Moses himself before too long, it was getting
ridiculous the way he was keeping on. I just said that he got what was
coming to him.

Then John asks us if I'm coming to the party tomorrow. I'd been
thinking about it and all of a sudden I said, 'Yeah, sure—why not?'

'That's the spirit, mate. Tomorrow's the first day of the rest of your
life, don't forget.'

That's good—he's right and I won't forget. I didn't feel so bad then,
but it's bad coming back to an empty flat and sleeping on me own's
even worse. I ought to have told our Mum and Dad I suppose, but I
just couldn't—they'd only make a fuss and make it worse what with
him griping and her crying. I know what it'd be like.

Would I have Tina back? That's what I've been asking myself this
last day or two. Tried to remember how I used to feel about Tina.
Well, we had some good times—some great times. We still could I
guess. It's making me feel bad just to think about it so I guess there's
something still there. I reckon I'd be willing to give it another go.
Can't say I feel much like going to John and Cherylle's party
tomorrow but I can't let them down I guess. It all makes me fucking
sick. Sometimes I want Tina back and sometimes I want to kick her
head in.

24 Oct.     Friday

Went to John and Cherylle's party tonight and it was really good. Kev
and Trev were there and lots of other people I haven't seen for ages.
Kev's being done next month for fiddling the dole but he reckons he'll
be miles away by the time his case comes up. 'On me bike and away
into the blue, kidder,' he says, lucky bastard.

Not only that, there was this really nice girl there who I thought I
knew but couldn't quite place her. Anyway, she's a really slim little
blonde and she's giving me the glad eye so I thought to myself, 'Hello!
You've not lost your charm, mate.' Then she comes over and says,
'Taken any good photos lately?' and gives me this big grin. Course
she's the girl from Boots that day I went to collect our holiday snaps!
She didn't seem to be with nobody so I asked her for a dance just for
something to do like.

'We was all killing ourselves about those photos,' she says. 'Are you a photographer?'

'No—not really.'

Her name's Debbi Hembrow and she's a cracking dancer. I told her so and all. She laughs a lot and we got on great. I really liked her, made me feel a whole lot better.

'They put up some of your snaps in the darkroom but the deputy assistant manager made them take them down.'

'Straight,' I said, 'What's it matter? The human body's the most beautiful thing in the world.'

'Was that a girlfriend or a model?' she wants to know.

'Oh—my sister's a model, but that one, that was' —too late, I'd already said it—'my wife.'

'Ooh, you married then?' And she gives a little smile.

'Yeah, but that's a long story.'

'I bet it is.'

'We might be separating soon.'

Then she tells me that she'd like to be a model, so I cracked that old joke about if I said she had a beautiful body would she hold it against me and she killed herself.

'You been married long?' she asks me.

'Ten years,' I told her—and it bloody feels like it and all. Then we danced some more. Spent most of the evening with Debbi, she's really nice. Then I took her home. I really fancied her to be honest. Hell, I'll say I did, I wanted to fuck her like crazy. She's small and slim and she looks so good she makes you want to eat her but I didn't kiss her or nothing, she's a bit shy and all so I reckoned to myself more haste less speed, if you know what I mean. Reckon she'd have gone though all the same.

'You know John then?' I says.

'Oh yeah. Who doesn't?'

She's got a great mouth and a really lovely smile.

'Well,' says she after a bit, 'I'd better be going, me Mum'll be wondering else, silly old cow.'

Christ! When I think of it . . . I don't know, I could always ring her, but I don't know. Maybe I'll ask John if she's spare—maybe that's best. She's lovely anyway. To be honest I had to have a quick wank when I got back, I had to relieve the pressure somehow and thinking of her made me come off in double quick time I can tell you.

26 Oct.    Sunday

Went round to see Tina, I reckoned she's waited long enough. Her Mum was down the health clinic and we had it off on the settee in their front room. Well, she wanted it and I wanted it but I kept on thinking of that Debbi. Then we had a cup of tea and I says to her, 'Are you coming back then?' and she says, 'Yeah—OK then,' which gives me a bit of a shock cos I didn't reckon she would.

Have to see how it goes I suppose. She come on back with me and she seems glad to be back. We had a good fry-up for our tea, she told me I'd kept the place nice, then we had it off again tonight. It was good, just like it used to be. You know, I reckon I'm glad Tina's back now. I told her it was pretty bad without her but she didn't want to talk about it much and just said we'd try again and see how things went.

'We still can't afford those chairs,' I said.

'Sod the chairs. I don't like them anyhow.'

Well, if she's prepared to be more reasonable then I reckon it might work out this time. And I hope it does. Yes, I reckon I'm glad that Tina's back. Funny thing, I never did get around to telling our Mum and Dad she'd gone.


31 Oct.    Friday

Went to a good Halloween party tonight. Debbi was there looking great. So I thought to myself well, why not so I went over and had a dance or two with her.

'Is that your wife?' she says.

'That's right.'

'She's nice.'

'Who's that?' says Tina to me afterwards.

'Who?'

'Her—the one you was dancing with.'

'Oh, that's Debbi,' says I and Tina looks as if she isn't interested one bit, but I knew better. I didn't say no more though, I just said, 'She's a great dancer.'

'I wasn't looking,' says Tina but I could tell she was, then she puts that look on her face again. She never looks very nice when she does that, makes her face look hard sort of.

Debbi danced with some other guy for the rest of the time and John said he was called Shane Troak and anyway he wasn't going out with

Debbi but with a girl called Chrissy Moggridge. Then I missed them at the end when somebody put all the lights out so's they could set fire to that pumpkin. Screwed Tina when we got home.

4 Nov.          Tuesday

Tina and me are splitting up. It's no good—we just seem to have drifted apart. It's nobody's fault, it's just one of those things. We don't seem to have nothing to say to each other, it's no fun anymore. Today when we was having our tea we just sat looking into our beans and waiting for each other to say something, then she says, 'It's not working out, is it, Andy?'

'What isn't?'

'You know—us. Everything.'

'Oh—that. No, guess it isn't.'

'Sorry.'

'Me too,' I said, and so I was. Christ, I felt awful.

We looked at our beans a bit more and I ate a few but they didn't taste the same.

'We'll go our own ways then,' she says. 'You can stay on here if you like.'

'Where will you go to?'

'I'll go to me Mum's for a bit, then find a place.'

'You could stay here for a bit I guess.'

'No, it's got too many memories. You happy to stay here?'

'Guess so. I don't fancy going back home.'

Then we went quiet for a bit again.

'Get a divorce then, is it?'

'Suppose so, yeah. We'll have to find out.'

'I'm really sorry it didn't work out, Tina.'

'Yeah. Still, that's how it goes, innit?'

'Yeah—guess so. No hard feelings then?'

'No—suppose not. You?'

'No. We had some laughs, eh?'

'Yeah!' and then she smiles at me. Made me feel really sad. Then I kissed her on the cheek—I really thought I was going to cry for a minute there. I needed a drink but Tina said she'd stay to pack her stuff so I went off on me own.

When I got to the corner I looked back at the flat. I can't say how I felt. Then when I got back I found her in bed with Angelo.

'Hello, mate,' he says but I was too surprised to say nothing, specially when Marilynne come out of the bog wearing no more than a grin.

'What—what's going on then?'

'What's it look like?' says Marilynne. Man, she's got some knockers on her.

'You're welcome to take an hand,' says Angelo.

'Er, I—' I couldn't say no more. I just couldn't take my eyes off it. I don't know why, I just stood there and couldn't stop thinking what a massive prick he's got on him—hung like a donkey with a pair of balls like bleeding organ stops. Tina looks at the wall and sighs, 'Oh, get out, Andy—just bloody get out, will you?'

Don't know when I've felt so bad. Didn't know what to do so I just waited in our sitting-room. About half hour later Angelo comes out.

'Hello, mate. You still here then?'

'I live here.'

'Oh yeah—course. Sorry, chum.'

'Thought you was under arrest.'

'Out on bail. Fancied a bit of an holiday, so here we are.'

'Yeah, I can see that.'

'All right, Andy, no need to get stroppy.'

I could have kicked his fucking head in for him. 'Was that the first time?' I said.

'Was what the first time?'

'You know—you and Tina.'

'You don't want to know that, old son.'

'Was it?' I said and I guess I must have been shouting at him.

'Now calm down, mate. What good would it do yer to know, eh?' he says, smooth wog bastard.

'I want to know. Was it?'

'Look, son, nothing lasts forever, does it? Take my advice—you take what you can and when it's over, then it's over.'

'You bastard!'

'Now, you ain't got no cause to say that.'

'I'll say what I like to you,' I told him and I did and all.

'Now I don't wanna have to slap you down, Andy, cos you're a nice kid, but you gotta watch what you're saying, you know.'

'Balls.'

'C'mon, Andy, no hard feelings, eh? C'mon, son, eh? What is it, eh? Just a quick poke, that's all. Tina says you and her's finished anyhow.'

'So we are—two hours ago.'

'Well, you're out of it then, int you? And you don't wanna cry about
losing her, do yer? I mean it's only like shaking hands, innit eh?' Then
he puts his great hairy hand on my shoulder but I pushed it off.

'All right, son. You think about it. We'd better go, we only just
dropped in anyhow. Me and Marilynne's staying at her old lady's
place for the time being.'

'Do the pigs know?'

'Don't be like that, man, it's not nice. You ready, Marilynne?' he
calls out and her and Tina come out. Tina and me look at each other
for a minute, then we looked at the walls. Fucking little cow, I wanted
to kill her. She goes as if to say something but I wasn't having none,
the little cow.

'Cheer up,' says Angelo. 'Not the end of the world, is it?'

'Fuck off,' I told him.

Then they all left.

'See you then,' says Tina to me.

'Yeah—bye.' I was choked.

'Cheero, Andy,' says Angelo and pats me on the shoulder again.
'See you, eh? Best of luck, pal.'

I slammed the door, then I hit it, then cos I'd hurt my fist I kicked it
and that hurt my foot. I was hopping mad. Don't know when I've felt
so bad. That little cow, soon's my back's turned she's on the job with
that fucking greasy foreigner. Not to mention Marilynne and all—
that's bloody unnatural that is. Christ, I wish I'd killed him. And fuck
to this bloody diary from now on too for another fucking thing. Shit to
every fucking thing.


9 Nov.        Sunday

Remembrance Day or something so there's my old man who's been to
some British Legion thing with his suit and medals on. Didn't know
you got medals for doing bugger all but he's got some. Stupid little
sod. Right off he starts with his 'I knew what it'd come to, rushing into
marriage like that.' I told him to shut it, then he reckons he wasted his
savings for nothing.

'Spell in the army'd do you good,' he says.

'Spell in the ground'd do you good,' I said to him.

'Oh!' says Mum and he's got his great gob open to come back again so
I said to him straight if he sounded off again then I'd clear off out of it but
not before I'd clocked him one, so he goes off upstairs and he didn't say
no more to me and it's a fucking good job for him he didn't and all.

'You mustn't speak to your Dad like that,' says our Mum quietly.
'I'll knock him down if he comes it again,' I told her and I would
and all.

'Oh dear,' she says and sighs like it's the end of the world. 'Is it all
over with you and Tina then, love?'

'Yeah. I told her to pack her bags.'

'Oh dear,' she goes, 'what with everything.' Then she cries a bit.

'That won't help.'

'But what will you do?'

'Get a divorce I guess. I dunno.'

Then she talks some crap like nobody in our family's ever got
divorced before. Christ! I couldn't take no more of it after tea so I
come on home.

Feeling really low. John come round and brought a bottle of scotch.
We talked a bit and he said Debbi was going out with some guy. Felt
like I wanted to spew.

'That's life, mate,' he says. 'You gotta take the rough with the
smooth.'

'Yeah, yeah.'

Then we got some more bottles in and got good and pissed. He
stopped here the night cos Cherylle's gone somewhere and slept on the
floor with some cushions and stuff. He's a good mate is John, a good
mate. 'Bloody women,' he says to me, 'it's never worth it.' And I
bloody agreed with him.

10 Nov.        Monday

Tina came round tonight for some of her stuff. She's got a fucking
nerve. She wanted to take the bed but I said no way.

'It's my bed,' she says.

'Get stuffed—but then you'll have no trouble there.'

'What's that mean?'

'Angelo had you lately, has he? Fancied a bit of black, did you?'

'What if he has? He's miles better than you ever were any day.'

That really got me so I said, 'Oh yeah? Least I don't screw with my
sister—or get people to take pictures of me without clothes on.'

'Trust you to bring that up. You're so childish.'

'Oh yeah?'

'Oh yeah. We used to have a good laugh about it, matter of fact.'

'Bitch!' I shouted at her. 'Cheap little bitch!'

Then she chucked a mug at us. I went to hit her one, christ knows I
wanted to.

'You touch me, you bastard, an' I'll scratch your fucking eyes out!' she screams at me—and I reckon she would have done and all, what with that bloody thing she's got in her bag.

'Bitch!' I shouts at her. 'Get the fucking shit outa here before I knock your goddam teeth in.'

I ought to have belted her. I wanted to, I know that much, little cow. All that shit about him being better than me, I don't believe a word of it, you try to tell me she didn't like it in the sack with me any less than one hundred per cent and I'm fucking Mickey Mouse, and she needn't try to make out she had that Ken neither as if he didn't have nothing better to do on his holidays than chase around after a fat-arsed little bitch like her when he had a wife of his own like his— no, that's just so much hot air, I don't believe a word of it, no way. She's not going to have me believing that jazz, no chance. Stupid little cow. I ought to have knocked her bloody daft little head off for her—if I could have been bothered that is. She can go take a running jump—I don't care, I just don't care. She can go out and get run over by the next bus for all I care, that's how much I worry about her. She's just a fucking daft little cow, that's what she is, and I'm well shot of her, she's just a boring little bitch, that's the middle and both ends of it. Shit to her.


13 Nov.        Thursday

When I see Tina in work these days she don't speak to me, so I don't bother to speak to her neither. All her mates stopped speaking to me and all so bollocks to them. Saw her in the pub today with some guy I'd never seen before.

Anyway, I had some shopping to do so I went on round to Boots to get some of that Acnestoppa stuff—it's the worry I reckon. There I am daydreaming I guess in the queue at the pay desk when all of a sudden somebody gives us a poke and I turned round quick getting mad.

'Hello,' says Debbi, 'you was miles away. I saw you across the shop but you didn't notice.'

'Sorry. I got a lot on my mind right now.'

'Yeah, I heard. Sorry about your wife.'

'Thanks—that's OK.'

She's got a lovely smile has Debbi, she just stands there smiling at me and I'm there looking at her.

'Here—you doing anything tonight?' I says.

'No—why?'

'Pick you up at half seven then.'

Magic!

There we are. Me and Debbi went out tonight and it was really good. She's dead easy to talk to and she's really good fun. She reckons we must have known each other in a previous life—in ancient Egypt she reckons. She come back here for coffee, said what a nice flat it was and all, we had a laugh about Tina wanting the bed back. Well, I just played it cool, we kissed a bit—she's got a lovely little mouth—and I fixed to see her Saturday and go and see that horror film at the Odeon, the one where the bloke chops his wife up with a chain-saw and sticks the bits in the freezer, it's called *Carve Up*. Sounds like a good bloke.

I can't help thinking about Debbi, specially her firm little arse—the thought of it fair drives me bananas—and she's got the greatest little tits on her. I can't wait to strip her off.

17 Nov.        Monday

Got a letter this morning from some solicitors called Ratchett, Paul and Co. who said they were acting for Mrs Tina Baker and claiming I've got to pay her maintenance or something, and with a list of stuff they reckon by rights belongs to her, just about everything in the bleeding flat, and would I make arrangements to hand it over at once and forthwith. It really made me see red I can tell you. If I've got to pay her maintenance so's she can go sleeping with any spade what comes along then I reckon I'll do what that guy in the film on Saturday did. Anyway, straight after dinner I went round to Dashiel Street where the lawyers all hang out and got an appointment to see this Mr Hurd tomorrow at half eleven. Hope it's not going to cost a packet. Passed Tina in the corridor at teatime—I didn't see why I should avoid her so I says to her, 'What's all this jazz about money then?'

'You'll find out,' she says and walks on, the little cow.

Had a great time on Sat. Debbi's really lovely. Magic!

18 Nov.        Tuesday

Saw that lawyer bloke this morning, he told us she's just trying it on but we got to split the furniture and the wedding presents. Asked him how you split a kettle, but you each get what your relations and so on give you he reckons.

'You didn't tell her to go or hit her, did you?' he wants to know.

'No—wish I had.'

'That's OK then.' Then he grins. 'Keep your hands off her and you'll save yourself a packet.'

'What about a divorce?' says I and he says we've got to wait a couple of years, more's the pity.

'Any children?'

'No.'

'Did your wife practise adultery?'

'She don't need to practise.'

'Hmm. Well, she certainly has no claim on you after that.'

'Here,' I says, 'how much would it cost for me to give her a smack in the mouth?'

'Too much,' says him. 'I'll get on to her solicitors and see if we can come to some agreement about the furniture and so on. In the meantime don't give her any money. Were you in the habit of giving your wife money?'

'Don't worry about that, she won't get a penny out of me.'

'That's what I like to hear. You'd be surprised how many husbands fall for a soft look and a tear, Mr Baker.'

'No way,' I said.

Seemed like a good bloke so I said, 'You married yourself?'

'Thirty-five years come March,' he says.

Well, that's sure one hell of a weight off my mind.

Went out with Debbi tonight—she's great. Can't wait to get her to bed and I know she's ready for it. Tomorrow maybe? Who knows? After all, it's the first day of the rest of my life, all of a sudden life's great again. You know, I don't give a stuff for Tina, I really don't.


19 Nov.        Wednesday

Tina's taken some stuff out of the flat, the fucking little cow's been round and taken some stuff out of the flat. I'd clean forgotten she still had a key. Anyway, she hasn't left me no plates and all the food's gone. Jon come up later, said he was sorry but didn't like to ask. Yeah, yeah. I reckon he could have had her and all. He says as I'm paying the rent on my own now I can change the locks if I want. So I went straight round to some bloke he told me about who's the janitor out the Tech and does jobs in his spare time and got him to change the locks right away for a fiver. That's five quid well spent though he said it'd take a bit longer to repair the bed cos Tina's sawed half-way through one leg, the little bitch. I nailed a bit of wood on it and it looks firm enough and we can always do it on the floor. Found some of her make-up she's forgotten about so I slung it in the bin.

20 Nov.     Thursday

Rang my lawyer first thing and told him what Tina's gone and done.
He said he'd get on with it. Screwed Debbi for the first time tonight.
Magic! She was ready for it all right. I can always tell. My God she's
lovely. I've never seen nobody so lovely—it was really fantastic. Man,
I haven't had a fuck as good as that for years. In fact I don't reckon I
ever have. She's lovely, really beautiful—she's like a doll almost, so
slim and nice. Her tits are like little rosebuds and her bum—man,
that's something else. I reckon she's got the most beautiful little arse
I've ever seen and when I fingered her hole she really took off . . .

   Well, there we are and the smell of her is just about driving me wild,
she's pushing her boobs up against me and I'm giving that great little
arse of hers the once over under her dress.

   'Oh Andy!' she says and, man, her knickers come of like they was
oiled. 'I'm not sure,' she says but you can't fool me none and she was
good and ready for it and all, but she's a bit tight down there so I give
her a good finger and she shivers and moans and her legs open up, then
it went in no problem—took her breath away anyhow.

   'Easy baby,' I tell her, 'just take it steady,' then I give it to her.
Magic!

   As for old Tina—well, Angelo can keep her, this is something else
and that's all I'm saying about it. I reckon I'm well rid of her. Stuff
that for a lark. What was I worrying about anyway? I mean we had
some laughs OK, but it's over now and that's it. That's what I say
anyhow.

   Saw her in work today, soon as she sees me she sticks her nose in the
air.

   'Cow,' I said when she goes past, then she calls us a rabbit. Well,
she needn't think I'm fucking scared of her or that Angelo, for two
pins I'd have smacked her in the mouth.


26 Nov.     Wednesday

Had that meeting with Tina and her lawyer today.

   'Now,' says Mr Hurd, 'let's try to keep everything friendly, shall
we?'

   'If your client is prepared to be reasonable then that should be
possible,' says Tina's lawyer.

   She hasn't so much as looked at me so I didn't look at her neither.
We spent two solid hours in that office rowing about this and that—
and we didn't have much furniture to start with.

'What about the sheets and stuff?' says Tina, on the make as usual.

'What about the knives and forks you took?' I says to her.

'Let's try to keep it friendly,' says Mr Hurd but course Tina wants a row so I give her one and the lawyers start on to each other about golf or something.

Anyway, we got there in the end and she come round straight after to fetch it all away. Some guy turns up to help her, don't ask me who he was and I don't care, anyway they go to shift the bed and the leg come off. Then when it's all over and she's ready to go she turns and we look at each other.

'Well, that's that, I suppose,' she says.

'Looks like it,' says I.

'See you then,' she says.

'Yeah—see you around.'

It was for the best, it was the best thing I reckon. Makes you feel kind of funny though—but to be honest I reckon it was for the best. Knew I had to see Debbi tonight. Magic! Had her from the back, she loved it like that—she's never tried it before. She's great.

5 Jan.          Monday

Well anyway, there I am looking out the window thinking of everything and that and in comes John.

'Here—you and Kristin coming to our party Saturday?' I asks him.

'Sure—hey, we'd best go down I reckon.'

So we went on down to wait and who's there but Tina!

'Hello,' she says.

'Hello.'

And there's that Janette looking spare as usual. Well, me and Tina just got talking I guess, you know what things are like—mind you, I couldn't think of much to say. She looks OK though. Funny thing was, we just stood there like we'd only just met or something, we ask each other, 'You all right then?' and 'How's Debbi?' and 'How's Rod?' and—felt a bit queer to tell the truth.

Then the hearse come along with all Kev's mates giving him an escort and John goes and says, 'Wonder what they done with his head, poor bugger?' and me and Tina sort of grin at each other, then Moses comes along and says it's high time we all got back to some work. Christ, he don't change!

And now I'm back here waiting for Debbi and reckoning what the hell am I bothered with writing all this down for? Anyway, to cut a long story short, as far as diaries go I reckon this is the end.